GW00937899

Freedom
from Trauma
in America

Bill Lemmer

Copyright 2015 by Bill Lemmer.
All rights reserved. Published 2015

Cover and text design by Jennifer Omner
Text set in Grafolita Script, Neuton, and Garamond Premier Pro

Publisher's Cataloging-in-Publication Data

Lemmer, Bill, 1942–
    Freedom from trauma in America / Bill Lemmer.
    pages cm
    ISBN: 978-0-9933370-2-4 (pbk.)
    ISBN: 978-0-9933370-3-1 (e-book)
    1. Travelers—Fiction. 2. Psychic trauma—Fiction. 3. Self-
actualization (Psychology)—Fiction. 4. Picaresque literature.
5. Adventure stories.   I. Title.
PR6112.E49 F74 2015
823—dc23

                                                    2015915007

Contents

Neil and I

I met Neil in my first school. He wrote with either hand. Once, on the way from school, Neil and I saw a red-faced man with parched hands and a stooped posture. He wore a maroon sweater that looked as though someone gave it to him years earlier. The man watched, through an open door, a young couple in the grass. His white lips moved slowly. He said, "There goes a boy and his girl. Similar to one I had. I liked to hold her and feel her breathe and hear her laugh. I don't recall the name. But I know the feel of her. I do remember her laugh. I had a young lady once..." A dog trotted past and the man stopped talking. Then, we saw a trio of teens rollerskate down a hill. We liked to watch and listen.

Green-sung spring days later, when we strolled again past the pensioner's window, I said, "Neil, Neil, you want things. You want to be a writer." Well, he laughed, but I wasn't making a joke. "You even have ambition," I said under my breath. Months later, we gave up ambition and lay down to rest on a pile of straw. Even then, we kept up our journals. Will the restless scratch of observation wear us out? What will be left of Neil and I? A witty remark at a party? A clever reply? And then? Four years of military drills, clean uniforms, salutes and sirs? And then? College? Relationships — those undreamed of? Next, a reunion or two, people I come to know and a drop or two of mineral water? If there is dirty water, is it possible to foretell in advance, beforehand? Do we live on after the waste is flushed away or explore the waste with strangers who are never entirely strangers? What will I do and how will I be while my friend changes?

One afternoon, we saw Neil's dog knocked howling into a ditch, by a car. Next day, and all the upset days after, the sun emerged silent on that ditch and even the dog's shadow was gone. Silver clouds raced the sky. We watched a friend's father, lustrous with water, pull a car from that ditch, pulling it out with a tractor. We were never loud boys, at least on the outside of ourselves, except for occasional shouting between ourselves. We investigated and duplicated most sounds except the sound of silence inside ourselves, a sound that isn't a natural sound for a kid. I think that Neil was aware of a quiet space inside, unruffled but easily stirred. We dripped some kind of moisture from our noses to the bottoms of our feet. We slid on cellophane and water-blacked cardboard down a hill, across a glossy pavement, off the rump-bumping curb and into the street. We laughed, grabbed the cellophaned cardboard and screeched to the top of the hill, where we jumped and jostled until the path was clear. After a peaceful few seconds, we screeched down again. Near the hill where we larked and watched beyond the periphery of our sniffing, a red and blue beer can lay in a well-scrubbed, often cut, leaf-raked front yard. Such a thing was not for kicking along the way, as we'd been chased by aging adolescent banderilleros, when tampering with their trappings.

This can was tossed by a gallant and dashing (and such was the toss, considering its distance from the road) service station attendant named Bill Hallidway, who ran after boys with a club, especially on Halloween night. Bill drove a re-bored, hyper-souped, hand-deluxed 1950 Chevrolet. Three of his cavaliers were with him when he drove. They just graduated from high school, along with others who seldom leave their home territory. They rode through school and down Main Street on the gilded promises of their parents. Promises that told of a good life and secure future, somewhere down the line. The great day of graduation arrived, with the sounds and songs of 84 mainly pink-faced and vaguely hopeful, thickly tingling youths. The road of life shifting gears. Going in directions somewhat unpredicted. By the law of averages, excepting Bill and his sidekicks, some will buck the odds and head for California. Others travel to Fort Knox or Fort Dix or Fort something-or-other in the olive-cloth distance. Some go away unannounced but most will stay, only grudgingly giving up their rural territories across the prairies of America—their patrolling and partnerships yielding to uncertain commitments.

Neil was honored on graduation day and went to college and so did I. College, away from hard winter nights, far from the giant mutations of prickly corn and summer that sticks to your arms. Away to a place golden and plush and waiting without expectations or planning. But those three in the Chevy stayed. Now, in that moment, disguised in the whiskers of night, they drove, and drank, and heaved their cans as exclamations of prowess. They picked up immeasurable beautiful women, in bobby socks. In these characters, there was a spiraling wind which rearranged them and never gave them peace. Their desire bored and frightened them. The taste of their conquests dulled them and set their appetites burning until they could not sit still. Always the next taste evaded them. Each hid this whooshing-inside thing as best he could — we knew this because we already felt it in ourselves. Each clung to the others' wish to exceed whooshing, unaware that the thirst for it is harder and harder to quench, so the more they tried the less free they felt. They grew into each other, these crusaders, but somehow they remained separate in and of themselves, especially Bill. When one of the wanderers returned to the mood of the others, their adopted unity served them well. They acted like things were pretty good right where they were in new spaces, provided their uprisings accumulated to strengthen them. Those who deserted found their efforts wasted. At night they convinced themselves to whoosh it up. This was how the beer can came to be in that place.

Their car coasted silently along the street, with lights out. The three guzzled furtively and sucked on cigarettes (which felt commensurate with a roar in times of discretion). One threw his empty can onto the road. The car coughed, smearing the night with its cleared lungs and zoomed into the darkest direction — a merging continuation of their self-absorbing search for personal liberation, preferably with multiple orgasms. Next day, in front of the beer can, a funeral progressed, its slow and steady winding round a corner and out of sight.

Neil and I shared our ignorance about the world which pressed and stayed dutifully on our explorer shoulders. A bicycle, with red and blue crepe intertwined through the spokes, came from behind the brightest bush and spread its wheeling flames across the sky. That was something, in the still pink lakes, between the estuaries and the enormous searing hoar-frost to come — the frost which roamed and spat. Neil said it best, "The sky is so many things."

Neil never told me what his adopted sister gave him, but it was always from the pill-bottle library in the bathroom and made him sort of mystic. He was like a wastebasket of pill bottles dumped in a larger wastebasket. Then the smaller wastebasket full again of papers and things until its scarlet coat of memory faded and the yellow body was forgotten and reduced to a night train wail. Next, another wastebasket. Neil said he often felt like a wastebasket. Kids cannot always explain why they think like they do.

One day of hot sun, Neil and I set off for nearby Henderson, one of the small towns near ours, on the J.C. Higgans bike. We took turns, with one of us on the handlebars. The heat lay coiled over sidewalks, waiting to strike those who left the sanctuary of shade. Neil was the first pedaler. The scenery was more magnificent and the air cleaner now we moved along, beneath a white puffy cloud which swooped as if to say, 'Here, take the controls.' We felt like reaching to grasp it, to steer the cloud, its brave co-pilots, to soar and dip, its spirit, flying with its energy. Easing back on our seats, the cloud roared its strength. Birds appeared to stop, puzzled in the sky. We leaned, chuckling at birds, laughing at wind in our eyes, steering the cloud through a rainbow. Pretending to stand in the cockpit, it hovered — a shadow for school old-boys to throw rocks at and a question to be shrugged off by parents with absent kids. Inside the cloud a prism lived. Sunlight pierced damp particles shining in a purple and pink honeycomb. In the shadow was a gold-backed blue unseen since a picture of Armistice Day. Stretching an arm, our hands changed color in the cloud. Vapor pillars surrounded us like colored stalactites and stalagmites floating in air, as though in a cave without bats. Light permeated the air, possessed and transformed it into every complexion of color. Another cloud blocked the sun — the cloud's decomposed light becoming red-glowing. "Promise, turn us inside out, then," I shouted, and the bike shook for a moment. Neil chuckled fondly and retorted, "and we'll watch outside-in." An obstructive cloud passed and honeycomb colors revived: purple first and then the rest, one at a time, lapping at and covering us until everything was in perfect balance. I saw clouds and sun, their form and sound resonating to my senses, in their connection to the rain and the effects of its watering. There is an abundance of sound with the cloud's windfall ear, with our musings and birds cawing flight. Then, silence brings some kind of clear view, as if everything is connected. That, to a kid, at the time, is unforgettable. I remember being one with the cloud, and Neil's hands gripping the handlebars, and adjusting my position.

We were in high ground and it was time to swap over pedaling. When I turned to Neil, the Cattail he was munching (a tall reed flower with a brown head, comparable to a big sausage) struck my face; we both roared with laughter, stopping to view the valley stretched before us: hill peaks and rivers on display. A river which at first appeared as something else nestled at the valley's end. "It doesn't seem to flow," Neil said, "just lies thick and browny among trees, waiting for us to climb on its back!" A game trail angled along the drop-off to waterway drinking sites where a stout, grizzled woodchuck drank, while sun squeezed leaves out of their branches. A blue heron stood in water, resting his bum knee. Closer, a red squirrel chattered a complaint and snapped a plumed tail. Gaily-dressed chipmunks bounded as though they had eaten several little rubber balls. The river, bulging like a tire inner tube worn too thin, waited for its long ice cover to fill and smooth the surface between waves, holding until another spring. "I bet the fish are just hanging there, transparent in the water," I said, "waiting, flitting into another pool, darting behind a larger rock." Hill peaks rolled in a purple glare which met the water, and morning's echoing haze crept back into trees. A cattle path unwinding into a pond. Jay shrieks minced in breezes from a morning to the west. Trees flexed their finger-mouths in soil and stretched their shoulders for a few moments. Pebbles on the river shore made drink sounds. A road fell in leaps and circles into the valley and dotted its other side. The fallen tree-boulder and snow-prone road was kept tidy in winter by council trucks. At the bottom, by the river, the road surface was loose, its verges gone to seed and its past worn smooth by traffic. The progress of its past was halted by speed, a smash, bang and clatter, by glass exploded into starlight and tiny drip sounds lost to the river and heard only by little animals who left tracks in rock. A silver car climbed through straightened sun rays. The glows ricocheted, giving trees motion, shadows self-regulation and a geographic perspective. A thick-wristed pickup truck with no loose eggs and another car started from the valley floor: crawling crabs. Telephone lines strummed on a peak about one quarter mile distant, breathing with users' needs.

A black spider ambled across grass right in front of us. White dots on its back drew attention from the rotating legs and eyes which bore holes in otherwise empty space, making sight marks. The spider, clad in straight metal fur, hummed with unmade webs and moved on the power of spider blood and spider-basic brain. Bugs were neither here nor there yet everywhere. These light-driven creatures weave an invisible net which connects them to the earth, materializes them, briefly, as part of it, until a future date, when they spring to life again.

A cloud covered the sun, darkening light in the grass. Instead of full green shades, rusty browns and striking yellows evolve into emerald veils. Before us was a genuine chaotic burgeoning; we loved it and our place and nature's frantic muscular growth — the way it spills over and redoubles itself, inter-reliant on everything around, with such potent nourishment as sky light and earth rooted beneath us. "It's frightening and thrilling to think that nothing stops the life which comes from light," I said. "A farmer or careless camper could burn this valley and in a few months it will be green again — only not as high." The suffocating weight of winter snow covers it for the better part of a year, flattened dry brush under a cold blanket. Yet it always comes back, greening. "Nothing anyone does will destroy this valley," Neil said, as we took off for Henderson again, with me pedaling. The sky opened more, cold white at its edges, while the earth glowed. Any color reflects the peace now. Soft grass is full of bugs that will tickle if you sit in the grass to lace your boots and push dirt over the fire coals. Another cloud blocked the sun. Grass hissed, whispered and grew in its unstoppable sure-force growth, yearning to

straighten its wind-bent boughs to the sun and suck it dry all
of every day, shouldering only rain and then drawing the water
to its mouth. Rain that wears away rock if not first cracked
and split by thirsty roots. Sun flickered through thinned cloud
cover and licked the grass as we bicycled near a goat trail toward
the foothills. The trail vanished in a shaded place behind rain
and sun in the earth's afternoon underbelly, which slid across
the morning toward us, from its high wooded spot near water,
where a meadow of light-stained leaves lay like toast in bent,
brown grass, luring the goats to deep purple hills with blue,
yellow, and dark red speckles. Valley dwellers at full power,
working to preserve their colorful condition, singing a song of
no reluctance. Their melody is a tune of instinctive drive and
they succeed one another. The valley tossed its hair in rollicking wind, rolling its sun-red eyes and roaring cheers to bones
roving and reforming in its belly.

We passed the bat caves on our way down. The last bats
had long sprung to grey boxes they hid in during their rock-
covered day. They spin, dart, flicker, clap leathery wing-hands
and dive off rock sides into airspace. The bats were in, resting
their crumpled leaf faces, tardy and bruised, but home. "Hey,
your ashtrays are full," Neil shouted at a car passing upwards.
"Did you notice that thing on the dashboard, Paul? They've
got a plastic idol to guide them safely into the sky!" From
their canopy on high the gods secretly frown on us, hoping
we will come to their understandings, despite our caginess
about being separate from them, and eventually from their
point of view, and become unattached to our fixtures and
rituals of home. We frown, too, at those drivers who cannot

yet see the great spiders in the sky who weave their imaginary webs. "Look at those bee rocks," Neil shouted again, as if he was slowly emerging from a long lapse. "In those rocks are trappings and inherited treasures of the beedom of all time. The bee palace rivals the Egyptian pyramids for vision — a granite-colored, air-conditioned honeycomb directed by one queen bee, constructed to her specification, probably with gun ports or exits or manufacturing plants, temples and even time. This rock is even time. Inside now is a bee kingdom. Bees are electing and disposing others at their discretion. All reproduced and protected to her desire. This valley and those rocks are miniatures of this — an outgrowth and substitutions for collecting nectar." This awesome possibility cooled his imagination. Birds put to flight as the sun lit more land and hills, making shadows fine and day more part of earth. Birds flirted, sounding like their flight, while no funny business pried off the last cap of day and feathers fell in weeds. Even the sun is part of a huge network of planets and systems designed by bees to help them in their work and to give them comfort as they sit watching it set: a bright, flowing replica — a marvelous super bee image for average bees to deify rocks they created, rocks designed roughly in the shape of a perfect rock but given individuality and set loose to entertain and awe bees.

As soon as we crossed the railroad tracks, a bright banner hanging over the road between the telephone poles welcomed us to Henderson. Most people we saw, pedaling along Main Street, were dressed in long gowns, or formal clothes from a bygone era. Sauerkraut Days is a tribute to hardy Germans who first cut and cleared the land. Men and women who prompted Indians to be wary of the immigrants' foreign dignity and culture. These stalwart folk, followers of their governors, misunderstood the barbarity of their Manifest Destiny but mustered up courage and self-satisfaction in the loneliness of untamed places, where crops are reaped from rich soil.

This day their descendants celebrated with eager bellies and perspiring faces. Beverage cans and Krispy Kreme Doughnut wrappers dotted the roads here and there. While a couple blocks away at Riverside Park, people swatted away flying insects attracted to stewing sauerkraut and frying meat. The festival's beauty pageant maidens and tractor-racing contestants mingled in expensive-looking garments, ready to be viewed in the eyes of the admiring crowd. Some of the children played, shrieking in a large shady lawn adjacent to the Otto Werner County Museum, set within the awesome harmony and hypnotic powers of the valley's wildlife and fauna.

Like an exploding bomb, the first motorcycle roared along the street. More followed from each direction. Soon, there were more than 30 bikes. Their beardy, dirtied and scary riders made the street roar. Slouched people sat upright. Children stood and gaped. Mothers clutched small wrists like the jaws of a sprung rabbit trap. The intruders gathered at the west end of town. Then, their bikes popping like a string of metal firecrackers, they roared four blocks to the other end of town. As they passed the first clusters of people, they shouted: "Fuck. Fuck you. Fuck a fucks. Fuckadoodledo," and other varieties of the obscenity. This went on for 20 minutes until a hastily-called meeting of the Civil Defense. We were outside hearing distance, because there was a ring of women around the mens' meeting, which broke up after a couple minutes. The most notable after-effect was that about 50 men were issued clubs and set loose in groups of four and five. Their duty was to patrol and protect townspeople from the imminent threat hovering over Henderson like a large unshaven cloud. The cloud and situation in general was complicated by the insignia of the gang: a Swastika — an emblem many men in Henderson had faced over loaded rifles. Henderson residents were noticeably frightened. This made them noticeably angry. The gang was already angry. The symbol was graphic proof of their attitude — a flippant obscenity. They defied society, for they had a society of their own. Their appearance was a psychic disappointment for Henderson. How would anyone be jerked, practically sobbing, in some cases, out of an anniversary dream to face a hostile gang? Yet, the local newspaper made no mention of the phenomenon in its evening edition. Indeed, people we watched refused to talk openly about it. Just one single town resident we spoke to agreed to their name being used in print. The others were timid and even feared voicing an opinion to a stranger. Evidence of tangible damage was non-existent. Nobody reported fights between Henderson residents and the gang.

The symbol of a Swastika worn as a badge by the bikers presented a clear problem, increasingly familiar in rural communities; residents reacted as though the hell-raisers openly favored disorder. Gangs frequently expressed their hostility to the fuzz and all that force represented. "We have been much maligned," a gang member told Neil. The member, a girl from the southwest on a Norton chopper, explained that they caused little or no trouble. "We are a club," she said, "only out for a pleasure drive." I think one member, a fellow who filled the saddle of his big Harley, tried to pick a fight with me. "You've been taking down license numbers," he challenged. "No I haven't; I'm not English," I said. "Fucking son of a bitch," he moaned to nobody in particular. Other gang members tranquilized him with psychological wampum. "Man, we could ride up and down this street firing shotguns through every goddamned window," another said in a talk-lull, "and if we wore white shirts, rode white bikes, were shaved and had Shriners' hats, they'd say 'Hi-Hullo, how are ya?' But we set foot in here like this," he snorted, gesturing to his unshaven face and dirty leather jacket, "and they bring out the rods." When I confronted a resident with the accusation that locals were toting pistols, one told me, "It isn't safe to have your children on the streets with them running around." Another, who refused to give his name, had a simple solution for the problem posed by cycle gangs: "Torture," he said, sticking his thumbs under the waistband of his Eisenhower jacket. "It's the only way to deal with some people. They should be killed a bit at a time," he added, jerking at a reluctant bolt somewhere in the belly of his car. Pressed for a definition of torture, he explained: "Chop off a finger at a time...Well," he began to amend himself, revising his technique as he worked it out and temporarily forgot the bolt, "one finger the first day, then two fingers the second day and so forth, 'til they're all dead." The man gave a final jerk on the wrench. It slipped off the nut. He yelled a hardy oath, stood and watched his knuckle bleed. We left.

I am opposed to torture. So is Neil; he doesn't argue or

fight, either. Even then, we felt that it wasn't a workable solution. Gangs are unable to accept compromise from a society they think is rotten. Deep down, we had sympathy in us for them. Everybody, probably, knew it was possible, under certain conditions, to be a converted Angel. So, in a drive for self-respect aimed at acceptance by reverse, gangs became or at least expressed their own love and compassion, which others witness as rottenness. We have to face it: society that harbors public officials who talk nonsense when something goes wrong, a society that tolerates this should be unsurprised by a few dozen cyclists wearing Swastikas in Henderson.

Neil and I reckoned that it will be an equal shock to the residents when bicyclists ride into town, clothed in peace buttons and displaying signs asking for an end to racial discrimination. That is a different kind of disorder. Peace preachers, preaching in public, especially on a hot day. What is the solution to civil distress? "The alternative to extermination of public pests is torture, equally impractical, and less brutal," shouted a bystander with a basketball. The imminent prospect of apocalyptic fighting exists, and we knew it that day.

Sauerkraut Days is already fast approaching (there are two per year). "Fighting is temporary," Neil stated. "They want to be happy in Henderson, even the strangers." Homeward bound, spurring the J.C. Higgans to speed, we arrived at a judgment, or two: "They need each other," I shouted. "They're all rebels at heart," Neil chanted. "So, they all do things that bring them the opposite result," I concluded.

The lower lip of the sun slid above the horizon, its rays hurrying back in time for the ascent, leaving a haze of ray dust in the air. The sun slipped over and then under. "Once upon a glorious and gunshot eve, a simple blacksmith and his simpler brother dressed in secret," Neil cried out, bursting into a familiar song-take-off of my last name, which we sang variations to on the way home. "You think there'll be trouble Paul?" he shouted. "Probably — where's my other sock?" I pleaded.

"How far will you ride?"

"To the river — Emory, are you wearing my socks again?"

"We're s'pose to whisper, Paul — if the neighbors hear…"

"To hell with the neighbors — if it weren't for them, we'd still be in bed."

"Here it is."

"Thanks — Emory!! It's got a hole in it."

"Finally with socks on, they laced the tall boots, donned square hats and shoved the tails of ascot-fronted shirts into their knickerbockers."

"The brothers Revere walked to a stable. Paul wore an enormous smile."

"Now, you remember the signal, Emory?" he said, laughing.

"Ah, one if by land and, ah, two if by sea…Paul, what's eating you?"

"Paul sits in the saddle, watching, and rubs his smooth, wood musket butt…" We burst into such laughing at that point, we couldn't continue and had to stop the J.C. Higgins and start all over again.

Our First Dates: Uprooting Desire

Neil and I tended to go our own ways, as far as the opposite sex is concerned, except for two in the early days. The first girl I dated was Nancy. Her mother waited for me with an umbrella under spring rain. Meanwhile, her prosperous-looking father tied his rope to a tree and tossed a grapnel through a basement window. Then, their boxy house was coupled with the tree, like a boat moored to a dock. Slurping rain coasted down our necks and dribbled inside. I heard Nancy, somewhere, bailing water. Along with Nancy's mother we returned to the house. I was a visitor and the subject of responsibility since there was a temporary curfew at the boys home where I lived. Mother returned because she was personally fragile, according to Nancy, and misconstrued by her 'control freak' husband, who in the face of madness turned his fear into yelling accusations at the rampant waters. We sat round the front room, on the edges, waiting for the rain to stop. Nancy's sister entered. She wanted to play word games. Nancy gave her a dirty look. Mother suggested that Nancy's sister go into the kitchen and make alphabet soup. The sister, they told me, entered three spelling bees and won them all. She was so good she was asked to endorse dictionaries. I watched from the picture window as torrential rain swept the street. First it only covered the gutters. Then it arched over the middle line of the road until lapping at the sidewalks. Nancy sighed and said, "Rats, I suppose this means no picnic." I was about to sigh also, when she had an idea. "It occurred to me that the original picnic was probably held in a cave and called a banquet. Why not a picnic in the house?" she asked, now that the rear of the motionless house was more or less safely bedded in the river's swollen shallow. Nancy's father returned 'flucked' (this means a pucker of disgust with nature's reaction to man's pillaging of its rain-forests). Flucking, Nancy said, is like mentally tripping up at being displeased — father's forehead laden with nervy frown overtones, his lips quivering and eyes rolling. Mother said, "Well, you're only young once..." "Good, it's settled," Nancy said. "Now, you and papa clear out of here." The parents glanced at each other. "We can't leave them in the rain," I suggested. "The basement," she replied. Father made a whining-sound. "They might drown," I hinted. "They could bail," she offered, pacing the living room like a great tiger; then she pounced: "The bathroom!" she exclaimed, pointing down a hall. Her parents, eyes low, traipsed along to the bathroom. As they got to the door, mother reached out and took her husband's hand. They held hands when we last saw them. "Touching," I commented. "Ecck, parents," she responded. "What about your sister?" "I'll just unplug her," Nancy retorted, entering the kitchen. I should mention that Nancy's sister was a rare aggregate of childhood disorders gone berserk, following furious medical interventions. She apparently needed a hearing aid because heart trouble weakened that part of her brain. Nancy said her sister's heart itself was weak from experiments to strengthen it and required a battery-powered pump. For the pump, she carried a purse slung over her shoulder. Sometimes in damp weather, the motion-battery corroded and then the emergency cord, which protruded from her left thigh pocket, could be plugged in when the batteries needed charging. Her right calf and foot were metal. Twice, during electrical storms, she said the artificial half-leg sent sparks up the ground wire to her purse and damaged the batteries. Nancy returned from the kitchen. "Ecck, sisters — I never know whether she's AC or DC. Poor dear, she's got so many problems and I am angry with myself for being harsh. So, I'm thankful to her in that respect because she helps me develop a better outlook on life. Sit with me on the couch." We sat on the couch, in silence. The rain slashed harder now and once when I looked out the window a red canoe was tied to a Massey Ferguson tractor.

Then, the picnic. Nancy brought a picnic basket into the living room. She dumped it on the rug and sorted two piles. Pepper and dark meat were in a pile with the paper plates. Light meat and salt were in the other pile. Eventually, two trucks arrived with equipment to shore up the back of the house, and we were rescued.

The second girl I dated was an intellectual. We met in the library and listened to music in a record cubicle. We heard Beethoven's Ninth Symphony. The composer's great black hair splashed over the grooves. His thick arms flashed on the wall like sky shadows. Outside, thunder boomed with the music. "Your misperceptions killed it!" she shouted. "Anybody could believe one or two of those things," she ranted on, although I'd not said anything noteworthy, "but not all of them at once. You can't distinguish things beyond your own vision. Or the things you can see have no bearing on reality-adjustment; you're bloody autistic!! You're too much," she sighed and turned in the cubicle, engineering a tearful parting scene. As she moved around again she stopped crying and said, "I can do better. You're nice, still unquestioning, just how you are. You could get money if you wanted, some day. You're more or less a potential leader, if anyone can lead in these heartless times when minds and bodies warp under the weight of sweet tastes and sleaze. But you don't fathom enough of the real things yet, apart from your boy-notions. You see what's outside of yourself but not seeing it through yourself, even when we're lying together, even during...right at the urge to violate each other's privacy, we pull away like a couple of unmatched animals, not like a huge glorious bird with sheets flapping climatically on its wings. You don't appreciate music. You're repulsive. No, it's not the way it should have been. Goodbye, goodbye, Paul." She jammed her palm into my chest and pushed open the door. Then she stopped, turned and shut the door again. "Neil is different. He's considerate at least," she said, with an emphasis that sounded like fault and blame. "Not a very striking figure. He'd never inflame a crowd to a peak of social passion. He gets fraught easily and is touchy and averse to a bed session. The wrong word, wrong inflection afterward, can set him stammering and enraged. He needs to be babied. There is no other way about it." Her cheeks were full and flush from words that she wouldn't release. Yes, she had to be careful with Neil. He did appreciate music, and she sexed him to the point of an epiphany. He told me how he met her in a park: her brown legs with white whiskers, next to the blue enamel of her bicycle fender — thighs showing soft as custard and her funny unruffled pubic point was all too apparent. These were the times

when we learned that emotions are painful. Once she penetrated his queer defenses and calmed his little-boy-about-sex,
she slid into a musical current with him: drifting, soaring,
thundering or skipping musical with him, although their
bodily instruments were absorbing obstacles. Yes, there were
always men around her — well, older boys. That was the way it
appeared and that was the way she wanted to think of it. My
childish belly and potentially manly shoulders were with her
now. "Music has always been people to you, hasn't it?" I asked.
"I can tell by the way you listen; you don't hear it. It's as if you
answer it. Your music exercises its own will. You haven't got an
impediment. You don't play; you merely release the music; that
is your gift." She smiled and revealed her waist. Chilly air from
the vent of her blouse sent several drafts across her skin, and
mine. At this point, I didn't want her to return to Neil. I imagined the outcome when she went, crying, to him, reporting
that she wished to be pregnant. He would cry and thrash in
bed, then leave, running away: California, Mexico, someplace
west, looking for a mother waiting to marry him.

The record cubicle darkened; the sun set behind the rain,
turning off the pink sky light. She gazed at a window without
reflections. She touched the walls of the cubicle with a finger
which lingered, like a kiss, at the corners. A plaintive melan-
choly verse to her music is in order — dedicated to her love for
musicians, reminiscent of a shepherd-boy-at-sunset verse. It
gained force, as simple urges will do. Her music washed against
and swayed me with its weight, growing to a larger sparkling
cloud which engulfed and swirled around me, roaring down,
dashing me, and its splintered pieces tore my face and set my

mouth in a picaresque expression as the music gathered up its weight and thundered, swamping, carrying me in its dark folds, hanging me suspended by and floating in its motionless currents.

The third girl I dated had desire alright. She did not pick her nose. Or cuss. Or smoke. Or booze, or anything else that would annoy anyone. She just had this desire. The desire did not show much in public. It was obvious in private. Especially when I was in private with her. I didn't notice it right away. She was very reserved and dressed in simple frocks. I attributed the desire to her withdrawal — a kind of reverse grasping in the face of an impending, and possibly harrowing, attachment. She concealed the desire in strange ways. Even diabolical. Diabolicalism is supposed to be uncharacteristic of shyness. I did know a reserved fellow — not Neil — who was diabolical. He liked to pull the tails of cats. He thought that pulling a cat's tail helped its predatory movements. So this fellow was called diabolical. More to the point, he was ignorant of the cat's gentle and genuine affection for human beings. His stupidity was in being absorbed in the diabolical.

Anyway, my first notice of her desire came the first time that she touched me — our fifth date. That fifth date with her occurred on one of those inhumanly cold winter nights: the solid cold earth, as in Siberia, but she was comfy. We walked among boxcars on a rusty railroad track. I half expected the parallel tracks to reach the moon, which broke out in shivers that reached the marrow of bones. We warmed to that illusion. She wanted to climb a Soo Line boxcar, which hung over another set of tracks. I said okay, as far as I was concerned. On the way down, she noticed a bull engine chug toward her and then treble its speed. She screamed and I leapt to the rescue, pulling her from danger, round the end of the boxcar. She looked at me and screamed. An engine 15 yards or so away tooted its whistle twice. The engineer waved. She jumped in front of the thing. I hollered: "You're about to be killed," or words to that effect. She turned away from the engine's path and gave me a look cloaked in abstinence, with an anti-boy gaze of utter celibacy. This was my first notice of uprooting desire — my interpretation of her reaction to me. I ventured a kiss in the middle of date nine. She fainted in my arms. I opened her left eye to discover whether she died or just passed-out. She drew a tear-gas device in the shape of a pen and said, "Unmob me, you handster!" I reckoned this to be a new game and unmobbed her. She fell to the ground and cried. This wasn't my first notice of the tear-gas device/pen. She always wore this item in a prominent, easy-to-reach (for her) place. I realized the device/pen held significance for her when we swam one night. She put the thing on her bathing suit. I felt my own urge looked after — that she wore a bathing suit at all, so I wasn't fussed about the extra apparel. I knew something was wrong on the night we swam. She oiled her bathing suit belt, for six minutes. I treated this as a come-on joke to prevent embarrassment. Once, in a spirit of good fellowship, I called her Miss Pittsburgh. She said I was immature but to stay that way. This girl I dated was an inspired player of chastity poker. Once when we played, I commented that I was grateful for my 'night with shining amour.' She replied, if my notes are correct, "Keep roundtable, or it'll be Le Morte d'Arthur." I told her my

middle name was Archibald, but can't remember why. She confused it with Arthur, a bad experience with someone named
Arthur. When I brought the subject of being intimate with her,
she wept silently. Tear blobs landed on her white taffeta blouse
and beaded at the tip of her tear-gas device/pen. She stared
with grave, fluid eyes. I felt an awful bore. She said, "That's
the way the cookie crumbles, bub." I offered to her and her
escort, an unmuzzled German Shepherd dog, that we could
safely penetrate our bodily impulse for sex by wearing a tender
approach to each other on our sleeves, like an ornament. We
forgave each other our obstacle about sex, tried to overlook it,
comforting each other, save for the precautionary hands-off
policy. At her house, when I was affectionate, at one point her
mother cuffed me with her whip. Mother was stiff-legged, and
I cringed at her curly-lipped suffering, moving as though the
legs were connected to her trunk by differential gears: a regal
march-move, following psychiatric treatment. I respected her
mother as all mothers, for at least she was a mother, fond of
testing the integrity of my intentions. She often appeared nude
behind her daughter, making seductive gestures, which made
me wonder that it wasn't just nature going crazy from exploita-
tion. The wisest course of action here was to treat mother like
any lady of standing who appeared nude before her daughter
and a caller. I invited mother to have tea with us, speaking
confidently, and unwhipped, expecting a refusal, but the
times when mother accepted were testing. Especially for her:
her monocle was affined to fall into our tea when she poured.
When this happened we all laughed red-faced until a servant
(also nude) came to fetch the monocle. The servant poured my

tea through a gilded-handle flour strainer. Virginia (the girl I dated changed her name to Virginia on her 13th birthday) never spoke of her father. Perhaps he escaped. Or fell victim to mother's cyanide-gas device/pen. Possibly, one of the potato-bagged carcasses they showed me belonged to Virginia's father. Belonged to him until, as Virginia put it, "We collected the deposit on him." Virginia probably inherited this mumbo-jumbo way of being with her mother, as she did the device/pen, or, like me, resisted bizarre habits which we're unaccustomed to. Virginia told me that she once watched her mother perform chastity rites with the goats in an empty old greenhouse. Ever since, Virginia said, she wanted to be like mother and made every effort to treat animals kindly like humans. She even performed chastity rites with a junior gardener, according to mother. That was her first try. She botched it. The gardener was really ruptured for overstepping the mark. The romance between me and Virginia blossomed sedately. Finally, I noticed she relaxed having me around. In fact, she seemed to enjoy my presence. At first I was pleased. Virginia returned my affections. She permitted me intimate liberties that she learned from the dog, namely petting, which were calming in a chaotic world. She was ecstatic when I licked her ears; however, she had pulled desire from its roots and spat it out. The last few times I visited Virginia, she coated her ears with peppermint as an enticement to test my own roots. This was just before her mother disappeared. Virginia said her mother took an extended trip, which was odd because her mother was never without the monocle. I guess we knew instinctively that it takes being the opposite of brutal to recognize innocence and beauty in another person and that Virginia's mother also fought to keep hold of herself. My intention in going over it is that I appreciate the lonely struggle to preserve our youthful innocence, that it often becomes cockeyed.

I was reassured about reuniting with my first passion —Nancy. Her fair auburn hair was lit by moon fire which reflected through her head and sea green eyes, her amber soul boldly absorbing and then penetrating space and time. Ambling toward the refrigerator for potato salad, her body moved with the fury of a barnyard's dew. She returned to her book, to the gently calling bed. I rose with lionic haste to shut off the television news. Out the window she saw a hostile land of disappointments and worry—its lights dankly yearned for her sweet and soda pop-flavored blood. Night framed land where lost souls clawed her unsullied eyes and plucked at her virginity with greedy hands—hands which pull her down to a coarse conventional life of supply on demand, and vice versa, to destroy her self-preserved holiness. Stars framed night, with music of lecherous vicars' tombstones shrieking in her unpunctured ears and piercing her brain from their core. "Night of fallen women," she exhorted, "come to me and be my brother." I smiled, accepting her gaze, clutching her hand. Again at her window, she recognized the thrombotic heart of sin and vice, listened to its secret calls and practiced her unilateral non-yielding. In us, Satan prowled, raving, panting to be released. A gentle gleam rushed headfirst into her eye. I was strangled. My bones echoed in Satan's mouth. I thought that a window burst, inverted. Shouts followed her, descending to the ground, lowering herself by her pure and untouched hair.

Inside the wall of her inner being, she felt the first heady wave of sin and danced in her new profanity. (Her away-for-the-night sister mourned, pledging to draw a mark on the wall and make an entry in their roommate's diary.) A wave of decency rose feebly to meet sin waves and was kicked groin-first into the hip pocket of her ethics, where it lay feeding on its own blood and waited for revenge. She danced faster and farther from cloistered walls, from pleading sugar-toned voices with steel in their pink sinews, from the warm spectrum of colors glowing of truth and beauty, toward the green and red-sparkling hilltop, into the silvery sin-gap. Voices glimmered a moment, then our enlarged space restored to untainted genuine pleasure of each other's company. A cold star flickered and with a sigh, also emptied, only to respray its light again. Closer, she ebbed to the end of rejoicing: the hilltop glow. A buzz was the only sound around her as she thrust through Hell fire's dark velvet brambles in the direction of light. Treading on infinity, she swam gaily to sinless sparkle, towing her petulant goodness by its puerile heel and zealously fervoring her way to conquer sin's peak. (Far in the flooded past, her relatives and ex-fellow saints mourned triumphantly, renewed by her quest and set strong in their ways by her fate, praying for her to the divine mathematician that she will revive the orbit of decency, restored on the throne and given another chance.) Heartily declining, she plunged on gleefully. Homeward. "Where there is life, there is more than desire," she chanted as her eyes threw out more moon flames between the twitchy, half open lids. Flames of rebirth and anticipation foamed hot behind the slits in our heads. Nearing the top she paused for a moment of regret, as was her custom. Then she dashed the last few yards at the light. Red-green flickers grew, illuminating faintly abrupt shrubbery and swirling leaves. Roaring close to the light, her saintly steps echoed on ground cleaned of sin. She fell on her knees to embrace the leap of faith with me, daring its evil height to floor us, to purge all morals from our spotty souls, allowing its light to shatter and remake us even stronger in its own sinless image and irretrievably purify the stains of all our mothers. She opened her eyes to purr, seeing the luminous source and heart for the whole of triumph. Groaning ecstatically, she recognized the reflection of a streetlamp in a wet dog's eye, and moaned, "For all our mothers."

She was undistractable. I told her that she was a moulded honor type student and she was entitled to one fling to bulldoze desire. Therefore, she could accept punishment and go back to her cage, rehabilitated. "You could leave me with a parcel," she pouted. "A tiny intellectual, beating down inside me, dark in my belly. A canker, eating away my youth. A rapacious parasite." "You are the image of propriety," I suggested, although she was quite at me: "You parrot. You're the first in your class to remember the prescript response and the last to forget it — or let anybody know you haven't forgotten it. You are fortunate. There's never a doubt, yet. You either have the correct explanation or you don't. When the issue is clouded by debate, you wait until a proper finding is reached. At this point, you integrate the answer into your being, where it's mixed with all the other causes and conditions in there. You are master of situations with a reasoned solution, for yourself and others. You're the one who can take charge at an automobile accident — the person who gives first aid rather than taking pictures of the scene. You can be masterful and precise. You've read much and are a good talker. Your presence is openly admired. But somewhere inside you a voice says: So what? So what?"

I sat on the bed in lamp's light, gazing at her among wall shadows. She looked out the window at night birds with cryptic messages, runaway automobiles, and poisoned snow. She was not really very experienced. Two men, even young ones, was a lot. It all happened so fast that it probably seemed there were no pre-sex days. Now was the time to think, before complete virginity was lost. On a couch, quiet, she drew up her legs. "The intruder could be watching this instant," she reckoned. "Could have spied during practice, anxious to get in from the cold. Later in the night, I might wake, the creature's eyes stare at me from inside, commanding others to keep a distance. God, if it gets its way...if, shit! You owe me. I'm yours now, but I swear I won't mother you without knowing how, you, you — even if I have to kill myself to avoid it," she screamed. As if kicked from inside, she surveyed her belly — pushed out more than normal, but not the unusual outlines of pregnancy. "I hear a new gurgle sound," she said, speaking to a potential foetus. "So, you're a plumber, too," she said to it. "You're more than a chaperone who drives others away. You're a plumber, too." She expressed the odd sensation of returning to her mother's childhood home, observing alien workmen remodel it for strangers.

Next day, we started. "No, I absolutely will not do it," the doctor said. "It's against the law, repulsive to me, and it wouldn't really do any good." The nurse — white uniform, face, veins, hair — entered the lecture passing across her face in frowns. "No, miss, you should have thought of the consequences before you started to flirt with boys you hardly knew," he muttered, completely ignoring me. "My task is to heal, reduce symptoms, to give life not destroy it. I could go to jail...Do you realize I could be jailed for what you're advocating? Jail!" Degrees hung in one line on the office wall: sheep skins jumping over conversations to induce the right decisions. "No, I've about had it. You girls go soft the first time you set eyes on the moon." Then he looked at me, mixing contempt with envy. "Then you come running to me to get you out of it. I don't care what the consequences are. You should have thought of them beforehand. Now you'd better vamoose before I call the police."

The minister was more courteous. "Of course I understand your predicament. And if it's any comfort to you, my dears, let me tell you this is not nearly as uncommon as you may suppose. But I'm afraid the only thing I can suggest is marriage." "Pardon me, reverend, but are you proposing?" she asked icily. "I hardly think this is a moment for sarcasm on your part, miss." "Well, he's against inventions. He's a poet." she said, referring to me. "I was about to suggest," he intoned, "that institutions of the church, while they're not designed to be bent to order for illicit pregnancies, can, when evidence of repentance is present, allow for certain moral...incongruities. I mean, if you were in love with this...young man, and if he felt the same, why of course we could accommodate you in a discreet manner." "But I told you, he's a poet. He'd feed it abstract nouns and revolutionary fervor. You wouldn't have this helpless babe fall into his hands, would you?" "Well, I hardly think that would be worse than what you suggested," he said. "I've not chosen a child; I want a career to receive my best shot." "No, there is no way. I'm afraid you'll just have to face the facts and make the best of them." "But they aren't the necessary facts, don't you see? It doesn't have to be this way. It's your arbitrary attitude that makes births necessary. You're as much a father to this creature as he is. When the plumber comes forth you'll condemn him for being born and tell him he's not as good as some prissy little prude who happened to find herself a dull man before her time ran out." "Well, I don't think your last remark was called for. I have four creatures of my own — I mean children," he said, wiping his judicious lips with a handkerchief. "In fact, it's not even doing any good to talk with you," he rushed on, "you'll just have to consider these things and pray for Almighty guidance. Now, if you'll join me, I'll offer up a prayer. Then I have some stencils to cut..." We left, thinking what interchangeable people they are — the doctor and the minister — moral cogs. They fit together perfectly, turn in the same direction. No wonder they have other people's children so easily.

Had it happened, her mother would be hysterical. Father angry, from his point of view, and betrayed. They would bear the cross well, never mentioning her to their relations, keeping the cross in their garage, between the station wagon and the compact car. Father would send money and long letters. Mother would pray. "I want to work on my geometry now," she said to me. "Yes," I responded, rising from the bed and putting down my book. "Paul, no worries, what is behind us can't be complete, because fragments will fit together in the future. If we've been cheated, I'm not bitter; others have been cheated worse." "Thanks. I am disappointed but not with you."

When we found out that she wasn't pregnant, I clutched at being responsible over my earlier remorse, angst, or fastidiousness, and unable to grasp a way out, so I climbed onto the closet footlocker in my room, bathrobe belt tied to the top door hinge and my neck, kicked away and hung myself. I woke lying on the floor, head throbbing, and tongue numb, and the big toe of my right foot was bleeding. An hour later I threw up. My tongue was numb all week.

Nancy and I parted, vowing to stay constant, puzzling about self-discovery, necessary for inspiration and formatting a view for the poetry of every day. She was sure that if I traveled and found momentous moments, my writing would become a less feeble art, although at risk of becoming a feebler person. "Watch out that the past and present and future don't separate, otherwise you'll be in fragments," she warned. Yes, better to be neither one place nor another. She taught me to think beyond just myself, even if that overrides my ability to write, and I become less sticky in the head and indulgent. It happens, this barfing complacency, when the circumstances to be absorbed in absolute desire appear unuseful and overwhelming. It was with this awareness that I tried to commit suicide. I was greatly relieved to tell this to Nancy and have her hand on my forehead, and content that we leave prospective plumbers to their own accord.

Roommates: A Special Breed

Neil and I grew and ventured outbound during our younger years, at the dormant airport in our town, playing around in the cockpits of biplane carcasses, growing and toying as the school years passed in a haze of teaching. Then, at college, we discovered that ordinary people, like us, can be just that for all of life. Unless, that is, they are somebody's roommate. Roommates are a special breed. Usually, being a roommate stirs a person's humanity. There are lots of roommates who are, in varying degrees, more than ordinarily human. Neil is among them. He lived in another dormitory. He took college life more seriously and moved in higher academic circles than me. He was extraordinary. Academic circles struck me as aloof and pretentious, at least during my first two years, before we began to understand each other. My roommates were Myron of Iowa, Richard Z, Clayton the mad Bolshevik, and Harold of Chosen Valley.

The names are unchanged to protect the innocent. We became less innocent, and no other names will fit them. "We could hang it here," said James of Iowa. He pointed to a spot of bare wall between Clayton's Russian flag and my poster, which read: MILITARISM IS FOR MILITS! I nodded. Clay went on studying. He was not speaking to Myron anymore. Clay was not speaking to Harold anymore, either. I was the only person on the whole floor of the dormitory that Clay spoke to and that was in Russian. Although his words were Greek to me, my listening seemed appealing to him. So I just said "Dyah" when he spoke to me. Myron tried to hang his print of Picasso's Girl Looking at a Mirror. At first there was opposition. So we decided to sit and have a sensible discussion about it. I liked our sensible discussions; they were fun. Whenever Myron wanted something we had a sensible discussion. Most of the time, they ended up with Harold, and a friend from the dorm, enjoying a water fight in the lounge, Clay playing wildly on a mandolin, Myron doing what he wanted and me talking to myself or Richard. The painting was an abstract. Harold didn't like it. So he said, "Well, I believe that if God had wanted us to look thataway he would of made us to look thataway." Myron, an art major, got worked up and butted in: "How do you know he didn't?" "Whadda you mean? You think I look thataway?" said Harold, raising his voice. Harold was not just sensitive about his complexion and his appearance.

"Well, I suppose you're one of those fundamentalist hustlers," said Myron, "who we're supposed to nurture because they've been torn asunder, poor creatures."

"Yeah, Harold, I mean Christ, floutin' the name of your hometown, I mean like Chosen Valley, gives a certain impression and then invoking the name of God 'n' all," Richard pontificated. "It's all pervading nihilistic materialism; its anti-Christ, really, all western society is taught that spiritless things matter most and that mind is only brain."

"They've outdistanced us in the real Thine," Myron shouted, "*That's* why we hate them! They'll rush into a lion's mouth in one gulp — man, woman and child. They do things with flair: family amusement makes their bones crunch at will; they can spew their intensities on the circus floor. In fact, they do it for practice in churches, don't they, *Harold*."

"I'll give you one thing, buddy," Harold said in a way which made it clear he hooked us into something he was in control of, "Fundamentalists have the glee. They believe in the nicest secrets of style most people lack and may never possess — even through lawmaking."

Clay rolled his eyes and Myron looked as though he could hardly believe his ears.

"You mean to tell me," Richard Z blurted in, "that we spent all this time and came all this way toward our last, final, ultra (boom-boom) bone-sundering, body-ripping end, and you're saying — alleging — we got the trigger but no glee?!"

"Yes, that's right," Harold said, "that's why we're still here: the glee is mishandled."

"If everyone has the requisite glee units to be applied to others," I offered soberly, "how has the formula for self-glee been bungled?"

Harold: "We can't conquer or admit that the earth must be cherished or worshipped," he said amid a crescendo of disbelieving howls, "for man, *times* are moments of longing for wealth!"

Myron: "We only have half the formula — the yes half but not the wow!" There was a silence, with looks of astonishment. "And we'll never get anywhere without the wow. Okay, we're trying, but it's a delicate matter of timing. We've got to catch the glee, match it to each person, pull the switch and go over the edge."

"But what if," Richard Z interrupted, "the switch is pulled

before we get the glee. Then, except for exercise, the whole damn thing is wasted, or boring. How 'bout that?"

"Yeah, how 'bout that?" I intoned. "It's not a dilemma of new morals or reshaping an old style to fit now — is it, *Harold*," I insisted, because he was yawning and we were actually friends, all of us. "It's a case of man getting his just desserts. Gleefully, despite western cultures' authoritarian social structures and corrupt rulers."

"That's right," Harold snapped. "Man's a spoiler. He ruins things, polluting earth, air, sea and even outer space. Even Clayton agrees that. He kills his children, parents, chums and lovers. Kills helpless animals. Abuses them. He breeds and suffocates and breeds again. Lord knows, man deserves what he wants but then wants better than that because he's duped into spoiling for it."

"Yeah, he's earned that end and now he's built it and voted to buy it or accept it," Richard said. "He's got giant banners saying THE END in 47 languages ready to stream across the sky and music pre-recorded to play after the big blow up."

"Man has, in all his national subspecies, justified the end to himself, his family, pious religious leaders and most important," Richard said, pausing to stress a point, "his historians. He has done this with an eye to himself."

Myron stood, taking a stance to pipe down the mutterings of others: "No, he is being cheated! Every day is waste, lessening the magnitude of new appetites. Each day chips off a piece of his greatness. But if man tries to prove glee with tangible evidence, the end will be a loud, wasted exercise. For although he has enough strength to succeed, he doesn't have the authority, the glee. Life is a thing of pure glee! Look at Picasso's Girl, she's reflecting his wish that all of us buck against all the imitators and emulators who will try to re-fit us into the machinery of industrial life. Anyway, you can't destroy the earth and eliminate a species without losing glee," he pleaded, crying. "It would only be another technological fact. And, man deserves more — the accomplishment of glee: the effects of perpetual curiosity in a way that causes him to realize a life beyond himself."

Myron looked defeated and stood down from the chair, which Clay had taken from the counselor's room, after he fell out the window. Myron turned to me and said hopefully and humbly, "Paul, do you think I look like a fool?" "You're appealing to a higher reason than me, but I really don't think whether you're a fool or not is the point."

"Well, I do," he returned sharply. "I think there are some very valid spiritual points here. And I don't think that just because you're a Communist that we can't be buddies," Myron said almost contritely, which meant he disagreed with me. In the first semester at college, he decided I was a Communist. First, I offered to be a Marxist, as he said must be the case because I painted the shower room orange, which he thought was a Marxist color. This was an offer to instigate his changeable views back from the brink of extinction. But, apparently, no. I even offered to be a socialist-pacifist. Myron stuck to his guns, convinced that I was a Communist. We eventually agreed a compromise. Since there was no question about my loyalties to the Communist Party, and the others wanted to be friends for the remainder of the college year, and as long as I held no

Party cell meetings in the room, whatever color I painted else-where, we decided the best thing to do was to forgive me and hope, with proper care, I could be cured. It was with this atti-tude that Myron and I proceeded to be mates. If there was any uncertainty at all, it vanished on the day Harold decided I was a Communist. He was sitting in the lounge watching Superman on television when I entered — Superman on top of infinity with his cape flared and trumpets blaring, a flag flapped in the antagonist background. As the camera zoomed-in you could see its Stars and Stripes and hear a stalwart voice saying, "Through Justice and the American Way." Harold looked flabbergasted at our laughing, as though part of him had just died. He couldn't even provoke a water fight because the water was turned off; at the end of our building an emergency evac-uation was underway due to pipe-bursting feces and garbage. This depressed Harold further. Also, he had a Communist roommate now, according to Myron, and another roommate who spoke Russian and was probably a Red. Harold always tried to be liberal, but it didn't pay that day. Meantime, Myron positioned his picture between his Russian flag and the poster. Truth, Justice and the American Way receded another inch into the dark ages of tyranny, totalitarianism, corruption, and finks. Clay's main regret was that he wasn't born a Bol-shevik. He seemed to try every way, but it felt useless. "Some people possessed the qualities for revolt and others comfort themselves as die-hard middle-of-the-roaders, ready for tribal patriotism," Clay mused. He sat back and looked up from an ed-psych book as though dreaming of the day he will lead a rev-olution in college. It was the way the day started which led to his reflections then. For Clay said, "God, do I hate bland days. They're so neutral. So useless. I'd prefer a blizzard to a bland day." Since this was early October, he received a few unfavorable glances. Particularly as Homecoming was the following week. Homecoming is a uniquely collegiate and jockstrap flapping extravaganza with cheerleaders jumping on dreams and a lot of forward passes. I guess that Clay realized every unfavorable glance and each acid stare brought him closer to his goal of total non-equanimity. Clay was really rebellious when he faded like this, and when he told us it was most interesting. During his first year fade, he was expelled from college. He wrote a short piece for the social page of the local town newspaper, complimenting faculty. Each short paragraph began with the letters F-U-C-K Y-O-U. He was expelled before he fully faded. Clay was reported to have no money and slept in heavenly peace during the winter, when his hands were too numb to open doors and he half-starved. Other reports said he wandered throughout the Upper Midwest, where he half-died from exposure. As there was a general lack of food, Clay was repressed from consciousness by those who resumed their bland routine of belief in the hollow clichés of the dime store morality which they inherited and he hated. Richard Z put it this way: "Here is the process. Your life is history before you've lived it. You find that you come and go, live and die, with no regard to the continuity of physical aging, which once governed. Instead you are dehumanized and what you rediscover afterwards is that what you call yourself in another form is different from the current me."

Then one day just before the spring semester, a door opened,

Clay walked up a stairway into the lounge of the dorm, where he was warmly welcomed. The protest was over. He remembered how he had been studying. "My sociology book is riddled with capitalist myths about the benefits of retail therapy and government propaganda about the destructive improvements in war weapons. It was conceived in the United States, written here, printed, sold and read worldwide. How could it be anything but Americana?" The global implications made him sick. "You make me barf, America," Clay said. "We live off the starving misfortunes of people in a corrupt Third World." Richard Z, who was learning how to be a librarian, heard the sound but no words and frowned at him. One of Nancy's roommates, who came over to our dorm to teach Richard, giggled. "You laugh! You laugh at me?" he demanded, then lowered his voice to a whisper. "You're so cute," she said, probably wanting to get it all over with as quickly as possible, on Clay's behalf, as if he really couldn't be expected to think for himself in the presence of a cheerleader. "Cu — *cute*? I'm a Bolshevik!" he said proudly. People started to stare. "I think that's so cute. What's a Bolshevik?" Clay put his hand to his face. "How can you not be familiar with what a Bolshevik is?" The girl shook her head with a cautionary expression, saying, "I don't know what *you* think a Bolshevik is." Her eyes beckoned to all the frustrated rebel and foolish man in Clay, who mistakenly took her expression for meekness. There was no question; he found her attractive, and on closer scrutiny, womanly, even if she was either inexcusably bright or stronger than him. His duty was to fight for control — that was clear. "A Bolshevik is a Revolutionist of the highest order. I want to overthrow the U.S. Government — preferably by force." He watched her awed reaction, but was glaring at the cynical expressions on the pretending-not-to-pay-attention faces of Myron and Richard. Harold went to the bathroom. "Probably by force," he continued. I want to set up a new social order in which all people will be truly equal and free and not capitalist lackeys." She was persistently in-awe, with no visible sign of aversion. "I want to overthrow the church…" he warned and then paused. "Gol," she sighed. "I want to abolish free enterprise." "Gol — I don't like it when they do things with cancer on mice and male-things," she added, helpfully. "Anti-vivisectionist? I am in favor of total vivisection — on human beings, with their toxic greed," he put in, with a flourish. Her stunned reaction filled his flailing arms. "Well," she said with a pinched brow, "I guess mice are no more important than men anyway." Clay seemed amazed by her rampant lateral way. This person was educable. With proper instruction, she could be educated out of the capitalist egomaniacal mire she was raised in. It might be possible. "Have you ever read any Hegel?" he asked. "No, you?" Then a desire for more specificity or less fight seized her and she said, "Huh uh", and shook her head. "Marx? Engels?" Negative nods. "But I'll bet I'd like them. I've heard about Marx — that he was a bad one." Clay sighed. Still, there was a chance. "I have a book here — don't let the CIA Gestapo catch you with it. Read it tonight if you'd like, and when next we meet," he added, very offering in his manner, "we can discuss it." He passed the book under the table and she accepted it. When she grabbed his knee and said, "Oh, hunky book," he quickly flustered. "No, it's in the other hand!" She blushed and said, "Oh," and we all burst out laughing. That was the start of it all.

Two days later Clay saw her again on the front steps of the library. "Hi," she said. He didn't recognize her immediately, although Myron and I were talking to her about a women's group she was forming on campus. Also, she dyed her hair gold and he claimed that it was obscured in the sun because it sparkled. "Well, did you read the book?" he asked. "Well — sort of... what are you going to do now?" "I have some myths to explore." "Greek?" Clay sighed, shook his head and started to turn away. "Why don't we study together," she suggested, "you might learn something." "Why not," he said, going into the library quickly ahead of her, and her following contentedly. From then on Clay had a pupil and the pupil had control. She intrigued us all. Myron said that her wisdom did not lie in intelligence of scholarly fields. "She displays a rare gift by knowing all of Clay's movements, probably everyone's, as if motion exists not as an entity but in relation to all our bodies at the same times. It's uncanny and he's obviously perplexed," Myron surmised. "You are inferring the data," challenged Richard Z, who was furious about her infatuation with Clay. "You'd be well advised to describe your observations and listen rather than behave like a medical student." "Anyway," I said, trying to come between the arguments, "he's pretending to take her for granted as the only possible way of changing himself, without fading. They're eager for each other but stuck in between his lectures and her arousing the latent free rebel in both of them."

"Clay, it's not that I don't comprehend your politics," she said to him when we were all under the willows one day. "I don't comprehend why they have to kill mice, anyway," she said defiantly. "Clay mentioned you missing half the formula, the wow. Nancy and I discussed it; the glee is mishandled because you're not realizing that the trigger for the other half is in the hands of those in need, who we help."

"The two of you inherited too much social conscience," Richard Z intoned, cueing me and Myron. I launched a not-to-smart, hollow and unheard monologue on capitalist tricks, maneuvers, spiritual materialism, and myths. "Yes, but I mean *really* why do they do it?" Myron pleaded, mimicking her voice. "Oh Jones..." I moaned. "Why do you always call her by her last name?" Harold whined, as we ignored the couple — still unsure what was happening. "We aim to embroider the Communist Manifesto," I announced, using gestures like Clayton's, "and make it applicable to modern life. We have this theory that surnames are part of the government's plotting and should be replaced with numbers. But since I have a lousy head for figures I can't remember the combination of numbers I've given her," I said, looking at Myron. "So," Harold pronounced, "*that's* why you called her by her surname, Jones!" "We worked out this system whereby everyone in the country will be renamed, by numbers with no two first combinations. Myron can be the last number," I said modestly. "And the identity of number one?" Clay queried. "Not for publication," snapped Harold.

"But me with my poor brain, oh, and she with the combination unshared," Clay narrated. Three days after the embroidery of communism was hatched, we stood in the ankle-deep maple leaves beside her dormitory wall. Jones was on the third floor, shedding a tear. "What's the matter?" Clay asked. "Why didn't you come to the river so I could tell you about Gus Hall?" "I won't talk to him. I won't even look at him," Myron said to an imaginary roommate. "Gus who?" said Harold, being the roommate. "The communists sent him over to start something, I think," Myron assumed. "He's kind of cute. I'll talk to him for you." "Not to worry," Myron said, wishing Jones' eyes dry. "I'll talk to him myself. I'll just open a window and see if he's still around. *What?* Where are we?" "A small cordon of guys from football practice gathered round us," I shouted. "Yeah, where are we?" Harold screamed, being one of the footballers, to the bemusement of Clayton, who now stood by good-naturedly, full of mischief at this demonstration of team spirit. "Listen, listen," Myron called to me, "please telephone me and we'll discuss it." "Hey, buddy, don't let her give you the run-round," Harold hollered. "Are you trying to give me the run-around?" Clay cried out, craning up at the vacant dormitory window. "I don't think we should talk about it with all those people here," Myron declared, using admirable sense. "Well, I want to talk about it now. And here, also." "Clay, please..." Myron pleaded. Harold giggled, in deference to roommate loyalty. "Jones — why weren't you at the river?" Clay demanded. "I *can't* talk about it and I'm shutting the window." "Jones come down here. Jones!"

I'm unsure of the definite point when Jones became a battle cry. But soon, a considerable crowd, led by the football team and approved by their coach, stood under Jones' room chanting: "We want Jones, we want Jones," Harold chanted, too. Feeling peripheral, I back-stepped a moment, thinking that dispersal was the better part of what Jones meant by inviting the wow to join the glee. Am I never to meet her again, lost to me in her equal affection for everyone? "It's funny the way you transfer yourself like this — you become so much of somebody, absorbed in them, that when they graduate, you find they've taken your experience of yourself, that you shared, with them, and grateful that they'd given you theirs." "And you are disintegrated when you aren't," Harold added, "bits of you all over the shared space. If you transfer yourself like this; you're so vulnerable that when it shows just how much, they take away and gather in this circle like a football huddle to switch-on again," he rambled, gathering us together, with arms interlinking, circling in the huddle. Then we ran off in our directions, laughing, as if a game was finished.

A Quest for Meaning: Pot

The taste is awful: bitter, acrid, stinging the eyes and burning the throat. However, pot is less harmful than non-filter cigarettes, certainly less damaging than cigars, or the phallic mini-stogie which glamorous celebrities inhale on public occasions.

Whether pot allows us courage to think differently is an open question. My personal view is that it's part of a search for meaning at college, growing up in a world that we don't understand. What accompanies this new condition? The initial loss of reasoning that comes with pot eventually opens up the world with a fresh pair of eyes.

We smoked pot dozens of times. None of us were addicted. Our spinal columns and nervous systems were in excellent condition. We pumped twenty push-ups a day and ran five and a half miles, on occasion, without becoming exhausted. We didn't rape young people or rob shops to steal money for a habit we didn't have. Myron grew pot right in the dormitory garden. Our room was not the only one. We knew seven other rooms which made discreet use of the stuff in our dorm. Admittedly, our brand was not as good as the best brandywine from Mexico and Southern California.

We asked each other to expostulate on what pot was like, for the benefit of any interested parties, including those working in education, should they seek to enquire. We hoped the college senate might legislate for its free use — a right to pot — and that the rest of higher education follows suit, and then local, county, state and eventually the national Congress. Also, we wanted to clear up a misconception, carefully nurtured by the FBI and other official groups who stampede the stereotyped view.

"Pot is no more harmful than any other tobacco," Myron expostulated, standing on his bed during a practice session. "It does not lead to addiction with heroin or other drugs. In my years of using pot, nobody I'm aware of became hooked on it, or on heroin. The two are different. Different types of people use them. Pot, for example, stimulates activity: dancing, running, playing and especially sex. Heroin gets people high, but leaves them relatively motionless. Pot is for kicks. Heroin is a way of life."

When we first took pot at college, I half expected to become hooked overnight. Myron enticed me to try it. A trusted friend is more precious than a rare commodity. We were so curious that we risked addiction to try pot. I was high for about four hours on two joints (reefers, the size of a cigarette), and high for another day on the memory of how much fun it had been. We sat round in the otherwise abandoned dormitory boiler house. A bunch of us, girls and boys — seven gals and five guys, plus a sixth fellow. This sixth, a so-called geek from the college literary magazine, took notes. He was not just chicken (afraid of weed), but was supposed to record events. Okay, nothing happened at first. We sat in a circle and puffed on a joint, passing it to each other. The object was to inhale as much as possible, until your eyes felt like popping out and your throat begins to smoulder. I watched others get high, becoming increasingly freer than usual from being fixed on what was directly in front of them, rather a kind of wider viewing. Nancy cried a bit. Neil smiled and laughed. Then he curled up into a foetal position, stuck his hands in his armpits and appeared to sleep! Richard Z stood and clucked like a duck, laughing wildly. Slowly, we became convinced that one or other of us faked being stoned, and they mocked us. I took another drag, felt none of the effects, and guessed that it was all a joke! I jumped to my feet, took a wild unco-ordinated swing at Clay and burst out laughing. Nancy tried to restrain me, although it was unnecessary. The second time, in mid-swing, I realized the drug affected me, but not in the way I anticipated. The pot made me paranoid, made me more self-centered than is comfortable. We knew it. So nobody was worried. Clay pulled me onto a couch and went away.

Then the fun...we were hawks, swooping high and low above a canyon and stream, gliding gently, so serenely, return-ing briefly to the couch and then outside again. Stars spiraled endlessly in the nocturnal sky: the way so august and near they gnawed at each other, bending out gyrations and adding phrases to the originals. Following them, my memory was fuller than sky and whirled for hours with the stars. Cows munched in the night, their old family eyes friendly to the earth. They wandered in shadows as though they were rocks gliding to please our eyes. At the hilltop, comfortable in fresh summer grass, I focused on the stars and said: "Oh yes, there you are." When the Pleiades — a group of seven — came to view and all at once my brain exploded.

Interior areas of my head flickered in response as a railroad semaphore is caused and affected by electric current — the stars spinning and shooting elegant sparks and dinging alarms, smashing, booming like surf in kaleidoscopic patterns: the astral motion split me in pieces and set me to new scores. One problem was the baffle-noise that lit pin holes in my head, which corresponded to the stars. The pitch grew so powerful with the fury and iridescence of constellations that I lost my awareness of where I actually was, then babbling, my tongue and jaw bobbing in stuttering waves of sound. The night show of star arrows began late.

It was set off by the magnificent dignity of Draco's Tail, growing visible with a rush. Wind fell around the dragon. Night sounds stopped. The tail swung with ease in a preparatory arc. Then the entire dragon gathered speed. Covering trillions of miles and volumes of light years, it pivoted on the tail and started a steady swing toward me, the huge jaws opening my subconscious. Inside, its throat was a cave, the distance and time of which covered our puny planet's history. Twisting to catch the stellar host head on (it stretched beyond and beyond), tears eased into collapsed eyes. On waking, the monster showed its left side. Legions of stars coveted my view and viewings, hanging sparkly in night's hide. The dragon's beautiful blisters turned me. A new beauty snatched a view. The entire side, which made me dizzy, rotated, as did my mouth with attempts to describe it, slowly, standing: "Pull me toward you." Both mouths moved again. Saliva at first evaded me and then streamed in a flood of tears and spittle onto my chest. Somewhere in my brain a fact cried for escape; my eyes could not be torn from the spectacle.

No filth or brilliance defined the sight. A moment arrived when I tried to look away, to avoid becoming a monster or its opposite, then farted and wet my pants. I passed a chance to bow before the storm, swaying as the hind end of Draco appeared, gurgling, teeth braced against saliva. Outstretched arms, white sweaty hands at the ends, reached to touch the windowless night, which swayed me until, falling in a roll, tumbling off the hill and crashing into creek rocks, I lay bleeding in cool water, snoozing in a peace that must be replicable in the world's daily doings. I'm certain that the clarity of those moments, not about being blank, rather being awake to a level of awareness without the adversarial nonsense of national pride, is also possible without pot.

This purring stream fed a flowered crevice in the earth, when suddenly Richard Z appeared. "I am going to do you a lessoned favor, fella. I'm going to take liberties with you." "Wha..." "I'm going to uproot your pleasures. That means you are here and your stupid formless soap bubble face stands out under your plantation-yard light. Bend over. You are Lenny Strange!" "Wha...?" "Not Lenny Wha or Lenny Ulp or Lenny Huh, but Lenny Strange. Now shut up and come with me. Stand, Lenny." I pry like a furious sage at a car's trunk plate while Richard hacked and jammed a lever under the seam and yanked it back and forth. "There she is!" he declared as the lid sprang open and revealed reels of Hollywood movies along with a small, worn projector which looked toothless in the splotchy noon-shooting of forest light. "Say...hey Richard, what do you mean by liberties? I'm Paul, you recognize me..." "You're no more flesh and blood than I am, boy. You've got to face facts. You can't ignore what you are inside, inventing a basis to evade taking part. Besides, it's unsociable. Now let's go find a hollow tree." So, we go. He skips over imaginary fences as if they're merry-go-rounds decorated with barbs for his lone enjoyment. For me, this is tedious overplay. "You're panting, Lenny. Try to keep up or you'll catch the barbs and crash down on occasion, as if you've never jumped before. Come on, Lenny. Is your nose a foot?" He runs off again, carrying a football and straight-arming all kinds of menacing growls and bushes that cry out for a god-like blow or even a Revere-leg or an eye-blinding plugged nose, eyes fit for coyotes and moonlit rabbits to subdivide and colonize and set in the shadow of raining dawn's old paint horse. "Here!" He stops: the jolt spins confused air around him as he twirls. A few birds he picks up as followers bump into and bounce over each other, landing and scowling and muttering at him. "Here's the place, Lenny, where I'll build movies and teach you to spin our shrine. Here, this small clearing in the wood with a fire scorched tree trunk standing out of the ground like burnt toast with a secret. At night two stars shine through the place during October, making it appear to be a dark gargoyle with electric eyes. Now, my lad, we see movies in daylight." He plunges what can only be a projector, judging from his theatrical mimicry, into a black leather case, then cranks a handle on one side of his case and studies a dial. "Twenty-two minutes. That's alright. This calls for the sage of the Indigo Powell." He rummages through a canvas bag which I carried. "Good of you to supply the film and stuff, Lenny. Or, what the hell. Now we're ready..." he continues, winding film around a spool, "...to get on with the show." He yaps a sharp flicker sound at the tree trunk and on its ridges peoples' faces emerge, based on the contours and heat of a long forgotten fire — based on those trunk parts which have the most water and burned first and fastest — I find myself visualizing the details of his enactment. The faces and bodies play out a scene. A lady who comes from behind the tree steps to our left and winks at us, strolling across the trunk with marvelous balance to the opposite side. Later she returns with a blouse in-hand. "Gosh, that's unimaginable, Richard." "Yeah, it's a good start." She takes off her nightgown. "Paul, uh, Lenny I'm beginning to be volatile. If the scene keeps up at this pace I'll have a root sufficient in size to feed the entire continent of Tasmania. That makes me Tasmanic. Or there-abouts." He drops his pinned up hair and sits in the ashes at the foot of the tree. In our stupor, we inflate with a classy razzmatazz breeze and embrace ferns nearby. A bird flies to the tree top, spying on another person with balance and two masculine, bark faces. A hand appears at the right edge of the screen, clenching its fist and opening, laughing like a Lilly. As rain falls, the lady throws something, peels down her tights and shuffles off with the hand into a grove of trees. Adjusting the projector, Richard says: "It's not trees but a bed, and the hand belongs to a man. That hand and part of a face are releasing their reservations." That task done, the hand caresses a buttock. It's a fine buttock, one which accepts a compliment. A third person enters and the bird flies away. This third is a person without a gender. Third has short hair, same as the lady, wears pants, same as any pants-wearing person, has a necktie, but also a truncheon, which Third reveals to dispel any doubt as to their apparent purpose, swinging it for two full minutes. A baryonic hero in an old opera, the once-upon-a-time Third who is neither this or that, sings with exaggerated gestures and pledges how they will treat the creature that stole their sister and led her into a life of shame. Then, Third pounces on the lady whose garments are covering the ashes, and they roll back and forth to confuse each other and avoid an indecent scene. The bird, at the burnt tree's top again, hops trunk-pecking into the picture. Sometimes the feathered detective pecks at the ash base, other times at enthralling people. Suddenly, a chair flies right through the bird and across the screen. "Johnny Apple-seed would be amazed, Lenny; they are like farmers sowing seed." Preliminaries over, Third yanks hair out of the head, yelling: "Demented." Next shot Third holds all their hair (a toupee and wig) and fingers their faces, smudging pancake makeup. As the faces are cleaned, they are not orangutan's after all. They are people falling on hard times. I laugh but feel cheap, taken in by this gross mindless masquerade.

They thrust each other away. While these two strug-gle, another person runs into shot and demands the return of an abducted sister or be derooted. It's like a dream with rekindled imagination to repeat it, and continuing like rein-carnation. Consoling each other as angels without sex, Third unveils lovely blonde hair and golden shoulders heavy as fallen dew. Richard Z is tripping and I am, too. The people in the movie yell in unison, "Ollllllhhhhhaaaaahahahahahahahaha-hahah..." They are crying with backs arched, balanced by the endless stretch of legs in front with blood bursting from their veins and the screen fills with seductive smiles.

"My, my, Lenny, I'm getting all fuzzy at the edges," Richard observed. "You're evaporating into the ground. You must be gone and ended and over. All because you followed me into a wood, where sheep play and no town brothers ever go, without proper nutriment and the obtainable flat barrels." "Nobody but a fool would believe any of this." "Oh you would. As one of somebody's heroes you're as virulent as the extremists all around us. Except, you're a demon, boy. We're set apart. But you can't dabble in a hero's crime and be free from your torture of everyone in your line of fire." Then there was a cellulose dialect. We were addressed as we lay on aging church grounds, Richard fading into his basic colors, bodily functions reversed. Striking a dramatic pose with his left hand in the sky, Richard's right hand pointed into space, the trees furred with afternoon sun. A voice spoke, celery-chewing, incomprehensible and I was too far gone. We just lay there; faces crusaded into a pond with millions of bathers and few waves: sunning people with songs, shouts and small noises made in a stealthy way, sounding as if they were yanked from within and speechless. They insisted others knew they were near and able to sire noises and to me it was an invention of our minds turned inside out.

My immediate after-thought was of Nancy lying on top of me on the couch. She was talking about a variety show. She had been the announcer, jokester, banjo player, dancer and satirist. I guessed it was her acted out fantasy without my involvement or what? Neil was still in a foetus position, apparently asleep but also busy. The sixth fellow, from the literary magazine, must have become less chicken, for he was driving a pretend race car in slow motion, up and down a road in the dining room. Nancy wanted to sleep but wake up at the same time. The chronicler got forward and attempted to show us his notes. We traced their patterns across the page. The notes became more and more rambley. Although the geek claimed he avoided taking any pot, he was high. He missed the boat. He was too late. Neil was sitting up now; everybody was coming down, getting straight.

I suppose those who feared their god and J. Edgar Hoover would pounce, saying, "Ah ha, if it's not dangerous, how come it made you delusional?" It didn't. We were that way before we took the drug, being used to our comforts and taught in our schools to pledge the flag every day, train for war, then buy and consume, before the next Great Depression, or else suffer consequences or indignities. A nightmare of perverse imaginings in all of us, merely because we wanted to be free of constraints, inhibitions, without pot, reducing our unbalanced worries into a self-radiant stable whole, unobstructed by the need for it.

Harold: Releasing Grapes

The letters which follow were discovered among little-known library volumes at a liberal arts college in the Midwest. Their discovery was made by an unnamed, unnoticed custodian during his unsanctioned coffee break. They came to me in my capacity as editor of *The Student*.

The most noteworthy library news, before this discovery and publication in the student newspaper, was the theft of a 12-foot plaster statue of Abraham Lincoln. The custodian, suspended for theft, liked and admired Harold as much as all of us; he was as puzzled as anyone, for similar reasons, about Harold's involvement in the missing president's statue. We were taken aback at the thought of colluding with his disappearance, without understanding his reasons, if it was Harold, when seen pushing the statue along on a cart.

We found a note under his pillow: "At one level I flee to shun the hasty-pennied anger of quacks who flock at me like light flashes, exposing my private parts," Harold wrote. "At another level I flee to release the Grapes: the contents of a vessel so named because if I call Grapes by a popular name it would be Angers or Fears. But Grapes is sweeter, so I cling to it." This was unusual for Harold. Our concern about him was written across Myron's mystified face. "Why are these Angers and Fears so important in his life right now?" Richard Z asked. "Grapes forbid me to see beneath the bread-like dignity of my fellows," Harold's note went on. "There will always be joys and sorrows," I offered, trying to think how to discuss doubt and anger. "Grapes is established by theft. It's repeatedly put in motion by stealing. I can't remember how it started. I believe it wasn't a mistake or deception or a whole bunch of sticky deceptive tricks. I've paused too long here and can't decide to relinquish the torch I carry, even though I want to throw down Grapes and destroy it." There were blotches on the notepaper, as if he'd been crying. "It's destroying my inner space; the fleeting delights are just not worth it." Myron's face reformed as he spoke: "I'm witness to a huge wild party, Harold—hear me, please—carried along by actions owned by others of all time and all continuing. These can't be controlled for us or by each of us because we can't acknowledge them, because they all exist privately and uniquely. The moment I lose touch with your vessel, within me, when it fails to strain out the Grapes, my torch is snatched away and I lose control of myself. There must be a condition for being where I am at one with us as well as my own hard-earned merit, if there is any."

Jones stood to speak, and it was just her demeanor which revealed that Harold confided in her: "He can't give it up and said he was afraid he'd cut the cord and short-circuit himself. Grapes is below everything and everybody, inside of him and taken over his nature like an addiction. It's impossible to deny access to it; his attachment to Grapes is self-destructive."

Richard Z tried to relate to Harold's dilemma. "My similarity to Grapes is that, sensibilities-wise, I hear light echo from across the world and hear sounds carried by oceans of current, connected to each other, if only momentarily. The echoes cast glows, absorbing this light, being overexposed in the cloyed lights of people who are at first blind to Grapes, and then re-made in their turmoil. Or if I don't discover how to stay in the light, I'm apt to drown in a sunny field while a farmer whistles and crows caw. So is Grapes universal and beneficial? Can we be aware how it illuminates and dims the way we act?" Jones said Harold broke down time and again. He made an unrealistic agreement to consult the college therapist with her, as soon as an appointment was available.

Part of Harold's dilemma and our involvement, or rather lack of it, in his private life, and with each other, is portrayed in these letters between a mother and son. Recognition, although short-lived, poured into the college. Most folks praised the college for its candor and requested information about their sons and daughters who, although they corresponded with home, appeared remote, matter of fact, and rhetorical.

The letters centered on a controversy caused by the son's public reply to a newspaper editorial in his hometown paper, *The Digress*. Records at the college indicated that Harold withdrew about three-quarters of the way through his third year. This was true. A resident administrative scholar examined the letters. Some argued Harold's withdrawal and subsequent disappearance from the area are explained in the final letter. Other observers, namely Myron, suspected foul play. His conclusion was based on the question: Is the final letter valid? Several weeks after their discovery, the Grapes still left us feeling empty of any inherent factual answer, without a solid foundation, empty of proof, each in our own way. This was Harold's legacy to us: there isn't a factual answer outside of us. Other readers drew their own conclusions. The custodian was fired, although he accepted a part-time job at the local town newspaper.

Letter 1 (from Harold's mother to Harold):

"Dearest Harold;

Well, looks as if spring is finally here for sure this time. Father is ploughing and the Derendiecks out Greenfield way have new tractor and plough. Will send you church bulletins as usual and am also sending you a news piece from *The Digress*.

Loving you, Mother.

p.s. Cindy sends love and xx (wonder what they are, ha, ha)."

The enclosed news clipping from mother was an editorial from the May 6th issue of *The Digress*. The editorial concurred with a policy adopted by the school board. This policy provided for the expulsion of pregnant girls from Harold's high school. Harold wrote a letter to the editor of *The Digress* — this we remembered because he spoke of it. He criticized both the editorial and the school board policy.

Letter 2 (from Harold's mother to Harold):

"Dear Harold;

Father says hello and I say why? Letter you wrote was certainly, at least not any of your business as you are no longer at the high school and also why did you write it? I can certainly understand that you have thoughts about your opinions and right to express such. But don't cotton on to why you have to turn whole town against us? Then to publish it in newspaper? Why Harold? Father wonders same. Pastor Canby called, asked for your address, said was hoping to visit you next time in town.

But worst was that Davis girl, probably will be next one expelled, called, asked about you and wanted your address. Told her you too busy to be bothered with much mail except what I send you. NERVE!!

Maybe should come and speak to you?

Cindy sends love, but not xx (???!!!)

Love and xx, Mother."

Letter 3 (from Harold to his parents):

"Dear Mother,

Glad to hear from you and father. Hope all is well back at the ranch. Things are pretty quiet here except for one or two scholarships given to fellows on my floor. I had the good fortune to be invited to dinner with my History Prof. (Professor Filcher, I mentioned him to you last fall). We talked about Pre-Renaissance culture of the Mediterranean. Most absorbing. He has some interesting views and I want to explore them further.

Hal.

p.s. Can you send me $55."

Letter 4 (to Harold from his mother):

"Harold, my son;

Sat up all night trying to think of Bible saying about what is happening to you, but couldn't — memory must be failing. Father says you aren't learning any but bad things there, asks if that is the place where all the nudos and pinkists are?

Woman's study club had meeting about Dead Sea scrolls and your letter. Bertha Krause says written in haste or you were locked out of your room again and so thought you wrote it. Her sister Clara said you always were bad; near cried, that woman is so EVIL!" (Editors note: Here the writer probably meant 'I near cried', not, as implied, Clara near cried. It is doubtful from what little we know of the situation whether Clara Krause would cry about Harold's fate. More likely, she would wish him god-speed on his way to hell and damnation. Clara Krause was evidently great grand-daughter of Emily Krause, first woman publicly scourged in Harold's town for criticizing the government's concentration camps to contain Native Americans. It was said that Emily tied strings tightly round the middles of carrots and then set them in the sun. The carrots, of course, exploded as the moisture inside them expanded.)

"Someone else, Selinda Schwweigal, I THINK, said possible you had been led astray by OLDER students; told her off her rocker as you are 22 and no students older. She said teacher then and not off rocker anymore than me. Told her you knew deep down own sweet way.

Harold, I don't get how we have failed you. Was going to say something more to that Clara K., but Rev. Canby said better we adjourn. Next week to study something about wicked movies shown in Chicago. Hope that Clara K. is there; will tell her.

Had long talk with Rev. Canby, said often things like this happen to young men before realize it. Said he would write one of deans there who went to seminary with him. Hoping you will see the light. Am sending pocket flash-light with Bible verse, to remind you of way out of darkness.

Love, Mother.

p.s. haven't seen Cindy lately (????!!!!)"

Letter 5 (to Harold's mother):

"Dear Mother,

I had a talk with Dean Noudle today. He suggested I take several religious courses and said according to Canby you and father were mad about our war efforts overseas. My friend Jones agreed. I shall write a letter to *The Digress* to explain my position and to clear up this apparent misunderstanding.

/s/ Hal

p.s. got the $55, send $10 more? Thanks."

Letter 6 (Harold's mother to Harold):

"Dear Harold,

Your second letter to *Digress* was oil on fire. Today two men from county hall came to inspect house, said someone told them it should be condemned. Wonder who??!!!!! Clara K. wrote letter to *Digress* saying you were reason communists taking over the country. Said also if you ever come back she will run you out of town and folks should not speak to us. Came to our house and father sicked dog on her. Father said he would sick it on you too, if you don't enlist until no Reds under the beds anymore." (Editor's note: It's doubtful whether the dog would acquiesce to Harold's father and sick for him, as Harold and the dog, crossbreed named Gamble-Skogmo, were long-time companions. Nevertheless, the sentiments expressed were plain enough. Harold's father will probably find other ways to express his disapproval of Harold's opinions.) "Then said he would do no such thing and he sicked GS on me. Becoming hard to live with, may come to live with you." (Editor's note: Harold's mother most likely referred to his father as becoming 'hard to live with' and not the dog. It is possible that Gamble-Skogmo, sensing the community's dislike of his masters, is as likely as not to be affected adversely and become meaner. At any rate, Harold probably took consolation from the fact that neither dogs nor mothers are allowed in college dormitories.) "Yes, will come to live with you, then you can get good food and ironing done. Not far, so will visit father on weekends.

Father just grunted when asked him if he had anything to say to you, but smiled when told him coming to visit you — think he really misses you.

Love and see you soon. Mother."

The following is the seventh and final letter in the series. Official records at the college listed a Harold Leroy Baumgartner as having withdrawn three weeks before the end of spring term. The letter was addressed to Harold's parents and was thought to be from an Army recruiter.

"Dear ____ Mr and Mrs Baumgartner ____,

It gives me great pleasure to inform you that your _son_, Baumgartner, Harold L. has been accepted in the modern Army's new training program.

Harold L. will be at scenic__ Fort Knox __ in beautiful ____ Kentucky ____ for several weeks completing his training as   tank maintenance _____

_____.

   Harold   asked me to tell all his friends in Greenfield about
the wonderful opportunities available in your modern Army.
   I am looking forward to meeting you and all   Hal's
other friends in the Greenfield (area, county, district, parish*)
   Sincerely,   M/Sgt William (Bill) McCarthy
   *to be used only in Louisiana"

As far as I am aware, Harold's mother did not hear any further
from her son. Neither did we. The Army, in an unofficial
statement, said it was not responsible for an unsigned paper
which did not constitute a document. Harold disappeared.
The Digress reasserted its confidence in the school board. The
school board extended its policy and ruled that "any student
who shall be deemed a father shall be expulsed (sic) from public
study to execute appropriate social responsibilities."
   I lost my job as editor at the end of that year, right after I
published the letters. I was not invited to next year's welcome
ceremony for freshmen, same as Clay, after his more-to-the-
point F-U-C-K Y-O-U article. Harold's disappearance was a
shock; also, we lost something of ourselves, as if slipping away
from ourselves, as if trying to collect ourselves for a whirligig
cycle of fast and faster unease around us.

Love in a Buffalo Head

The sidewalk was white in the jagged blaze of sun. The windows of the Lincoln Memorial Building, where we meet with a circle of fellow students in the Bel Air Cafe, glared blank at me. Others are immersed in studies or watching baseball in the campus lounge. They read like all of us until eyes burn through the night and try now during our rendezvous to revive from the fight against sleep.

I was fired as editor because of "misuse of a computer" and deciding to reject a psychology professor's proposal to publish a series of articles. His idea was that students need to realize that college is an oversimplified pipedream for profiteers and cornered neurotics. He asserted that students "are victims, not so much because of eating alone in carousels, without sleep, or the bowing, but a lack of opportunity to become worldly-wise. Student satisfaction," he concluded, "is boned on past thrills. They are almost as dreary as scientologists, just not so obvious." The articles which he submitted were a variation on an old log-splitting theme, trying to shape us into something without our discovering it for ourselves.

I was welcomed to the caffeine-buzzing group without verbal acknowledgement, as the conversation was in full swing about some art exhibition. Jones and Clay pulled me onto a stool in-between them. "What a painter, the Dutchman Vincent van Gogh," Myron was saying. "Now he was a man," Jones teased, "with a hairy chest and hot breath in his lungs."

"Well, this is just it," Myron snapped. "He wasn't witty or polished. He was undoubtedly a bear at smart parties, and made teachers shake in his presence. Every minute was real to him. He had no use for clocks; van Gogh sealed time behind a glass face, drove a point through the heart of time and displayed it. The hours restructured in glowing colors for him." "Probably he couldn't comprehend a week or longer," I added, "because each instant was different and more exciting. To comprehend a week's worth of instants is like trying to look at a mile-long stained glass window." "Every bird touched him," Myron said. "Each is an echo in his psyche and in his painting."

"Paul, did you go to that exhibition last week of the French sculptor, Rodin, and his countryman-painter, Degas," Myron asked. "Yeah, I was impressed with the visitors, too." "Paul and I went together," Neil said, jumping in while distributing mugs of Bel Air coffee. "For instance, there were these two guys in thin puce suits with broad dorsal flaps and brown glasses standing outside the exhibit. One of them said to us: "Yes, I believe they did the same thing with Degas' stuff" and the other fellow nodded as if he knew a secret that others were unaware of. We just burst out laughing because we didn't even ask them anything." "What impressed me about Rodin's The Thinker," I said to Myron, "is that The Thinker might have been wondering about a person's place in the universe, or about where he left his grocery list." We all dissolved further into laughter. The exhibit was devoted to Rodin, with a few exceptions: a large statue called Warrior with Shield and five paintings of washerwomen and ballet girls. The statue had an arm (holding the shield), one leg and a face without features except for two nostril-like appendages which jutted out a couple inches. "Then we got inside," Neil continued, "and a pale gent turned to me and said, "It doesn't have any affection does it?" And I responded "Yes, biting isn't it." He smiled and strutted off. "I appreciated Warrior with Shield more than any other piece in the exhibit," Myron said. "It's the best comment on the inhumanity of war and the nature of heroism that I've seen in a long time. The more I observe it the more I realize its truth: empty face with symmetrical nostril-like growth, warped sternum, four fingered hand and the bravado dignity-with-stare." "I was interested in the spectators too," said Richard Z. "They seemed bewildered coping with the problems of assessing its value. As if value is realized at a glance only." "Warrior with Shield has a stiff neck, twisted to one side," Clay said. "If the statue had a mouth I'm sure the jaw would be firmly set." Then Jones put-in: "Instead of a facial expression, it's limited to holes protruding from the face — as if they are rope or chain holes, so it can be put anywhere for people to admire." A person to my right said, "Ah, sublime." "I began to have the impression that the sculpture was a being," Neil said, "and remembering, Warrior with Shield was reminiscent of…I couldn't place the action, but it was something I'd seen before. The entranced expression on faces of the statue observers remained whether they stared at it or not: then I remembered. The monster warrior is near to looking like a hobo knelt on a railroad trestle, using a grounded pigeon's nest for a pissoir." "Yes, it was impossible to study this statue," Richard offered, "without the rapture of spectators and sentiment that emerges like smiling or crying. Possible to hide

the laugh or cry, to keep it inside, but impossible to prevent it."
"What's important is the way that we are, not the twisted psy-
chobabble of your rejected professor, Paul," Neil said urgently.

The person who asked me about Warrior with Shield's fer-
vency chuckled knowledgeably and faded back into the crowd,
which bubbled in front of Rodin's The Citizens of Calais.
Small girls led a chorus of noises, giggling, telling mothers'
ears about exposed rectums and nipples. Tight-faced men
with tight grips led their boys to restrooms. A bearded genius
descended from somewhere to oversee a low humming sound
affecting a misunderstanding of a dear colleague's music. Near
Rodin's Balzac, a young lad cried, while embarrassed crowd
stood in awe by the bronze thumbprints. Around them, steel-
nerved, uniformed curators eyed with a rush the statues
which might topple and pictures that leaned. Richard continued: "Behind a cluster of look-alike school boys, a janitor
cleared his throat. The gym emitted a wild animal smell: the
odorous sent of a beast rarely seen by man, now disturbed by
this crowd. Without notice, panic seemed to flex its muscle in
the crowd's eye — The Thinker had to be left. It was as though
despair thrust its fist into high air and the crowd couldn't
absorb The Thinker's thoughts. Mistrust and Doubt slapped
hands," Richard yelled, banging his hands together, and we
suddenly realized that other Bel Air aficionados were either
intently looking or quietly talking about us. "Yes, and the
writer's fragments remained shattered," I said, off the top of
my head, "scattered between innocence and man." "What the
hell, Paul, you're quiet and then you say something like that?"
Myron insisted. "He's lost his job," Neil said, "accused of one

thing and mishandling another. But it was really a personality clash, huh, Paul?" "Yeah, it's not really a deluded thesis, just self-absorbed misperceptions. I'll give academic pursuits a rest, free from scraping for money with an editorial job, and find a place in the real world. But I, in my infancy, shouldn't complain," I said, "a little one in the greater scheme of things, baying for a mother's wisdom and a student who struggles to be free in a bestial world. Scattered between are fragments of whatever it takes to be a writer, ranging from metaphysical poet to autobiographer to humorist."

"If writing comes out in painful spurts, similar to a broken pop bottle being defecated," Jones began, "how do you aim to unify the fragments if humor evades you. Because this usually means you're upset." "Apparently, when I need raised spirits most, they find me: they constitute a sunny weather type mood," I said, but Myron used my slowness to put in his own two cents' worth. "This is an error," he expostulated. "Humor is illuminating; that's more to the point. I know this because when the same, or at least similar, temperament abandons me, I feel the world is unbearable without it." "When humor wears thin, I try — with staunch belief and all haste — to rip myself apart," Jones said. "I'm immobilized when I'm with self-hate. This is why I think everyone should stop being the writer or whatever they are and be a person first who cares for other people and then proceed again to that position when humor is lost."

"What about that night, Jones, when we were over at Myron's studio and you came in a rage?" Richard asked. "The hate then had an intensity I never felt before," Jones said. "Myron asked me to help mat some of his drawings, which is a considerable achievement considering my egoism at that time. When I got there and found that you and Paul and Richard were there too, I, for whatever reason, grew sullen and morose, glaring at a wall, hardly aware of Myron, until the rest of you left. Gradually, I told myself to quit and act like a human being, rather than a cannibal with a taste for its own flesh. The harder I prodded myself, however, the more frustrated I got. My anger increased. I think you really tried to understand," she said to Myron. "But you being familiar with my childishness added to my abuse." "You should have gone off when I attempted to drive you away," Myron told her, "that was my first thought. But then my moods disturbed you. And when you ripped your knuckles open against the wall, I finally felt as awful as you must have, but at the same time we both eased the rage within each other." "Yes," Jones agreed, "and we sat holding my bloody hand, the blood absorbing in my blouse and running down your arms." I was thinking of the way we appealed to Jones and Clay on a previous occasion and that now I, too, was being appealed to in a way that might have mutual meaning: "I feel now, when humor leaves me," my plaintive voice trembled, "that the irritation at everything I don't understand about why people are as they are, then anger, won't be so acute. I try to unify the fragments — uniform only in that they deal with the incoherent whole of me — which I guess includes resignation, pride, guilt, black humor, mockery, faithlessness and many other unhelpful elements." "How then," Richard chipped in, "to describe an ailing nation? We're a product of that deep corrupting system." We all laughed solemnly.

All the banter, all the gossip, so much fun, but in some way it's like intrusions that veil what's sticky in myself. This is scary, because it's impossible to predict, if I'm opened to what's really under my skin; how will that awareness, of my own homelessness, the absence of a baseline, affect me? "We should be more open to those who secretly wish, even for their own sake, to be friends with us," Myron insisted. "After all, Paul, your moodiness on leaving the paper; I mean nobody really knows you like Jones now knows me and me her! We can sit on the table with a megaphone and make our observations into a diary too!" "Yeah, we can say something like this," Clay proposed: "This is for Lewis and Clark and Abigail Van Buren, and to the journals and diaries approved by Duncan Hines, and blessed by Archbishop Michael L. Flaherty. They will happen by on errands, our prospective audience, or be curious, pause, step off a walkway, move to the fringe of our sound, stop, put a bent leg in front of the still-planted one, hold their elbows and listen for a moment. Their numbers will increase as we bring them and return them, after word of our words spreads — in regard to the amusement and empathy in our speeches, long soliloquies and narrative poems." "But generally though," Richard interrupted, "except for their insistence on seeing us and after a few comments about our clothes, we'll be left pretty much alone in a world of suppressive digits, concrete, and desirable things." "I agree there," I said, "Lewis and Clark were right; Abigail Van Buren was just hungry for money." "Oh, alright, alright, Paul, give us an ode then," said Clay. "Give us something from your orange head space about carp," Neil challenged.

"The carp, yes. That color was the name I gave, age five, to a space, as Neil called it, when my mind was luminous, or at that age on the edge of conditioning, to be like a free spirit, after many beatings-up, and later, age 10, changed to international orange when I learned that other kids in the world were beaten-up, too. How long that space in life was inhibited, obscured by the yelling and welts. The carp, fishes with scales, in another life they breathed out of water and, well, they glance at us with their left eyes (it's as plain as everyone's face that the carp's right eye is only decoration, much the same as an extra bureau drawer and knots on trees). Hail to you carp, I say. Good old friends, they are — if not for their vanity, they'd surely walk and in all respects be equal to man!" "Come on, Paul, don't fart around," Neil pleaded. "Okay, okay, this is the carp ode: Scales of scales, whales of scales, flashing in your river like graceful knives. Tails with scales and flash wills which dart least or regained 'neath every wave, waiting always to be found so anybody can have the sun in a bowl, and the only short breath of the good-luck-piece carp is that you can't live in a front room bowl and watch television, but can only find your wealth in the mud." There was robust applause and chortling-on afterwards. "When I laugh so deeply," Myron said, "I have the sensation like a lighted bulb in a chocolate belly and the inside of my mouth is clean." "What I like about Paul's odes," Neil said, "is that they aren't composed with concrete meaning. They're part of an unsuffering ethic." "Your odes pay homage to both pleasure and pain," Jones revealed, "but they don't humiliate subjects by celebrating pleasure without pain. They create substance and attempt to close wounds." "My odes attempt to prevent blood and thunder from both colliding and merging, or from running out the door altogether to find new ways to repackage themselves for their next visit to the supermarket for more Saran Wrap," I said at the same time as catching a glimpse of Nancy walking into the Bel Air. As was my habit, I looked at her in an almost captured or capturing way. She was slim, yet muscular, with a handsome frame, and beautiful mind. She turned towards our table, which was also distracted and breaking up now, and looked back. "Hello," I shouted, leaving to be with her. "How are you?" she asked. I shrugged. "Can't you talk?" I shrugged again. "What are you thinking?" "I said hello didn't I?" I was always susceptible to Nancy when confronted by her, and preoccupied by it. She smiled, but then frowned and said: "I have a secret." My face must have seemed too inquisitive, for she gazed slyly at her feet. "All right, what's your secret," she countered. "You told me you had a secret." "I do." "Well, what is it?" "If I tell you, it won't be a secret any more." "I won't tell anyone. There is nobody to tell," she said. Now I frowned. "If there is nobody to tell," I reasoned, "it can't be a secret." She grinned and laughed. When she laughed a vacancy became her eyes and she looked as if something very pleasant was happening to her. Nancy leaned against the table and began to pretend-prattle about her adopted cats. Most of them had been dumped in the country and some run over or shot, mauled by dogs, or snared by little boys. I guessed there were too many of them. After she told me about her cats, I mentioned my boyhood dog, Pooch. Then there was a lull and I was afraid she would go away. I started to talk about the new phone book, and running out of witty things to say about it, I improvised and talked about the phone book crisis, telling her about a shortage of paper, and then stopped in the middle of a sentence: "...this is ridiculous." "Yes," she said. I knuckle-dusted the edge of our table, being prone to act on sudden impulses like this. "Do you want to share the secret now?" she asked. "Can we go for a walk," I said, offering my hand, and we went off. Descending the front steps towards the campus road, Nancy skipped round me twice and said: "I am the gentle and beautiful fairy queen. I am now bewitching you; you are not cross anymore. Look into my gentle and bewitching eyes."

She took my left shoulder and turned me so she was looking right into my eyes. She stared until her eyes were large and seemed to exist independent of her head. I looked into the eyes and then out, at her (by comparison) ridiculously smallish face and smiled. She put the heel of her hand to her nose and wiggled her fingers at me in a hypnotic way. I just chuckled and put my arm around her; it was such a tiny privilege but felt such a great honor to be able to be meticulous in our admiration for each other. We skipped on the sidewalk and laughed until we were out of breath.

"Do you believe in ghosts?" she asked.

"No."

"Do you want to hear a ghost story?"

"No."

"I'm going to tell one. If you don't want to hear it cross the street." I walked on. "Listen," she insisted, "there is a curse on this ghost story. Persons must not hear it unless they want to."

"Let the curse strike me dead."

"All right then, I'll cross the street," she said, and she crossed. "Do you want to hear it?" she shouted. I kept walking but glanced at her. She looked pretty and I wondered why I felt mean. She lowered her voice to a whisper and began to tell the story. She bent low and then sprang up. I heard her whispered excitement. Then she gestured to the trees. I stopped and watched. Once, I caught myself listening for her whispers. She took great long steps and swayed her body, shaking her hands like Al Jolson, jerking her head back like he did, ya-yaing. She stopped and caught my bemused interest: "One doesn't laugh when one hears high grade ghost stories. One turns purple and raspberry with fright." I laughed again, louder than before. She cocked her head and I crossed the street.

The self-doubt and confusion, which had been in me since losing my job and agreeing with her to spend time traveling on my own, was gone. I said: "You're crazy."

"I am imaginative and nervous, not crazy. Do you think I could be a great actress?"

"You already are." She put her hand in my coat pocket and we walked this way for several blocks. I relaxed and her warmth gave me goose bumps. "Who are you?" I said.

"I am sent to aid geniuses. I come to earth once every seventh century. I stay 48 hours, on an assessment visit, and then I leave." She made the sign of the cross.

"Where do you go?"

"That is my secret."

"Is that the secret you wouldn't tell me?"

"Partially."

"Tell me where you're not from then."

"Fool, even seven centuries ago they had inductive reasoning."

"You are a gentle bat, the kind a birthday girl would like."

"You have potential," she said gravely, "and I am sent to give geniuses strength to live between inspirations because you're vulnerable." She sighed. It frightened me, wondering if she was supernatural. I need to go my own way to face myself but question whether she will wait for me, afraid of seeing things through childish eyes, living in a life of constant flux, where, in the background, people lose or attack each other. These thoughts passed and I asked whether she was hungry.

"No, but I am curious."

We went to an all-night restaurant. I ordered root beer and a hamburger; she had the same. We finished another beer. She belched and held up two fingers for the waitress. After the third round we talked of personal things. Nancy's sister just married. Her husband, a French legionnaire's son, beat her. After the fourth round I vowed to write an editorial about the husband, or rather family abuse, if ever the villain recovered from being electrocuted by Nancy's mother. She kissed me and I nearly cried. I caught a glance from a waiter and that stopped me. For a while the conversation veered to civil disobedience and then we spoke of fresh air and its benefits. As we stepped outside, I felt thoroughly kissed. That was the rest of the secret. The great questions eluded me and I was fool and philosopher enough to let go of them. She, happily, had wisdom. "Despair is a greedy concession to conformity," she warned, and belched. I definitely have insight into my preoccupation with concepts, aware that they're something to be let go of, preferably in the practice of writing, in a job of some sort with people, or otherwise the concepts turn to conflicted, contradictory, spineless progress as my journey unfolds. There is a tempered steel character beaten into me by those who reared me, and I feel like sex would not dignify how I feel about myself and Nancy. It's as though she is too purely genuine to be tarnished by my feeble sufferings from their puny imaginations. We walked for several blocks.

Houses became fewer and streets more run down. Eventually we came to a park. Across the lighted horizontal town a siren wailed for an emergency. The darkness closed, closeting us in cubicles with moon gaps here and there. Stars spilled like acid to eat at the depth of darkness, revealing nightlight holes with overhead lamps often hid. By dawn the stars will succeed. A great mound was in front of us; it was a fallout and bomb shelter. Through a narrow wooden door hung a framed sign, which read: SEE COUNCIL MEETING 4005 FOR DETAILS. Peering through a window frame, it looked like a solemn cluster of forms, with one beating another, while a tuna fish loomed behind. One form made continual trips into an alcove with a big sink. The courier blocked light which festered and whirled to escape their shadows. Beating and whickering increased. A perforated man-shape approached the pane; his face shown like an over-exposure: dots on-screen. The forms appeared to beat their heads together and fall over exhausted. Behind the mound, a line of boxcars bore the label: WHEAT AND POP BOTTLES. "Where's the wheat gone?" she wondered. "Dunno," I said on top of the question, thinking, as she was, that we crossed one of sanity's borders. Gazing away from the mound, my eye intercepted a still green and white ceremonial flag. We made our way over, casting a worried look back toward the mound. Beneath the flag, in a bandshell, were two young kissers, a lively set of warts alone in the whole park. Inside, the bandshell hummed from a sudden but slight rain, while squirrels dozed in dust-scented trees and rain dropped from the armpits of limbs as the air grew darker. Rain dripped on benches, bird-washed drinking fountains, hissed on grease and pinged on chain swings and sheet metal slides. The kissers made their own acoustics, overwhelming the hum. As if they forgot to breathe. Underneath the pants of one, a new nation emerged, forming like a capitol. The new nation pressed forward against its jacket walls: "Oh, oh Jimmie, you kiss." The girl, a cutie with ants in her hands, sported soft openings and friendly lines, where Jimmie was probably first to travel. They peeled one more layer of reserve. "Ummmmmmmmmm, Jimmie, there's two people watchin' us." "Hmmmmmmmmmm." Rain stopped, but the ground slobbered, heaved and cracked with apparent anticipation.

A town work truck with amber headlights straddled the curb and drove right up to the bandshell. The two kids full of sperm and eggs stopped necking and froze. For a moment everything was steady in the moon and in smells of fresh-cut grass. Two men dressed like city employees were armed with new nets. "What the hell is going on?" I complained. "It's the night butterflies; they're here to catch them," was the whispered reply from Nancy. These were no ordinary men. These were adventure men within the context of a cause. The pair wore denim uniforms and leaned on a large chrome coffee pot, between them. "There's one, George!" The machine swerved, cutting in front of the bandshell near the kissers and veered into the park. One hunter jumped out and chased an ominous bug. The creature flew and curled in the sky. The netman trotted in pursuit on manicured fingers of park lawn.

"Watch 'im, Lewt."

"Uh!" He swung at it. "Shit, I missed."

"Try 'im again, Lewt."

"Uh!" He swung at it. "Shit, I missed."

"Uh!" An angry varmint's zing accompanied each swoosh of the net. "Shit! Shshshshshshshshshshshiiiiiiiiiiiiiit."

"Duck, Lewt. For God's sake duck, man, here he comes."

The warrior moth careered off the truck windshield and in the commotion the driver's window shattered, spraying glass on George's lap. The bug's crumpled body lay in rubble; dark slime oozed on the side of the engine hood.

"Quick, get in the truck; I'm gonna start the spray."

"I'm comin' Mother of God, I'm comin'; wait for me."

"Hurry here." George grabbed Lewt's arms and hoisted the fagged and nearly fallen netman, whose apparatus hung about his shoulders like an extra organ breaking through his body. "Quick, put yer mask on. Here they come!"

A brisk hum filled the air as they came from far off. Against moon flicker the murky night's creatures lined up on telephone wires along the residential side of the park. Then the attack: the bugs purred and darted at the truck. They buzzed around the vehicle and charged through the broken windows.

"Start the spray, Lewt. Start it man; what you waitin' for?"

"Can't get the fuckin' flame lit!"

He chiselled with matches as if the spot was marked: STRIKE MATCHES HERE. At last one ignited. A brave leader moth zipped into the cab's soft illumination, making a pass at the men. Lewt moved match to pilot and lit the spray. A second moth flickered in intermittent light mist which filled the cab.

"That'll stop 'em, huh Lewt?"

"Yeah."

Another moth entered, circled George and dove for Lewt, apparently seizing him by the throat. "Aaaaarrggghhh. Aaar-rrrrhhhgg. Aarrh. Oooohhhoooooo. Get 'im off! Get 'im off!! Yeeeaaaaaah." George hit the insect on its back with a barbed swatter. But it grabbed Lewt again and the two rolled. Lewt attempted to escape from the insect and George tried to kill it. The workmen and their assailant scuffled onto the floor, rocking the truck. The moths' sound increased until the mist boiled to a crackle and the scuffle noise was lost. Even the turbulence stopped. "I got 'im, Lewt. I got 'im. Lewt?" The truck lights shone back at it through the bandshell's basement window.

During the fight, the kids had continued explorations. They lay on wet ground, at the other side of the bandshell, and gazed at the sky. Each star possessed singular motion through the Big Dipper, Milky Way and the swept scope of super stars to the west.

"Oh, Jimmie, you kiss."

"I do more; wind me up and you'll see."

"Tehtehtehtehtehtehtehtehtehtehtehtehtehteh."

"Hahahahahahahahahahahahahahahahahaha."

"Tehtehtehtehtehtehtehtehtehtehtehtehtehteh."

"Hahahahahahahahahahahahahahahahahaha."

We crossed a wide grassy field with a baseball diamond

on the edge of the park and buildings on the opposite side of the road. By the streetlights a sign read: THE HENNEPIN COUNTY MUSEUM. It was closed for the winter. We walked arm in arm, kicking through leaves and found a dry pile under trees to sit in. Her warmth rose around us as we lay in the leaves. I kissed her back and neck. She has a love that transcends her. And I trust her. She sighed. I worked her coat loose and she put her hand on mine and held it. I caressed her with my hands and she spoke: "I would like a buffalo skull."

"What?"

"A buffalo skull; I've seen one in the museum."

"For Pete's sake, a buffalo skull." She responded with a meek smile. "It's all locked up in there."

"You're technically cunning and physically strong, break the door down."

I sighed; one hundred percent of me wanted to — anyway, if this was love in a buffalo head, okay. "What will you do with a buffalo skull?"

"I'll give it to my poor sick grandmother who was a pioneer. Or I'll make a lamp out of it." She set her eyes on the haze from the nearest streetlamp, while I found a dislodged back door.

"Here they are," she snorted, after we'd been inside only a minute. She knew the place like the back of her hand. As I groped toward her voice on the other side of the room, I felt an unnerving undying quality about the vague objects all around. "Grab that Indian tapestry," she said as I neared; "we'll wrap it up in that."

"Hey, the teeth are falling out — hold it the other way," I said.

"Anyway, he won't care," she said.

"Who?" I asked stupidly, and turned round. "No, no, silly — the buffalo," she giggled.

My laugh caught me off guard and I felt as if the wind had been poked out of me. Then I laughed louder, with new wind, and she joined me, laughing at her own joke. We leaped out the door and trotted to the dark edge of the park. We rolled on our backs in leaves and laughed. When we stopped, the stars seemed several miles away. A faint mist hung over the piles of leaves, from our breath, and whenever we stopped laughing, it dissolved.

Then we left and I carried the head for a while. It was as heavy as an old typewriter. The idea to go bowling was mine. I bowled a few times, years ago when a man was a pal to me. I had no particular interest in bowling, but thought Nancy might like to go, listing the advantages, not forgetting it gave me a chance to watch her move.

The bowling alley was a plastic coated and tiled cavern, where machines stood out as much as people in a cave during a storm when even the thunder was manmade. We selected balls and shoes and went to our alley. "I'll keep score," she announced: "I only want the score when I get strikes," and flipped her coat onto the bench. Next to us on both sides, and as far along the line as I could see, were bulky men in short-sleeved knit shirts. Behind them in the rooting gallery, several people sat, knitting and smoking.

Nobody noticed a few teeth that fell from the buffalo's skull, through the Indian tapestry.

Consorting with Cows

As I moved with the darkness, a vehicle rushed to a place where proper nouns saved and redeemed, where proper blanks on proper forms, correctly filled out, give life again. With the same darkness, my body wore a musty soybeans and wheat smell, arriving in a town, alongside a prosperous well-groomed street. A few hours later the street will buzz with children and power mowers, a street which heaves when a car comes and goes too fast.

At the town's edge, cows stood in one of their off-hand groups, having arranged a direction for each cow to point. Light lay on the trees so softly, it swayed my eyes on long strings, and darkness hugged. The glow created patterns as if skeletons of designed cities drifted past while curled light under bark drew weight from the air around it. There was an instance of noise, which stopped. The cows moved sideways, rectangle-shaped sails with spots and highly-divorced eyes. Stopping their group chew, the cows gazed my way. The chew process continued in the farthest parts of their bodies while they watched. One cow snorted and her white saliva floated downstream. Another dropped waste in the river; it splashed on her leg and she bucked. Several stood groupfully: feet in the green, faces to the moon, in a rain-rich pasture. (They do more than merely stand. Cows whizz, lope, bounce, crawl, trot, sedately walk or dejectedly bustle, and they mill, nosing the vacant wind.) A few were on the ground, their udders sticking out beneath haunches as if the cows sat on pink rocks. Other cows scratched on stumps or branches. One worked a branch up over her cheek and forehead like cockeyed antlers. Mallard ducks slept in the inlet. Crayfish were as unobtrusive as acrylic or Plexiglas. Willing to take pot luck, I walked into the center, which melted without a glance from bovine all-day eyes which attracted light like roosters. I chose a cow. She moved away with rivers and hills of high-hipped pelvis and shimmering ribs and no apparent motion, as if repelled by magnetism. Coasting around the cows now and pointing with my chest, I wore the scales of hunger and uniform of thought, attempting to hold them rapt with my chest and elbows message. They maneuvered to a thicket with some humanoid sensitivity and extra advanced sense-ray of cow ambivalence. The group was parried. I tried to guide them with an easy going presence. Udders hung: fruit of ungainly trees which flow before sun and appear only on misty nights. Two cows slid into a thicket as fish through a stream, or as shadows into day. A cow with a bleeding udder cruised alongside the thicket and balanced on the edge of a trot, delicately slowing its mechanical hoofs in a lovely restrained motion. Their silent vigil presented a pos-sibility of cow-jumped-over-the-thicket flight. A cow might develop, or have in reserve, deer traits. For instance, she can bound along, except in the physical form of cow, wrap herself to fit impossible thicket shapes. Cows inside the thicket, even in tree ribs, emerging almost whole, then merging at their necks and heads. Cattle which moved plain as light or near light, through slanted shafts of Alders, forms taking shape like living puzzles.

My eyes reflected in cow eyes: a face in three horizontal moments — our eyes mirroring, an arm chopped in two and separated from the body. Then, our bisected eyes darted into each other — scooting away from the eyes. An enormous hip scalloped in dust came into view, with a black spot-area sculpted in three parallel shapes. I looped the cow's neck with my rope. Primitive reflections whirled in those bulged eyes. The other end of rope was wrapped taut around a solid tree branch — one with textured bark. Her tail swished as I smoothed the flank and polished the sides and curlicue of a protruding haunch. She resented any contact with nipples, kicking at me, bucking against rope. The soft teats stretched and I captured a rhythm of sorts. (It's a pull and squeeze at the same time.) My hand warmed while thin streams of milk shot into my stale mouth, splotching my chest and head. A relaxed belch rose through heavy breathing, then the cow sat. Stroking her side again, I flicked an early dawn fly off the cow's neck and fed her corn.

"Do you see why I'm doing all this? Well now, tell me madam cow, do you sense what's behind this pursuit? How in hell did I get way out here? I'll bet you're dying to sympathize," I murmured in a rhythmic and quizzical manner, pausing to dig at a tick from the cow's back. "Well, if the reasons were secret I'd say, but there are few secrets, mainly misconception, uncertainty, ambiguity, and I'd rather be unconfused."

Unleashing the rope loop from her hide, and as the muzzle was eased free, the cow flinched, as if thankfully, bucked, backed and after a half fall she trotted away. The animal watched me from a distance. Then she grazed.

Along a road with cold air ditches, were the carcasses of bug splattered time. Sun-gleaming machines which built the road left their gleam in asphalt that sat on the earth, the empty road not yet sharing the glow of fields where grass bowed this way or that, and nobody listened. Ditch grass is thick and wet and permeates my clothes when I lay down, permeates me if I lay long enough. Permeates itself, and with nothing left to permeate, grass eventually evaporates and becomes sky. An empty tin can, poised half on and off the yellow line, whizzed into a ditch at the touch of a car tire. Several feet away were the hard entrails and car-flattened skeleton of the largest locust since the seven plagues of Moses. The rusty tin can rattled along in the wind, unevenly because of dents. A screech owl, startled and attracted by the can, floated quietly to investigate, glided, then dropped into a near swoop, just in case. This owl, probably no stranger to the road, ate many fine meals thanks to cars that used it, although judging from widening cracks, cars hadn't used the road for some time. The main sound was the can. Whatever rustled in the ditch was quiet. Somewhere, a car passed? No — only flat sun sliding on the bottom of sky. Sound faded, as it does; this is certain when it's gone, because of knowing the silence.

No matter how far we appear to be different in this world — and at the moment I can only describe it this way — there is a greater presence in the way we're the same: a breathing which shines through aging, through convention and instincts and which permeates all of mind and matter. This breathing essence is, I presume, the substance of life, even while people cling to their screaming, striving, volatile age. They are, in the silence, a sky reflected glow. With them, even strangers, I've a chance to figure out how best to be, finding the whole, reflecting the light of billions of lives. The silent essence is above bustling streets and in the sloshing waste pipes, on each piece of grass-cracked sidewalk. It's inside the face of every hurried person who rushes to their family or apartment or job or to jump off bridges or make love or fix something. This timeless breath of life, a small gleaming part of it, is my own being. Why should it dawn on me now? How does it stay with me, over hills and across the prairie? Who or what put it in streetlamps glow and in the taste of warm coffee? Why will even a mouse fight for it? The periods between this still awareness is marked with lapses of concentration, breaking the silence. Returning is the important thing, to silence, through the breath. Life is spotted with these lapses in returning and that is confusing and maybe even sickening for those unreturned: "Yes, I understand and am awake with this silence." When I open windows and let the world in, will it emerge through the silence as an opening space to reclaim myself and everyone else? If the radiant silence is gone, will the bitter and white washed past return, rigid and cold in the lapse that strives to alienate me?

An owl flies through space. Owl wings aren't magic; one wing is their wisdom wing and the other is their skills wing. Air crossed by the owl hums gently in reply to the bird's music. Muddy water under a bridge then reflects and shines shades of colors, each one alive to its causes and effects — the life force water ever-changing.

The cohesion of nature unclutters the dirt, dissolves it, reconstitutes the past, lingering impish pulses from my father's early beatings. Those flushed tremors are less unpredictable when I'm just sitting and letting the fragments fly. There is one way to overcome the angst when it interferes. On the one occasion, I painted my college dormitory room international orange. One of my roommates said he would transfer to another floor, although he moved into a girlfriend's apartment. His replacement agreed to cooperate with a number of projects and even to help paint the shower room that color; it's a flag for being out of control for convenient intents and purposes, yet liberating when I'm writing. In any event, eventually, the dorm administrator, when told that a roommate was a subversive, said, "Howdyios amigo" and booted him out.

Things went well for a while after college, after Nancy moved to her auntie's. I lived with Peggy Sue, a friend from junior high school who worked at the college library. We settled down, first in the Midwest, and then in a Frisco suburb, surrounded by families with children — this was after our three week trip across the markedly warmer States. The West Coast offered the best prospect for fending-off the flatness of Iowa and the odious indignities towards Indians in the Badlands. Afterwards, there were journalism jobs back in Minnesota and the humdrum of the court beat, the easily exposed bumbling cover-ups by city officials with their hungry fingers fiddling public money. Peggy Sue decided to complete a Masters degree and I just dug-in to 17-word sentences (a near fruitless aim) and wrote my butt off, writing the articles assigned by my editor. Neil, and Nancy, migrated to the West Coast. She went to bed with a white-collared churchman and we didn't like each other after a while, but we agreed to be amicable. I was judgemental and unpleasant, that was the truth of it, and the seclusion of writing didn't help.

It was in Nebraska on a New Year's Day that the Toyota's pistons went through the engine head, in the middle of nowhere. Peggy Sue bought a Maverick and drove through Denver. The Rockies, Utah, Arizona, Dinosaur National Park. I stripped the threads of the drain plug while changing the Maverick's oil in the middle of a desert. Finally, up through Yosemite, towards my first big job, with Associated Press.

It was a humdrum time, being with Peggy Sue, as companions. There were the usual tiffs, of course, to supplement television viewing and excursions to Midwest relatives and surprise visits to Greater Frisco friends. Then, I had a relapse, as we called it; she said it was a breakdown, when I lost control of my imagination, having assumed that everyone has a limit that they deal with in one way or another. The strain was just such that it was, with hindsight, my avoidance of a lone traveler's journey that, rightly, prompted her to take a leave of absence. Incidental and innocent aspirations became crucial to me, to maintain forward momentum. I dropped out of everything, started to write stories on my own, returning to Sister Mary's Friendly Home for Boys, where I slept on the porch. I heard that the poet John Berryman jumped into the Mississippi River and died. Nancy and Neil helped me during this time when Peggy Sue and I reunited and lived near the university in southern Minnesota. Nancy became known as a West Coast feminist, and Neil was a copywriter for an ad agency.

Next door to where Peggy Sue and I lived, the children were badly in need of paint. Their swing set was decaying, unnoticeable to all but me. The rust ate great holes out of its strong steel limbs. The structure became seriously weakened by the moon. One fall night, I knew what to do. All those innocent children. They played unsuspecting on a treacherous swing set which blew in the subtle currents of the afterschool-winds across the prairie of suburbia. Night's cold winds slapped me. Bird-empty trees watched while blown leaves listened and covered my furtive paint sloshes as I decorated the side garden, shivering in my PJs and splashing myself, covering the prism of autumn grass and the swing set, set off in the orange.

There was a row alright. At our last neighborhood together, there were as many cocker spaniels as children and one started to yap. The neighbors were curious about what I was doing playing with children's toys in night clothes, as they saw it. Peggy Sue flashed with anger. Then she brought my bathrobe as I stood chilly in the flashlights and autumn air. We waited for the police. Charges of disturbing the peace, misuse of private property, kicking an animal, which is really preposterous, and theft, were dropped, or so I thought. Somewhere between the Midwest and the West Coast, coming and going and vice versa, I had deteriorated. I should have started traveling without a companion, as Nancy insisted in the first place, rather than avoiding the test of exploring with myself.

I was grateful living there and to have a newspaper job, mostly feature writing, regular pay, weekends off. Peggy Sue became an aspiring lady. She smoked tobacco, drank gin, made love to people she knew, overate, overspent. She fought it. However, she helped me when I said the wrong thing to people living next door. She agreed to have her living room painted orange. If my notes are correct, she even admitted that was the only color for a living room. Did I holler at her until the word holler was unpronounceable? Or did she holler me? She was speechless on her return from a weekend at her parents' to find her bathroom and half the kitchen also painted with that color, with nearly matching towels. I never did finish the kitchen. That was what started the argument. She yelled at me again, about the kitchen. She challenged me to paint the bedroom that color. She never mentioned what color. She just said: "That color." She called me a disappointment. The eggs she was beating splashed on her beautiful face along with chicken stuffing in my bowl. The sight of her then broke me. I left the house. Events intervening seem irretrievable. You begin to wonder whether harsh words are a criminal offense.

Plankton on a Shadowy Sea

While I sat on a greenwood bench, pausing in a town where I once lived, a dog walked, its steps leaving hungry tracks beside the park's asphalt path. Next to me was a rubber, peppermint-smelling teething ring with a baby beneath it. The dog's skin was chafed, from lying flush on the bone. His mouth became an organ of respiration, the teeth resonators. The mongrel searched vaguely through his dog brain-nose for food, dog-sniffing eyes to the ground, but there was only the rain. He barked, as though disappointed because each raindrop was hollow. Why is a dog or a raindrop unique? What about the plumber? We agreed that Nancy will parley with her auntie out West. The bark returned; he got up, raised a stiff leg and peed on a smelt brick. The dog stayed in the jaw of the alley across from the park, but moved to a grassy lip. His hind paws scattered turf and his forepaws then dabbled and delved. His ancestors listened, dabbled and delved. Under his brownie-speckled coat, he peed from beneath a locked leg onto unsmelt rocks. Apparently tired of searching, the dog lay in a pile of opened raindrops and closed his eyes. Probably he dreamt about golden-olden days of meat-fruited trees and steaks on every corner. Above the dog's yipping dreams, rain clouds coated the sky and carried the sun in their pockets. Clouds powered by all the light shifting and reforming. They prayed in a thousand voices, like lumber floating silently down to the Gulf. The dog rose and shook. He glanced at the unattended child — one of those oblique ways that dogs glance as if to conceal a primitive dog thought, of stealing the child's dummy or, worse, leaving his pungent scent as part of accepted dog logic. He watched moisture float away in the air and passed to a new zone of smell. I jumped from the bench to the ground and followed for a while, but could not keep up with the inconvenient-for-me turns around garage backs. The dog was lost to me, like some crafty twin. I stood idle at a street corner and thought, briefly, of a mackerel sky. The semaphore changed. Crossing the street, back to the park, the baby was still asleep with the dummy still inside her mouth. People I passed in the crossing disappeared into the shadow of buildings. They left behind the sun's restrained glare. Even a kid can sense the futile struggle, between seeing things in flux as permanent, wishing to own a moment that is fleeting. A blue-capped person, another child, with black boats, waded in the park's mud-brown water. Two bleached clouds flitted across the polished puff-blue sky. The rain song finished. There was a before and during, but it still appeared like before and now at the same time. The grass grew golden-haired from its brown gilding to a spring green in full tufts and thick families (colonies) which covered the ground, while the sun also bleached the drift of winter. The grass was bending and humming in full illumination. During the afternoons, football players come to the park with iron feet, padded shoulders, solid heads and plastic-coated groins. The sound of their charges and impacts might wake the baby, float across the park and fade at sunset, when their thunder is silenced by bird song as night blots the sun. I listened to her breathing and smelled the precious breath.

(I remember this most, like a child, as a flow of energy felt rather than made into some concept. Nobody sees the combatants come, or if they do, without noticing, or with so many different unfriendly backdrops that the whole experience can nevertheless be free in a field of being present attending to a child.)

In the morning, tracks and shredded ground evidence their presence — the presence of a crowd...of the full-strength fascination with force and sweaty beauty: cheerleaders, snappy breeze, clashed pads, murmurs, brutal roars, oohs and ahs. As the groups form, silence is cut into little pieces and hauled away and more people become yet another crowd. Their presence rings the plastic droppings which are shreds of the players protective limbs.

While walking, the baby touched my ear, tenderly, running through me in a way that will be unwashed whether we are dry and wet with sun and rain, whether savagery ends in debauchery, whether morality becomes senile, all of which can take several thousand years but which can also happen in a day: amorality to immorality and vice versa. Looking into her eyelids, I doubt that it starts savagely. What is her secret?

Something, I don't remember what, jarred me from thought. It was another dog. There he was, under a tree, his dappled fir lit like plankton on a shadowy sea, and by a breeze which shook sun from waves of leaves. The large, tan dog stood. Across from the park, he was chained beside a garden. These yard-gardens are mostly the same: garage offset behind the house, access to it from the street. The alleys were lined with rubbish bins and kids' tricks. The dog stood patiently, his jaw half open, watching us. I moved behind a bush now to avoid irritating him, observing him in the way prescribed by the Boy Scout manual — unobtrusively crouched behind the nearest bush, figuring-out, reasoning, trying to stay sane in the whirligig. We stalked the dog, observationally, in fact a Doberman-cross German Shepherd bitch. If she charged we could be between the massive biscuit-smiling, man-grinding jaws. Uncertain death. I felt the knife in my pocket and bit my lip. My heart beating woke the baby, in my back pack, also peering at the beast. She accepted my water and bits of Snickers. There were leaves on the ground by the dog, and on the other side was a pile of dirt, where the scrawny animal leisurely dug a dog-sized hole, next to the garage. I took a clod in my hand and threw it sideways to distract the dog. Then we sneaked to another boulder-like bush, but nearer now, near to the edge of the dog's chain. She giggled, or guzzled. The dog watched us, impassively. We were so close I heard the great dog's bellowed panting. Saw an occasional wisp of steam from her mouth. Yellow teeth sat in the jaw like naked people in a church pew. (The shaking thought of naked people made us giggle.) When she yawned, a black speck appeared on the inside of the dog's muzzle, unveiling anvil molars, over which the drool flowed. Her bone was out of reach.

As I stared at her, hoping she had not seen us change bushes, I thought of the time, the first time, I tried to rescue a dog. That was a hot day many summers ago, when feeding a near-lifeless dog for several days, gaining her confidence, rubbing on lemonade, and waiting until the dog licked my face with an enormous sandy tongue, using the dog's licking as a chance to rub lemonade under her neck and ice cubes to complement the soothing smell of lemonade, and then the wind dried her. I hadn't anticipated the wind. But, can wind be anticipated? So I fetched more cubes. On my return, the dog owner, an elderly gentleman, took her for a swim. I always remember that dog; she opened me and eased my own meager bruises.

A couple of weeks earlier that spring, on my way to school, I noticed a dog that was chained. Two older boys threw rocks at him. I punched one in the eye as they grabbed me; he must have run home to mama. The other fellow really thumped me in the head. I kicked at his taut groin and ran into an alley, hiding in a rubbish dumpster. Once at the house, I was not only late for supper but had coffee grounds in my hair.

The place that I mentioned, Sister Mary's Friendly Home for Boys, didn't actually have a name, to be honest, not one that I knew of, anyway. We called it that because it wasn't friendly. It was a bunch of kids without folks. You had to leave as soon after your ninth birthday as possible, to be housed elsewhere. The burly Dutch woman who fixed the meals rolled her eyes when I entered. While washing my hands in the kitchen sink she said something appropriate to that day. "I don't know. I just don't know. How anybody could get coffee grounds into his hair."

The whole popular idea of throwing rocks at dogs filled me with trepidation. Why did I join in, when their wonderful curiosity and companionship is such a gift? If as boys we were doing any good by throwing rocks, then dogs would want us to continue. So I stopped throwing rocks at dogs, because my heart wasn't in it and I came to be on familiar terms with dogs and wondered how long the need to redeem myself would last.

Lifting the baby out, as she seemed bored with dogs, I explained that Franklin Street was my first route; how a few of us neighbor boys strolled along the road to our favorite years of school, admiring everyone, in awe of everything. The sparks on Franklin Street will, no doubt, grow and flower inside me — those innocence days when we were oblivious to the dog-eared world around us. I left my second home, as a teenager, realizing how little I understood about the way adults behave. She burbled, as if to say: "It's just pride, look what's happening in the world."

My rocks hurt dogs, I explained to her, wondering what kind of a life there is, to be a fragment of a person, defined by a group. "Just do it," I expect she said, and I moved a washtub across the alley from the dog, carrying it nonchalantly, then dropping the tub at a place where we could watch and hide behind it, to consider why the tan dog was chained. We were a few feet from the dog when she barked. Sitting back on my haunches, wide-eyed and breathing heavily, I gave the dummy again as the baby finished my snacks. Again the dog barked. An infuriated man looked through a back window of the house. The venous outline of his one-eyed face fixed on the dog. We crouched and observed him and didn't move. At last, the man disappeared. He probably saw boys throw rocks at this dog and kept a bucket of water by the door, to throw on them. Inside the house, being hardened by unchanging habits, he must have muttered to himself and wound a clock. Being still for several minutes, one of my feet was numb until, while rubbing it, I suddenly swallowed twice as the man leaped at this dog, with a knife to her head, snarling. The dog cocked her head. The baby twittered and chuckled. I brought my feet under my body and took a deep breath. The dog stopped panting and closed her mouth. The man lunged forward out of the blue and the dog screamed and leapt back when a knife struck her shoulder: she yelped, staggering and running the full chain length. Scurrying forward on hands and knees, he rammed the knife into the dog's belly, or so it seemed or my vision was putting things over my eyes. The dog roared and pounced on him. The man grabbed her neck and held his knife high-poised over the shoulder. Growling, the dog kept spinning on her hind legs, trying to throw him off. With each jerk, the knife slipped in his hand, cutting his own hand more and more as the blood spread. I was alarmed at how frightening this was and that I felt out of control. Unleashing my pack, and as if galloping, I pointed my pocket knife at the man, but his shoulder-blade hit my hand and deflected the knife. When the dog spun, a massive paw smacked the man's face. I rolled out of reach, crouched low and feinted with my left hand. The dog snarled; her scruff was straight, then swerved, exposing the shoulder. I leapt on the man's back. I knew his face and abdomen were bleeding. Was I crying because of the dog's agony? I plunged the knife between his shoulders; howling seemed to ease the man's pain. Then he turned on me. I was caught between dog and man. With the dog's meaty breath in my neck, I used my hands as shields in front of the man's bulging eye. The mongrel broke her chain, lunged, hind teeth ripping into the man's hands and arms. With his left hand stuck in his mouth, the man was butted against the garage. I leaped and hit my head on the garage, saw stars but held on, grabbing the animal's shaggy mane. My knife was still sticking in the man's back — the dog's chain wrapped around my foot. I couldn't tell which foot, in the struggle, but was conscious of the sharp ankle-strangle. The dog released his hand and bit my face. Blood and saliva ran down my mouth and, for a moment, I wondered vaguely of what the staff at my care home would have done if they found blood on my shirt. I grabbed the collar and tried to take hold of her nose. The head motion of the dog made the collar hit my face. The impact felt like a few of my teeth came loose. I clenched my hands around the dog's nose. She pushed me against the garage and chewed on the man's shoulder, jerking the clothes away, as he grabbed at her face again. The animal stood back and barked, then roared and sat. At this moment, I heard the elderly man begin shouting.

I wrapped the dog's wounds with torn clothes. The sun shone white, cold white, over our shoulders. The intenseness of the moment clashed so hard with the washed-out white of the garage that, after being in the man's shadow, my eyes hurt. I held the dog and said: "Dadnammit, girl! What was he trying to do?" I stood, whimpering and unraveled the chain from around my leg. The man reached out. The dog wanted to lunge. I glanced to my left and saw a passerby putting on a green sweater and running towards us. The man called to her: "You know who this is? Tried to kill Becky." The woman seemed too shocked to answer — at the sight of my bloody face and the knife stuck in the man's torso. The man knelt, pulling timidly on the knife. The neighbor arrived to help him. I eased the dog away to our bush and picked up baby, and the dog simmered-down. The lady shouted and the man looked up

and waved his hand, saying, "Come back boy, with my Becky."
Then they gazed a bit. We returned to the alley, leaning on a
telephone pole to catch our breath, kneeling to ease my gid-
diness. My nose and mouth stopped bleeding, tricklings of
blood drying on my face; the mouth opened only more than
a crack, then froze, and I couldn't breathe through my nose.
Coming to my senses, I noticed a lady with a sack of rubbish.
Our eyes met and she opened her mouth: "Oh lord child,
you look like you was hit by a car?" Trying to stand, my legs
refused to work at first and we both wound up just raising our
hands a little, because all four arms just dangled. I finished by
being turned on one shoulder with an expression of trying to
push her away from me. She dropped her garbage and started
towards me. I wanted to lumber off, but imagined that after
a couple yards, blood would splash out the side of my head,
shuddering, holding my mouth, vomiting. I felt like throwing
up a dozen times. My disgust for the man's attack on another
being was so intense that it made me ill. The dog's suffering,
like the baby's openness, took me to the other side of meaning;
it's as if we share some kind of refuge, because we are at one
with each other.

Clouds covered the sun for a minute. As we walked through
the park, toward the dog hospital, our path filled with grey-
blue shadows which grew visibly. This park sloped downwards,
and then rose into thick bushes. There was a fountain with
four nude nymphs cavorting around a large bowl. The nymphs
were frozen in stone. A pool at the bottom of the fountain
was boarded up for autumn, with leaves and burlap scattered
on bushes nearby. A leafy place to hide baby, briefly, was what

was wanted, while I dropped Becky off, to heal at the rescue center. Baby went too, bob-bob-bobbing along. The park was clean like a church carpet. Ahead, there was an outline of a boy riding a bicycle across the hilltop, silhouetted against the sky like a silver bridge. Going up the hill my legs were buoys in water. At the hill's crest, sparrows flitted on dry ground. Several large trees stood in a yellow-dotted meadow. When the clouds swell, they throw a screen across the sun. Shadows beneath the trees grab what little light there is and press it to the ground. We went to a creek near the greenwood bench, and washed. If nobody comes, I will take baby to the home where I lived. We lay on the grass, some of the inhibition gone from us, sleepy. My thought was fixed on the futility of abuse to dogs — throwing rocks, hurling insults, and worse to children who fall from favor. A siren wailed in the distance. Ordinarily I would have thought to investigate or speculated about events. The world could learn from dogs to be open-hearted rather than self-obsessed. The siren went on for a long time, as if the vehicle was going very slow. Across the town, traffic buzzed — so removed from us that it passed in the simplest short-lived terms. From this hilltop and the lake beyond, cars rounded its shores, which were filled with swimming and shouts in summer. In the autumn colors, while the lake waited for its cover of ice, we returned to the bench on the hill in the park. Afterwards, Matron seemed pleased to look after the baby whose name I said was Becky.

A lifetime passes and the hill is changing. There is some resistance, against people who want to build on it. Is it a pity, their aversion to change, or an opportunity for others to preserve the hill and its creatures without being degraded by human life. I can see, even now, how uncertain I was about standing up for dogs, even before my observations from the greenwood bench, when genuine acts are heartfelt, when the need for proof doesn't come into it. Across the lake, between the houses and trees a mile away, two schools played soccer in spotlights, red fluttery cloth, cheerful music from bands that stay in formation and teams that clash with grunts bulging their cheeks. A chain-link fence of rainbow clouds hovers over their arena like a sizzling vine on a leash, waiting to eat the space around spectators and participants, waiting to eat the space in them and leave them the size of cubes, waiting to eat the space separating them from the crowd, when they dare to stop for a minute to think or by mistake fall into contemplation, waiting to reduce the distance between Becky and I and them and between them and the sky, waiting to reduce the space of our nostrils and shut off the breath between them and leave us shriveling blobs joined in the park's shadow. As if a person can be fenced in during their own quest for the true narrative. Far away, there are voices. A crowd of mothers and children, with a few men, spread out in the park. Branches near me blurred my vision, becoming, and then turning into, bright beams, as the sun, gooey, like sticky caramel mantling thinly, glowed warmly behind a glitter of cloud, but luminous branching light was always present.

One Hundred Days in Jail

Each day in jail there are more stripes across my skin. The stripes mirror the ceiling light. One hundred days leave mental stripes, too. So much solitude; I feel as though my bone marrow is reduced to effluent by the effect of being an entrapped animal. Stomach cramps and my legs resistant to unfolding, with sinuses reversing, draining into lungs, affecting my eyes and mouth which lock open, emitting kindergarten sounds. The face-side of my head is like a discarded bag with little air left in, until late afternoons, when sun splashes into my cell and melts the stripes.

Aware of being drugged, I feel the tyranny of fantasy, different than being stoned on pot, hopscotching around the past, absorbing the present and nightmare futures. Fantasy happens most often when I despair, just as humor wears thin — then I imagine changing form altogether. My body moves in segments, a lobster on a string. First the head shoots forward, belligerently, examining space that surrounds the next step and relays its agreement to the right side, which lurches ahead. My body's left, exclusive of the arm, hangs for a second, then follows in a series of chop movements like dominoes falling in a row. Finally in an orgy of grace, my left arm swings in a semicircle and propels the head again. Reaching a peak, I crest, fall over backwards, and shower sleet from a green-bleak sky, coating tree branches until they shine in the web of a streetlamp. Such was my first day free from jail while my case was assessed.

A halo over semaphores, glistening sparkly on sidewalks and turning to brown mush sheen under car tires and ricocheting off pant legs, lay on parked car windows, causing them to be opaque, laced headlights yielding a square and bent glow, hobbled daintily with clouded glasses, a moisture ring around hat brims, the distain of fashionable people who saw me on my shuffle as a pauper on a corner. They wanted to grab and twist the secret of life, to say "Why death?" or "What is death? Quick pauper, here is a donation; can you tell us how to stop death?" Sleet fell on them in straight white lines. What am I to them but a relative of curiosity? I tried to pay attention, attending to appearances and how receptive I am, careful not to miss my stride. Pace is important when you are on a string. I crept, lurched, trembled, shivered and jerked along the red brick streets. Sky lay cold, shining above the howling clicks of every neon sign on earth.

An automobile penetrated my fatigue, its sodden driver yawning straight ahead. Outside the car and inside the driver, a child walked alongside. Artificial lighting turned the driver's skin a mottled chameleon green. Lights exploded demurely along both street gutters, casting their half glows almost to the middle stripped yellow line, which shone in darkness beneath a city of iced snowflakes. Three separate body motions fused in a rare physical unity. Branches crackled under the collected works of breathing beings. Alleys shivered under unknown billions of neatly stocked stiff and sanctified snowflake ancestors, securely seated, salted and preserved for far away thaws of not yet conceived births. My fingers locked on sleeping houses and covered lawns, barring light. Holding streetlamps in view, garbage bins swirled, hanging soundless with threatening benevolence near fall-washed storm windows. Devouring timid furnace fire smoke and infiltrating cracked basement windows, I seeped into fathers' bedrooms, through cats' eyes and panda paws to erupt and pounce. While they dreamt about oceans of their own sweet childhood goo, I cleared the fallout from their bruising arguments, leaving them when they yawned to steal into youngsters' rooms, penetrating unoccupied key holes and under fur lined door bottoms, rolling in rugs, cracking bedposts and purring through the infinity of sleep. Dogs snarled and trembled. Cats hissed. Potted kitchen plants wilted and steaks paled. I swept across night skies, praising the harvest of rescued children while owners abstained.

In fact, no abstention materialized, as the fantasy neared its end. Life was divided into three areas: passion, fear, and misjudgment, as if in reality it is divisible. Confinement was responsible for shaping the fantasy, or illusion. The unreal effect of jail was more perilous because it became credible to the keepers in seeing me as a mentally discursive case. Are reflections on jail any different from craziness in the world — people on the breadline, vice, wars for the sake of religious beliefs, attention deficits gone berserk, Americans killing each other in America while leveling much of Europe and Asia. I was given a framework in which to live, as needs be, a prodding elbowing thump-crunch deal. Being confined brought me to think that my castles in Spain are like the skewed orange order of events, built and rebuilt in my head for no good reason and more flights of fancy each time. A glowing pauper under corners of increasing light and among wet branches, I dared the jail to dim my best intentions, to dimmer and dimmer and flicker away. I was trapped like a Cobra in a cage with one barred window, confined in a tiny space with stale air to breathe and barely enough room to coil against their invincible can-doism.

A whirlwind seizes inside me. Little time, precious time, is left. Why is there limp and elusive meaning — so much for liberal arts college — or is it my desperation at having to guess why I am at the jail's assessment paddock? Why do adults hack at others with axes and newfangled weapons? Why are people islands without weather? Is it only arrogance and vanity that causes this and can I ever be rid of it?

When my subvocals became audible, in the cell, I was jabbed by the wardens and their innocuous, infuriating mockery. Also incredulous was my response: parting my lips the width of a grain of rice, breathing in their monkey business: "Let my silence curl and settle in the sea bed of your storm, for we are embedded together as fossil to rock. Take heart as you fill in the form of your blank space, empty it with the sea tides and let it fill-in again." This is what I said to them: "Stand on the observation deck and watch yourself strut in the iridium sun, ride to blue mountains on the seventh moon of Saturn, split trees if you must, but avoid at all costs blistering the skin off babies. Pieces of our form are shared between our heads and our hands. Pieces of it are in wallets, banks, spiritual darkness, plants, oceans, and civic departments. Please remember, wherever advantage is taken, disadvantage is given."

"Hey!" shouted a voice wrapped in bubblegum. I jumped up,

scattering some papers waiting for my signature. "When does the action start?" "Yeah," another teenage inmate joined in, "We ain't got all day." "Right you are," I chuckled. "You haven't got all day," she promised. "For myself, I'm in it, in the sun as surely as if I'm part of it, beneath a waterfall or an open shower head. I'm as much the shade as the undersides of birds."

A haircut was needed since the first week in jail. I remember being escorted across the jail grounds into a long cell-lined corridor, catching myself breathing through my mouth. My arms swung across the front, instead of at the sides. My hands brushed through the shaggy growth. Glancing nervously at a man of Chinese appearance walking in front of me, I noticed that he wore his hair like a white cap with a hole in the middle. It bobbed on top of his stiff step. Hair was never so unruly before my time in jail. At least once, when taken away from my cell, I was pulled by the hair. My speech then was appalling, as if noise on behalf of a few tortured people.

I tried to cheer up my incarcerated brothers and sisters with interest and hope, for example, with a drug warped anecdote about the navy — 15 rubber life rafts, armored life rafts — being seized. Whatever happened, I said there was a buffalo skull, too. My last words were: "We can't let them get even one in our ocean. It's just like letting Big Brother in the bathtub — soon all the waves topple like dominoes and then they'll land on Kansas City and then where are we?"

I'm unsure of the nature of the criminal charge against me. Knowing people as I do, one of them, belatedly, probably turned me in for smoking pot. Or Nancy's parents tried to sue me, or someone made a citizen's arrest. Maybe there is more than one answer. Perhaps more than one person snitched, with the crime taking some time to be defined.

I felt the weight of hair on the fringe of my sight, on the balls of my kicked heels, and in the burned palms of my hands. Little brown stains on my arms and chest marked the entry of little attitude-changing electrodes. My hair felt like it held my head like a clamp. "Well, it's over my head, all this," I said to the back of another pauper inmate waiting for his assessment, tottering forward, traipsing toward the mall wing of jail. "I've been on the seventh floor for a hundred days and missed the worst of winter. That's something. The worst of winter is gone. I'll soon get rid of this hair and be ready for spring." Then, on the right, the bright-striped barber pole appeared. It was a cage in glass, harmless and forever turning. The barbershop was downstairs. Entering, I glanced up and saw through part of the windowed roof, partly topless, lost in dazzling sky reflected sun, as if from the ocean bed looking up, bright shafts fluctuated from the surface heaving like a human conscience, then settling steadier downwards steadier and vice versa.

A tuxedo man sat in the corner of the shop. I looked at the two barbers and thought they probably employed him to shine shoes and buy grandchildren ice cream cones. There was also a lady or a guard or a prisoner inmate in a pink floral frock, sitting in the barber shop. A convict in black and white striped clothes was having his head shaped like a little league baseball player. (The habit of estimating people is an unsavory condition fostered by being victimized; it's like an abreaction, as if someone else is at fault. Estimating people is most likely tantamount to being out of bounds mentally. People won't like it, even though they are aware of doing it themselves. So afterwards, they are likely to state their misperception out loud about whoever they estimated. This is why I'm in trouble.) The barbers cut hair and talked about sports to each other. Tuxedo man appeared to be unoccupied. Was he related to a barbering family? Who knows why the pink person was there. Whoever it was looked the epitome of fertility, radiant with joy.

Pink's skin was a multiplex of fawn-speckled under brown with the bosom and knees sticking out a bit and the legs were out of view. Or were they taken away during a scuffle with jailers who raided the shop to reclaim the appropriate role — of visitor, convict, genuine person, inmate, guard? Her long hair, though, from what I could see, if that was hair, or if it belonged to her, was pink at the ends. A scotch-plaid scarf, in blue, covered all but the bottom hair on her shoulder blade. The hair was bunned and wrapped in a thing. She really looked sublime, sitting down into one of the plush red barber chairs. Miss Rio: that was who she reminded me of — the dog lady, who chained her animal behind the garage every day for years, until I freed the creature.

"What'll it be, sir?" "Huh?" I said, startled by the voice and simultaneous reflection of his face in a mirror and the grimaced barber's smile and his absolutely waxed head.

"How would you like it cut?"

"Short, cut it very short, please" I answered weakly.

"Any particular style?"

The pink floral person watched. She stopped reading her magazine, if that was what she was doing, and looked at my eyes.

"Ah, yeah, like yours. Only without the fluff on top."

"What fluff?"

"That little upside down bang." (This was the longest conversation in one hundred days and I wanted to prolong it.)

The smile disappeared inside his yellow smoking mouth. He swatted a long comb against his breast pocket. The other barber leaned over and appeared to evaluate my head with some concern. These were barbers out of an ancient slick age of togas and perfumed gestures. They were in their forties and had the bleary eyes of combat on the front lines of the television lounge. Like most barbers, they had long and curly, but even, arm hair.

The electric clipper buzzed around my head. It whirred into the hairy sphere that protected my brain. My ears whirred with the noise. I felt the hairs fall dead on my shoulders. The barber slashed through the thick of the clump and dabbled at the sides.

Miss Rio slipped her magazine into a handbag, intent on watching the barbery. She wore Stiletto shoes and blue tights up and under her dress. The buzzing became less harsh, droning further away. I closed my eyes and sighed. There was a pain at the edge of my eyes, a burning sensation and a smell of lemon. I thought of the barber pole stripes falling toward the floor, with my hair. The stripes appeared to peel off as they rose to the surface. Opening my eyes, Miss Rio's pink hair was piled in a bow now, behind her neck. There were wavy wrinkles in her forehead as she frowned.

The barber behind, smiled at his conquest over my double-crown. I said to myself, is he thinking that he's giving it to the Jerries at Cologne, catching a glimpse of the sharp-bladed scissors slash within an inch of my inner ear? "That's all right, I don't need that ear anymore," I said out loud, "they're taking everything that isn't bolted down. I've lived with a captive body and brain for one hundred days. I can manage without that extra ear."

Chop, chop, chop, with an eye on my eyebrows next. I bet with myself that the barber crops his wife's hair whenever he returns home; marriage is cutting and recutting a shape. The pink lady smiled. Chop, chop, chop. "Cut it shorter, fluff," I insisted. Chop! Chop! Chop! Hands, scissor blades, fingers and a Mason's ring flew around my face. They dove and soared now like heckling birds at my eyes and ears and the back of my neck. Then an electric clipper defoliated the top of my head. All painless. No pulls. Not even a nick as the siege continued. Pain or blood is bad barber form.

"How's that, sir?" the barber asked as he whirled the chair around to face a mirror.

"You're not even started, Fluff. I asked for it to be cut short."

"If I cut it any shorter, sir, you'll be bald."

"Cut it short, please Fluff; cut it as short as you were taught to, please. Cut it as short as yours will be in ten years. Then we'll polish it. We'll put a fine sheen on it. We'll wake up that tuxedo and ask him to kindly polish it."

"Okay, bud. Okay, cool down." Chop. Chop. Chop! Whirrrrrr. The barbers' smiles drew mine out of confinement and overcame the irritation welling up inside me. The short-winded laughter spliced between the whirr of clippers and the chop of scissors as the barber worked fiercely. His wrists perspired.

"See what he's doing." the pink one said in a voice flecked with warm metal. "He's trying to chop off your head. Hahahahahahahah..."

"I see now what he's doing with my head," I punched in, finally on firmer ground, with the laughter, "but who cares? I've got an extra one hidden away in a very safe place." We all laughed, laughed until we shook, while the barber walked on the dying stripes and slashed at my final still-standing hairs.

As if in a flash, part of me is missing, dying on the floor, and there is a sense in the flash of beginning afresh without it. My only desire now is to be alive and without condemning anyone for what's happened. I recall a youthful spirit, defamed as a tattoo, and ashamed. I need to let loose boyhood-buried courage, to overcome the crudity which sucked early innocence with the back of a hand, or the front of hands, or the belt. At moments like this, there is a wanting, not to be saved from being beaten to death, but to lose recriminations and forego estimations.

Two-Eyed Dana's

Something sounded like glass clinking; also a truck and I sat up in bed. There was Pete, still asleep, and the sun rising. Pete, a fellow traveler, was also detained at his majesty the sheriff's pleasure. I went over to the window, shivering a little from the breeze, nude, thinking of the bed heat, too sleepy to turn around, and the soothing breeze was cold comfort. When the sun is low, its pink light peeks over the periphery of dawn. It was that part of the day when the world is divided into two sharp zones: light and crimson. A homestead perched on a distant border, where the sun was yet to reach. The crimson glowed; its streak of light flowing from each side beyond the window. The light shone on Caesar, Dana's jalopy misfit-collecting van, its barred windows sneering from a reserved bay in the parking lot. The way the outline of this van was lit by sunrise made it look like a steel skeleton. Streaks of light met in the windowed wall of a greenhouse, quivering water in a glass. An oak tree stood proud on the large green, still holding most of its leaves, and now the sun grasped it and changed it to a crimson torch, the trunk a deeper shade in that light with young branches, sprouting like eager fingers. Then, leaves around each branch glowed scarlet.

I never remember daybreak being so spectacular. The sun crept higher in the sky, white light seeping onto the road. My hands moved from the left leg, transferring an itch to my nose, which made me aware of absentmindedly itching it. When

I concentrated on it for a few moments, the itch vanished. "Amazing," I said softly, not wanting to wake Pete. My arm was unmarked, no small burrowing creatures from traveling rough.

Turning, without thinking again, about the turn, I snatched my clothes off the chair and crossed the hall into the dressing room. Dana was there. I jumped into my jeans, pulled the shirt over, grabbed the boots and tried to leave. She stopped me, waving her syringe, motioning me to sit while she did her mime. Two-Eyed Dana loved her monkey, his little furry eyes, the balloon over his head, and he loved her right back, never biting her in a fit. Two-Eyed Dana fought the forest, the rangers and the state governor's helicopter, to build an assessment center in her woods. She said he loved his helicopter, but rules were rules to break, the governor told her after the affections Dana bestowed on him and his copter. She fought to keep her monkey, too. "Booming cannons echoed from the coast," she beckoned in a clear moment. She won her case, against opposition from those who petitioned and lived near the woods and refused her invitations to tea.

"NO!" she begged, "You runt, after all I've done. Anyway, you've been there before." "Eddddddkaboeggallge," insisted the monkey who put his fists and four thumbs into a profile, like the others, as if going to the coast to join in the war. There, he saw grinning horrors and bloody arms. "He thought of me in his own way," Dana narrated, "and missed my comforts and shrill voices. Buildings smashed and wreaths of purple noodles on the trees." The monkey blasted the enemies and skewered their memories and chased them back, into the lake. When it was over he returned to Dana, living in her woods. It was not such a long war, but she said her joints were rusting and oil generally was in short supply. There were lots like her, Pete told me on my arrival, lots of rural scatterings to place crazy individuals, war veterans returning with fried minds, the generally misunderstood, those posing a threat, and down-and-outs.

"I'm on a journey to help dismantle the scaffold surrounding me and be independent of it," I explained over tea and brownies. Pete said that Dana's mime irritated the infections he suffered with since he fell while cleaning windows near his last residence at a half-way house. He claimed to be covered in snow and left until spring when the ground thawed.

The three of us walked to the day room, for the daily cinematic treatment: the first film was called "Darkness Down. Down on the Road." Lord knows who made it, probably the doctors — the only time we saw them clearly they were knitting something together, with eyes on the eye of a needle, probably as part of Dana's staff development program. Credits were missing at the start of the film, if it did have a beginning. Every time we are ushered to the dayroom a film is in progress, now with two lonesome Jaguar-haired shadows, passing by a line of Jeeps, the lights shining blue on their faces. Like clouds frozen and nailed solidly over eyes, they passed often, by light, in the light of the speeds overtaking, had eaten and slept and traded on this road, with fancies on it and in its terms. The films are hallucinatory, as if encouraging madness will cure insanity, as if losing our minds will free us from the preconceptions that caused us to follow a reified world in the first place. Fine for the monkey because, from his point view, this nightmare is real.

The Jag-hair were driven by fear of a limitless hole at the end of life, destined to live in constant sight of the road, watching for Jeeps. These shadows never strayed from the road when the moon lit the fields around, and geometrical shapes with eyes popping in the wrong places gazed and moaned at them — everywhere the moving of shadows. Geometric shapes of past and family, folks traveling on a crescent and never coming to touch the road. Never revealing themselves to its lines — to the webs which hung above — and in the darkness to the shades and past tenses of shapes. So, they lived on the road, or so it appeared in this film. In all their days, they never left it. The Jag-haired shadows came out from their shelter, from their cave, from their living places only at night. One night over the telephone and power company automated trees, the Jag-hairs watched the migration of the fog animals. They sat by the road and whispered as the herd passed. It was maddening to watch — which was Dana's point, in keeping her place in the woods, to evidence insanity. There was only the silence of the road. The fog lay down in shifty shells on the lake road, over its own layers and deep in its own wake, soft and silent.

Then without a break, a film sequence called The Wreck in Jag-hair Territory — a vehicle shattering drops of moisture, splashing the snowflake purple and gold of the darkness and voom shhhhhhissssh through a dent in the night, past shadows and shapes and the translucent herd. Those people with muted faces and visions, committed to the path ahead, by the lights and not noticing any of the differences in the veils and canyons of fog, whished past, untroubled, passing through a herd of the fog sheep, then a silent passage. The shadows and shapes watched the herd, without noise, without hooves touching the ground, without young calling to mothers, without brays, without shuffles, without apparent thought or conventional sound. The herd breathed its way past. Two roadside hunters watched for moments of clear poaching opportunity before they realised the herd passed. They had only watched the fog. Darkness swirled round them; their thoughts, sounds, and meanings inside the audience. Then one of the vehicles passed, roared by on the mushy road, its dizzy tires grinning. The couple listened to it lacerate the fog, listened to the moisture close around it, before, moments later, a crash: a minibus smashed through a wooded thicket and screeched to a stop, the doors clunk-locked and double-clunk locked. A scream turned to blood and ancient gargled sounds like frogs make in early spring, under water and mud, traipsing about to breathe, coming into daylight when nothing is apparent but the certainty of light. For a minute, only time and a primordial reflection inside, holding safe frog meanings whatever they were — no more of the stained glass heresy from cathedrals, no more of the holes in the mud, with their own veins traced in frog trails.

The herd exploded into vast and everlasting light. This is what we imagined that the shadows and shapes heard and perchance tasted sparks left by a hubcap as it skittered, as if of its own accord, on concrete, although Pete and the few others appeared to be locked in a hypnotic sort of trance, absorbing the film show. Finally, the herd rested in front of a whirly crescent, slowed and stopped by fog. Beads of moisture grew on the hubcap, as temporarily as veiled questions about what their madness was doing for us during the movie. There is an intermittent connection between us as the subjects of treatment and to the film as an object of Dana's experiment to readapt misfits, where cartoon TV failed us as children. So, we watched the walls and cities built on its surface by the reflection of fire from the wreck. At last the camera instructed its medicated audience to watch the pulse of its chrome-softened and cloistered speed, cut off from the wreck and the crash scene, if it was ever observable, surrounded now by fog. There was a dark, silent interlude. Next morning in the film, a crash couple emerged from the wreck. Fog cleared and the road emptied. They crawled on all fours, trying to be unseen, to the hubcap and make it a trophy to their survival. Fog passed distant swamps at the next waysides where two more frightened occupants rolled up their car windows to reactivate small circular muscles straining now to open the vehicle's doors. Then they raced through lowland to escape fog, in the distant hills. The road was designed as a swift passage when the sound of motors ate the air raw. The other wrecked people became less discernable and then unseen. As they passed, the screen blanked in diamond-white color and strobe lights belted us with steely shining that felt like coming from the inside out.

One thing which was not spoken about was the actual film therapy. This was what Dana called it: "Film therapy with two eyes" which described our assessment, so the name stuck, Two-eyed Dana's Assessment Center. Privately, we usually talked about the last night's TV thriller. What was it called in Denver? Thriller-horror double bill or creature feature. "I rooted for the kidnap-killer's family all the way," I said to Pete. "They should've been honored with the key to Denver for their tolerance and generosity." Pete squeezed down a mouthful of smuluousch and eyed his lover, leaving smuluousch residue on his face. "Farm boys with big guns might've given him a sporting chance," he said. "Yeah. But in their hysterical reaction to the kidnapping, they lost one or two lawmen and a perfectly good psychopath, who was alright until city hall drove him to distraction," said Phillip Blockdon. "He was no less meaningful in his pursuit of happiness than any of the agents who tracked him, or the girl he kidnapped. But he did not; I repeat did not, much to the disappointment of reporters, molest her."

Blockdon was a pediatrician on the outside. The way he recalled it, the sheriff came for him during a tiff-de-tiff at his office. He was carrying an unmarked calendar to his desk when his knees started to jangle. When he sat, the jangling ceased. When he rose the jangling started. This caused a furore. It apparently upset two hospital trustees at the Coke machine. The trustees went off to the bathroom and the machine became animated, he said, lifting its skirts and also fleeing. Later, Blockdon's nose buzzed, such was the aura of pell-mell. His coworkers handled the situation with aplomb, one of them fetching water while a second offered him a paper bag. He held his head in this bag for ten minutes and the buzzing stopped. Philip developed immunity to paper bags and for a long time after his admission for film therapy assessment, he sat at a table with a watermelon husk on his head. Eye and mouth holes had been punched out of it. At the end of the 49th day, the watermelon fell off. A horrible whining sound coiled from his chest. One of the staff rushed for help, returned with a mop and hit him in the head with it. He said he was never the same since, but is anyone the same after tripping too much into hallucination?

"The therapist is a specially trained agent of the mental health team..." Philip blurted out. "They train people as a profession to kill off individual spirit," as I put it, more or less sliding into my own conversation, "and when they detect the spirit arising, they suppress our capacity to regain sanity. Then we revert to injecting what we think are their healthy bits, like TV celebrities with breast enhancements, or morphed hormones, bigger lips, and emasculating muscles until there are erections in biceps."

"And as they're dancing," Pete said, as he and Phillip stood together on the table, "Have the therapist, as they do, seduce him. With love or sex or professionalism, or whatever the occasion demands." "He'll forget about Susie Q," Phillip shouted. "Then she'll be removed from a danger." "He'll give up his weapons, now that neither of them is afraid," Pete yelled. "...And...he could...be treated." We shouted and jumped on the table. As the tears dribbled, we realized the pitiful indignity of our resuscitating caricatures of Dana's full-term residents, just standing and gazing into the chest of others as if new life can be breathed into another person.

There was something of the adage of quarreling sisters here: every day was a gift for faded flowers. What holds them together, their wish for fulfilment? Or shortening mortality and the sisters' awareness of it? How many will learn? It's clear: people are outstanding, like Jones. Can they inspire us to be awake to our cartwheeling antics? Give them power and they are egomaniacal, unlike Jones, shaping us in their image.

Philip's postulate: "There are many preoccupations worthy of an unmarried person on a fine afternoon such as this. I chose one in particular, an unwise favorite fixed since child-hood — reactions to the events of each day, which berate anyone else are unwise and therefore futile. Daydreams are better than nightmares: it's easy to identify the nonsense, whereas bad dreams are hints of deep effects from being mad at someone. Anyone can live a nightmare life like this even as a daydream because recovery is in the loving rather than berating."

Pete's postulate: "How interconnected the world is, com-pared to my fractured boyhood and teenage view of it. The flow of leaves and the air in trees, above the rigid-headed in war zones; nighthawks and wet bats in the oozy fall sky are commonplace. Behind the lights of mechanized transport and beneath the flashy neon diner signs, there is a need for reshaping and brightening, at least to my uncultivated way of thinking."

Dana's basement tavern is a watering hole of all due cries and sentimental barf — the place like that room under the grade school stage where students go for peace, unless a lecher-ous teacher is there waiting to grope. One petition to use the chemical baton with film therapy is that mental illness is pro-tective because we become oblivious to socializing pressures, like wearing a straightjacket, taking in World Series baseball games, the meaningless starvation of a billion people. Subject-ing us to loose construing, the aim is to expel the gross effects of consumerism in ourselves, turning worldwide poverty into acceptable enigmas, ingesting the subtle effects of Two-Eyed Dana's view of democratic fecundity.

Downstairs, in the smoky tavern, its green walls, muted multicolored people seated at booths, there, a paunchy bartender wore a frog mask, without warts. I was convinced the tavern would teach us more about a path to free us of unspoken upsets, to begin what the therapists called normal activities. "George, look at this place," I said to the bartender, nursing what they referred to as beer. George, resting his backside on the counter, squinted at me through eyes buried in fog. He seemed to breathe the stale air sideways, as if through gills. Did he, too, begin an impossible journey before, nothing more provocative than a few beers? "Yeah," George said. He looked around and remembered the start of a nationwide campaign to use parks as a natural place to start courses in practical nudity, forestry and herbal medicine. He sighed, "Yeah, what about it?"

"It's green."

George glanced at the place and then answered, "You're right, green."

"You're not encouraging me, George. Did a gentleman tell you not to encourage me?"

"No, I ain't seen one for a month."

"He could've phoned you. He knows I come here, damn him."

"He didn't," George anticipated.

"It's green, George. If you painted this place a bright color, if you painted these walls orange and the woodwork black, you'd have released something. You'd be released."

That was it, simply, my occupation was to write about universal landscapes, inside and out, in the spirit of being orange-free from childhood baggage, and before, for instance, a nuclear bomb goes off in a scientist's bathroom at the secret underground Nevada White House and blows the world sky high. Or before the natural magnetism of earth evaporates, leaving us dwellers without gravity and unable to swallow. Or before Porpoises learn to speak English and invade the London Stock Exchange to help Britain earn legitimate profit. Or, before the external landscape turns to a color of its own accord.

Now in the tavern, I was deep again in plans for renovation. "The place has been through a lot, George, and all of it green. It's time to change. The green belongs to another age. Adapt to changing times or you'll lose your customers. Look, there isn't much of a crowd here tonight, see?"

"Never much of a crowd Wednesdays."

"Well, there could be — look, why do you think there isn't much of a crowd Wednesdays? Because they're all in the lounge watching colored television, that's why."

"Hmmmmmm."

"Man, we don't have to accept fate. We don't have to just shrug and resign yourself to failure. We can be successful. All we have to do is realize that what the maddening public want is warmth, light, excitement. They're like moths, George; they go where the light is."

"I got lights here, just had 'em installed last summer. Expensive, too."

"Sure they're expensive, George, sure they are. They're fine lights, too. Look, I'm just saying that with faith we can go all the way. We can't be content just to lip service these days. How do you think man got to the moon? He was willing to take chances, that's how. And in the blink of an eye, the moon is going to be orange.

Then what'll guys like us do? We'll be stuck here on this green earth in small green places. Sure."

I sipped my lemonade. George waited on a few more customers, youngsters filtering in from the new admissions reception room. Did George feel that he had to admit it and concede that much? I guessed as he glanced back. Sure, the place looked dull to him. Of course, he was there nearly thirty years. "What about these kids with blankety-blank faces and scar punctuations on their arms. They wouldn't come here if they thought the place was dull, or a possible exit, would they?

"It's something to consider, George. All schemes are something to consider." Talk about nudity in the lounge almost cost George his license, a cunning plan about buying old racehorses to breed new ones, so he would think twice about a new proposal. "It can always be covered, next time under a blue. Yes, blue is a good color."

Whatever George proposed, he remained to serve Dana's pick-me-ups to increasingly subdued customers. Pete and Philip were sent to halfway houses. Two-Eyed Dana's Assessment Center rubber-stamped the jail's desire for custody and I was transported to a mental asylum for rehabilitation.

The Balloon and Shower Room Escape

A plan dawned, for a few of us, during winter afternoons when we were all gathered in the playpen. Around 45 of us lived in Cherwell 1A, following our stay in the Hole, for what they called intensive care. Newcomers arrived and others left, but it was usually about that many. Before activity outside the ward was introduced, the staff corralled us in this big room we called the playpen. Regardless of the moods, when the daily state of emergency was declared, everyone stayed in the pen, from the time we were taken from bed until the time we were put back again. Now, after a new charge nurse, Victor, we just use it for play, except during random states of emergency. Most often, the staff are at the front. They try to organize the noises so that everybody is engaged in some sounds, music or otherwise.

Recently, the stand-in doctors put me down as actually ill again, being disorganized and confused; more to the point, staying out of the pen too much, skipping too many meals, missing treatment groups and ward meetings. The theory was insane. The more organized these practitioners, the more primitively they viewed us as internal and external distur-bances. Being under intensive care meant solitary living again in the Hole, where a person becomes a more viable human proposition, thanks to the drug-fingered and crab-faced staff.

The playpen was about twenty yards square. At the far end were two doors which separated the pen from the sleeping areas. At the near end, where the attendants gathered, were two doors leading to the place for eating. Men slept in a dormitory off the far end, women through another set of double doors at the near end. Very large windows at either side kept the playpen well lit. On one side was a porch which overlooked a walk-in aviary. There was the odd Cockatoo, but mostly parakeets, with a small weedy vegetable garden, and a view beyond of grass and trees. Cherwell 1A was reputed to be the only ward with such a view. The others were surrounded by buildings with addicts, blood ailments, dementias, spaced-out children, psychopaths, terrorists, brain surgeries, police cases, teenagers, celebrity rehab, staff, indigent elderly, quarantined microscopic bugs, and crippling manias of all sorts.

That afternoon when a plan dawned, a show and sing-song game was in progress. Two thirds of those present were encircled in the middle of the room. There was another circle at the near end. Several people were off to the side, where I was, reading or knitting or other individual things. "A female with red lipstick to meet this man with a stocking cap and sing." Everyone looked around for red lips; a husky nurse hoisted a fawn-haired lady from her lounge chair. They shuffled toward the fellow, who was stooped and seasoned with grins. The lady's purse bounced gaily off her hip as she met the stocking capped man she'd met a thousand times before. "A female now with gold earrings to meet this *other* man with blue socks and sing." Everyone looked at ears.

Then, out of the blue, Abel strolled into the pen from the far door. Where had he been? What did he think he was doing? I put down my biography of Beethoven and walked quickly to where he was. Abel was sufficiently unique to be a permanent

Cherwell 1A patient, or, and more likely, the staff were insecure and defensive enough that, after such a time, they could
not let Abel grow. "Abel, what the hell?" He smiled, placed
his hand on my shoulder and eased us toward the tea trolley. I
squeezed his elbow.

"What?"

"The plan you mentioned at breakfast?"

"Yeah, what about it?"

"The shower."

"Whadda ya mean, shower?"

"There's something about the shower I think you should see."

"The shower?"

"Yeah. I think the balloon plan is best. But we need to feign
another route..."

We slurped tea in silence. The game was really funny now.
People singing a dozen songs in a surreal way — hundreds of
dreams and goodness knows what being verbalized. Abel was
older; I loved him as one does a true friend. He claimed to be
the first pacifist, brother of Cain. The rest, including Albert
Einstein, Bertrand Russell and Prof. Harvard Winston Dusset
of New Jersey, followed in his path.

Abel was about six feet two, stringy but sleek and very
strong. Blue eyes were the prominent feature of his bespectacled face. The smooth olive skin was stretched across his face.
His forehead was high with thin blond hair tousled on top.

"How often do you take a shower?"

"Oh, once a week, I guess," I answered in a bemused tone.

"Well, try for twice a week. And tell me what you think of
the diagonal corner."

Abel liked this oblique approach to things. I knew by his tone, he had made a discovery. The shower room was a place of intrigue and controversy. First, the enormous space with shower stalls, sinks, unused bathtubs, and toilets, was the most unobserved area in the place. (Female hygiene was separate.) Inspection was difficult due to poor ventilation: if the showers were on, windows on the shower room doors were steamed.

I stood in one of the five shower stalls and looked around. The door was straight ahead. To my left was a row of high and narrow gym lockers. Two long wooden benches fronted the lockers and three little tables occupied a side wall to my left. One corner of the bathroom appeared to be cut off intentionally — for all we knew, a ventilation shaft or a bricked-up chimney.

"But Abel, if it doesn't lead to the outside, it won't get us anywhere."

"All the same, it must lead somewhere," he said without a chewing pause in his sandwich.

"Okay," I said to Abel, as we sat on the dining bench, "what if there is a space behind it? And what if we actually get out before the balloon is ready? Then what?"

"You can't be flexible when you're rigid, Paul. That's your problem. I've conceded that to you many times. You are one or the other. That's why you're here.

"Look, we go. Chances are, some of us will be caught. So, get on with it for the sake of experience. Theoretically, we'll escape or at least be more free for trying. We concentrate on the intention and not the outcome and make ready the balloon. If by some fluke, escaping from the shower room isn't discovered and if there is a way out, then we go if your balloon plan collapses."

Abel started a record of shower room use while I tried the weights — useful to me in both escape plans, as a device to strengthen myself with exercise following months of the hospital's bone-narrowing diet, and as a trial to test whether the staff allowed showering after daily exercise. The weight lifting initiative was something of a surprise to everyone, evidently bolstering self-esteem and confidence generally. During the two months which followed, Abel organized a list of workers and tools; I lined up resources for the balloon caper. We sowed the idea in the minds of a few key people. Basically, the entire plan will be ritualized — a secret affair allowing each participant to keep some of the secret private.

"Naturally, the escape will be a comic smokescreen," Abel said, introducing the idea to others, "a joke played on behalf of everyone trapped in lunatic asylums disguised as hospitals. We might all escape downtown, more than a few, possibly in all directions. Behind the façade of escape, we show up the confidence trick played by psychiatrists, taking their salary in exchange for pretending that they incarcerate people who are dangerous — allowing us to flee this madness and find our free will: their toil at the expense of fruitful lives brutalized by their business."

By spring, the basic crew numbered four: Murdock, Jimmy, Nadine, and Mrs. L, plus the two of us. Abel was to supervise the shower room and help me with the balloon in his spare time.

Jimmy was in his mid-30s, confined as a juvenile and still

wearing his hair in a tightly-cropped butch style. His diagnosis was undisclosed — apparently in his case due to the rarest category of undiagnosed mental disorders which occupied the inn of his body. Jimmy was placid and sulky when unmotivated and became vaguely remote if annoyed. He was a natural to start lifting weights in the shower room. Because he was an appeaser, Abel said, the escape plan grabbed him, with a contagious enthusiasm and quietly fearless commitment.

Nadine's presence was another reason we were confident about Jimmy. A most beautiful girl, her love for Jimmy was an endless poem to watch. Several years younger than him, her short straight blonde hair always comforted the shoulder of the puce sports coat that she usually wore. Nadine was a cheery person in his company but a haunting introvert when upset. Abel said her fault was the lack of dimension to her love for Jimmy, which was boundless. Yet, she didn't touch him a lot, didn't fondle him. When she smiled and tilted her head, their blue eyes reflected an incomparable compassion. Her sense of quietude comforted him. Only when Jimmy's nerve collapsed, only when he was introspectively diffident about her, did he loose control of his limbs.

Murdock's story, as told to him at his trial, was near to being monstrous, if the innuendo was true. He was one of the fathers of four battered children, according to a social worker who testified that two of the babies died. Murdock was about age 40, bespectacled, thick red curly hair, smooth dark skin. He became agitated by any mention of violence. He was easily provoked even though he lacked the spite to direct his resentment against staff provoking it in him. Although Abel was ostracized by Murdock, his unresolved amnesic quandary was somehow turned to good effect with the basic team by stimulating his interest in them, after the routine of the escape was established.

Mrs. L was hunched and swollen at the joints, malnutrition having taken its toll. A woman of about 55, thin white hair stood like slender reeds from her swollen head. Her evasive eyes irritated Abel, because his were shifty, too. However, Abel's broad face, reassuring smile and calculating repose tended to mask his abhorrence of cruelty — a disgust so revolting that when he became aware of it, he turned to raving tirades against the Hole, dictatorships, priests, insurance companies, and supermarkets. Mrs. L was extremely focused, intelligent, especially in her perception of other human relationships. She was scrawny, like scrapes of many people pasted into a living collage, and Murdock found comfort in the presence of her puzzlement.

The hospital notes stated that I was 25, serpentine, addicted to Winston cigarettes, a five foot nine inch stock frame with short legs and thick brown hair curling at the nape, usually stubborn, communicable when awake following treatment, abnormally independent and extremely outspoken when unrestrained, resorting to stirring things when other people reacted to threats or humiliation.

At the hospital, every day is similar. In fact, the days are so much the same that it is difficult to distinguish one staff-controlled event, if there were any worthy of that label, from another. Odd, how one group of people, in loco parentis, act as if those they are responsible for are too insecure and effete to be gainfully employed. It's as if the staff need to experience their unpleasantness towards us to convince themselves we are best kept as empty vessels. As if their mind-numbing regime will make them accepted by the environment they work in and the organization which feeds on it.

Although most people I knew and watched appeared disillusioned with their existence in Cherwell 1A, they possessed a capacity for sudden excesses of energy. Some people were at times beyond reach, appearing to exist like hollow facts. Others, like the basic team, were, like me, at various stages of waking up from bedlam and inch by inch regaining mental stability. Our plan aims to channel what power of recovery there is to our advantage, each person giving their own energy and meaning to the escape. Our collective aim will humiliate the punishers who dehumanize us, and in so doing unmask the unvirtuous acts which demean them and surely damage them, too. The escape can be an antidote, energy for clear thinking and strong character, a monument of conversion from a drug reference number to an open-minded human being. At least this is how Abel and I were thinking of it.

Nadine cleaned the baths in the women's toilet and the showers in the men's toilet room every day. So it was in the spring, when hygiene starts in earnest, that the basic crew started work. Murdock began hanging around the showers, helping Jimmy with weights, and taking two showers a week and then three, which was supposed to be the limit. Mrs. L spent a lot more time in the men's lounge, serving tea and coffee. She was in there from about ten in the morning until eleven or so and then from about two in the afternoon until three o'clock or so, which was supposed to be the limit. These were good times, because the playpen was busiest and the people in the lounge were knotted with uncoordinated bodies and disoriented brain-firings. Jimmy said we were all Pisces until one day when Mrs. L said her eyes stopped seeing stars; it was then when we all laughed that we realized that it was our time to act. Mrs. L fainted in Jimmy's arms, which made us all sense the danger of her penchant for near-enough boiling baths. A man with a signet ring came and tried unsuccessfully to pull us apart.

Each member of the basic team enlisted others, known only to the basic member, to avoid the mixed messages caused by mixing in groups: the staff found mixing confusing. Mrs. L's participants started keeping some of the newer chronic admissions in clean pinafores, for each wide-eyed inert-spaced day in their laid-back chairs along the playpen walls.

One humid summer evening, Murdock started to peck away at the diagonal wall in the corner of the shower room, using a little metal peg that Jimmy gave him from the weight lifting stands. Murdock chipped into the plaster until he outlined a square on the edges of the brick. The opening was going to be about three feet high and a couple of feet wide. Jimmy watched through the steam, as though preparing for a shower, while Murdock worked, and the outline was soon finished.

This beginning was a pleasant surprise to me and Abel, who had been on hunger strike for a week, as we prepared ourselves to be a low-profile three foot by two foot shape. I was drafted in to chip further into the outline. Abel established a tunneling routine for the basic team. As it happened, I had plenty of time to gather canvas for the balloon.

My big problem was to shift the canvas from the storeroom, which was behind the dining room, to the unused balcony. This meant smuggling canvas pieces through the dining room and playpen to its opposite end, where a stairwell led to a boiler room. The plan was to ask three people to help me bring canvas to the stairwell, then out a window and onto a balcony just above the porch. There is a solid railing so the hot air device can be worked on there.

The canvas was draped over a stack of folded tables. During late winter, we amassed enough pieces to begin sewing them together with needles and cat gut from Mrs. L, then concealing it between the canvas pile and a wall. Abel suggested assembling the blower first, to allow for success in the shower room, depending upon which escape route became the diversion. The most dangerous part of the balloon escape will be gathering the heavy and bulky canvas on the balcony and firing up the blower without detection. When discovered, the balloon will be in the air, creating a distraction for those wishing to use the shower room tunnel.

Murdock usually operated on the hole, while Jimmy or Abel kept watch, with Nadine and Mrs. L keeping the staff occupied with her suggestions on calming for the less able patients. Jimmy sat on the end of the bench, weight training. Abel stood near the door, inhaling, waving his arms and hugging his expanded chest. This enabled them to look out into the lounge and through to the men's dorm. Murdock was to crouch behind his lookout, Abel, if there was a warning of staff coming through the dormitory, for example, giving Murdock plenty of time to enter the veil of steam.

Work in the shower room lasted fifteen to twenty minutes each episode of chipping. Then Murdock and the lookout took coffee in the lounge or pretended to fetch soap or towels from the men's wardrobe lockers, so as not to arouse the suspicion of personnel in charge of the area. We gained confidence when, after three weeks, the shower room work remained unnoticed.

We all took turns in the playpen during afternoon sessions. In the late mornings, we made toys in the shop, which was above a storage room. I made sculptures of Don Quixote on an undernourished nag and his squire Sancho Panza on a donkey, the small work being soldered and large pieces welded. The incessant variation of sculpting intrigued me, in the form of the pair mounted, bust of Quixote, the head, and mounted, as if always refining the expression of personality. The plan was to remove sufficient iron and sheet metal scrap from the shop to the balcony. The metal shop was in a large circular alcove off the main shop, where on occasion Abel and a dozen others also worked. When I'm on the anvil, the shop is closed off by a large sliding concertina door so that segments for the hot air blower cannot be recognized. The basic crew helped prepare the surprise, as Mrs. L put it, albeit in a rather abstract nature because of constructing it bit by bit. Abel made cloth dolls of a holy family: Judas, Jesus and Mary, Peter, John and the rest. Others made such things as wooden bowls, tapestries, and jewelry. Most of our products were sold somewhere, and we received coupons each week to buy stimulants or depressants.

Nadine worked in the laundry and Mrs. L in the kitchen. Nadine was really our coordinator. She was the only person any of us communicated with confidently. Mrs. L was to dispose of debris from the shower room after wrapping it in pinafores.

Meantime, treatment, whatever its intention, was administered by an omnipotent and ubiquitous authority. "A real strength of this induced illness:" Abel announced, "our incorrigibility, our immunity to the deterrent effects of treatment or possibility of treatment, lay not so much in exploring the opportunity of getting away with it as in the crude autocratic philosophy they live by. Once you accept the virtue of being reduced to a grain of sand and crazy at the same time on overcoming..." he paused, "how would you say..." "Duality?" I offered. "...their dualities; then, the possible consequences for them remain like the chances of getting gored by a bullfighter or of the risk of crashing for a racing driver. While we just leave their twisted thinking, leave a hole in it, leave it where it is and leave them with their folly."

When the shower room work resumed in September, Murdock broke through the wall after two weeks of chipping, only to find another partition wall of brick and mortar. I noticed through the skylight over my anvil that leaves flew past in bursts and strained to hear the honks of Canadian geese. Mrs. L ferried a chisel and a hammer, wrapped in pinafores on the bottom of the tea and coffee trolley, as she made her rounds. I won't forget that day because that day Abel preached again, pointedly, on that day.

"I noticed how you always say thought-out things," he

warned. "The only reason you play up to Mrs. L is that she says what she thinks and you haven't got the ability to do that. You admire that quality in other people. But your admiration is only for what you lack, not for whole individuals as they are. You throw out what doesn't appeal to you. You don't admire people, not the person. All you see is parts of people. That's why you don't actually see anyone.

"You want to express yourself genuinely, with originality, but lack of spontaneity drains from your face. And the guilt is always there, left on your baby face to rot it, as if you don't want to wash yourself of it. As the years go by, the effect of violent tirades by your own in loco parentis leaves you faceless, sometimes, as a result of your own self-deprecating reactions, the ones behind what you actually do, like kicking the imaginary tin can of yourself the length of the road of life."

I felt pulverised by his perceptions of my inhumanity towards him, and it was a moment, similar to those moments with Becky, that I once again felt opened and free of what he observed, having been opened by other strangers, some less strange than others, and when I take that to heart the openness reappears.

Jimmy asked me to give him a hand with the weights, giving us a chance to gauge the chisel noise, with Murdock hammering tentatively. When he needed to bore in a bit, he signaled Abel with hand slaps, in turn signaling Jimmy who knelt down and pulled clangy weights that were tied to a pulley, alerting Mrs. L in the distant background, who performed diversionary jumping jacks. There was one hammering session each day, while the rigorous exercise was in place. Mrs. L maneuvered her trolley to the shower, after showering finished in the mornings and evenings, to collect chippings in her pinafores. Each of the basic team's recruits dutifully perpetuated the ruse among other showering patients, and the ever so gradually increasing chipping sounds became another background noise, like the wheels of the night shift drug trolleys.

Murdock worked round the first brick in the lower corner of the frame ahead of Thanksgiving. By then the daily grinding routine became tedious and boring, reducing our efforts with the escape to three sessions a week. Our enthusiasm was first replenished when the first brick came out, and then diminished, exposing another brick.

There were further difficulties. Nadine's concern for Jimmy was now obvious, threatening the escape scheme because she worried about Jimmy being hurt in some way. Abel figured that Nadine privately condemned the plan — not on its own merits — but because she was afraid for Jimmy's involvement. Nadine's reservations led to her being suspicious and this affected her involvement, and her holding back was latent, which evidently caused Mrs. L to be incensed, in part because Abel was morose. If everyone was affected by Nadine's doubt, the plan could be immobilized.

Nurses speak of an enormous underground complex of wards where people in conflict with life are made to live with monsters, like the one in Loch Ness. We lived under threat of this monster's punishment, meted out in the wards below ground where the most feared inmates are political fanatics, poachers, terrorists, the plague-afflicted viruses, dementias, and those nearly comatose from electric brain experiments.

Snow makes the ground in front of the ward like an enormous lily, flexing its petals in the wind, being transfixed by the many faces of winter. There is warmth in the snow that was obvious to us in the basic team. Especially in the early morning, before breakfast; we stand with others who gather near the window, watching. Our attendants look astounded — that we can be still and silent, beholding the warmth of snow, the warmth felt inside a person. This change of mood on the ward set us to work again. Murdock started first, with fresh tools wrapped in Mrs. L's pinafores. The next two bricks to come out were on either side of the first one. It was quite an occasion when they both came out on Christmas Day. Murdock was keen to extract a top and bottom brick so he could have a crack at the inner brick wall.

During the glistening winter months, Abel and I thought that even if the actual escape fails, the plan we carry out will ignite the dormant flame of sanity which gives rise to being sensible in the practical moments of enacting the plan. On this note, I forgot where Mrs. L hid various parts of the balloon and bits and pieces of the blower. Hospital routine changed with the snow and, with spring coming, everybody became restless. Sedatives increased at night.

The sun starts to rise earlier, adjourning to a lobby on the second floor. We look across treetops, watching the sun emerge behind hills, its kindly heat on the glass around and inside us — we gaze at the light and the land and it gazes back, telling us that it exists how it is within us and not in and of itself outside, meaning we're human beings, each at home within ourselves. There are always these moments to see how things really are — when the light hangs like water over the treetops, houses bleached from view, filtering through leaves; then the first details of buildings.

Time appeared to manifest our disillusionment with escape routines and the screwed up stubbornness in the gas that noised in Abel's abdomen. He walked about gasping, really sucking in the air that he whipped up with his arms and jumpy steps. Nadine told me in a letter that Abel felt he had to take in air to cool the burn of indigestion "that fumed when the acid came up." Abel was finally put in the sick ward, exhausted, the effects of an ulcer which, after his sermons, probably knocked the bottom right out of the oozing sore in his stomach. Word was that he sat in his bunk and gawked at a television the whole of the spring. Abel always said, when asked why he liked TV so much, "I read through my ears and eyes."

I noticed fresh papier-mâché on the rectangular wall, used to disguise the hole once a chipping session was completed, was painted, to resemble brick. When Murdock was in the playpen one afternoon, his face was locked in a grin. What affected a rise in his usually dormant sense of ambition was beyond me at that point. Nadine was near the porch door, intensely at work on Jimmy's hair. Jimmy was buried in an old comic book, with pictures of Zorro and the Green Arrow on its cover. Jimmy's absorption brought a smile to everyone's face, reminiscent of the way us kids were captivated by those films at the YMCA, and the amazement at first sightings of TV serials about Boston Blackie and Captain Video.

While trying to maintain the hole as symmetrical as possible, we worked on the first five rows of brick from the floor, taking out two on either side. Two bricks out during one session made easy work of reaching the soot and rubble lying in the shaft, which narrowed upwards. A lighted match showed us that the breeze was from below, which was the planned direction for an escape route, if ever we could maintain the shape of the outline. The scooped out soot was washed along the overflow channel of the washroom, running in the floor gulley beneath the wash basins, but we needed somewhere to dispose of stones and brick bits which were shoved inside the tunnel walls, wedged with socks to make good the walls, covering them with papier-mâché to the level of the plaster and then painted with emulsion. This looked like an infection by fungus, which plaster develops in a damp atmosphere — nevertheless, it was more or less a dead end.

Abel and I were unexpectedly overcome by a hot flash to see the light as it really is, and at our basic team meeting around Mrs. L's trolley we discussed trying a simpler path. Our co-conspirators covered for us while we laddered ourselves with ropes through a skylight above the workshops.

Standing on a small flat roof, with only nine feet to the top of a wall, we heard noises from a road which ran around the wall of the hospital and beyond it a patch of open common ground. Our knotted rope was around my waist as Abel climbed with me coaxing him to rest on the knots that bound the segments together. I was right behind, my head constantly stuck into his backside. We were about sixty feet up in the air and below about a dozen people milled around. "Whadda ya think?" I asked Abel. "Well, I'm going this way," he said, pointing down a roof line. After about a couple dozen yards the roofs became lower and below lay the gardens of terraced staff houses. Finally, crossing a number of flat roofs, we were fifteen feet off the ground. Everything was quiet when we dropped to the ground — then, a clatter of shoes on cobbles and a group of people appearing at the back of the gardens, and we turned into the night.

We sprinted past the end of terraces and turned into a T-junction. To the right was the road around the hospital; we turned left, really hitting on the road, over a humpback bridge toward a well-lit street. We'd done it.

"Do you want to come, Abel?" He hesitated. He was the wiser and formed close relationships with Murdock, Mrs. L, Nadine, and with Jimmy. As I started to repeat my question, Abel moved closer, leaving my sentence hanging half-dressed in the air. "Only to the corner," he said softly, then asking, "Where are you going?" "For a walk. Let's find some wonderful Nadines," I said. We both laughed, walking slowly, taking the sidewalk a slab at a time. The cracks between slabs were still fat with swollen tar from early summer's heat, prominent enough to trip up anyone daydreaming. Abel dragged his feet, and tripped. Behind, the hospital, Cherwell 1A's barred windows, small in the distance, punctuated by lighting within; we hadn't gone all that far.

"Where are you going?" Abel asked, as we stood now at a corner, sensing this was our last corner together.

"Walkin', just walking, I'm going westwards."

"Will you be back?" Abel asked.

"I don't know," I said, slightly raising my voice. Glancing at a Robin breaking into the soil with its beak, glancing back at Abel: "I won't be back, Abel." He eyed me straight, started to speak, opened his lips, and began to turn. "I'll be with you in spirit, Abel." He nodded, stepped off the curb and walked across the way towards the hospital. He was also afraid, in his wide proud shoulders, for the basic team, the reflection of a medic's glaring eye on Nadine and Mrs. L in particular and that in a moment they could be called back for advanced treatment and put to bed, or into the Hole, or downstairs.

I walked a few blocks, winded, stopping to wipe my face with a large pink part of pinafore. Two kids played across the street. A dog barked. Sounds and sights and smells came, as if I had just woken from a blackout. An insect buzzed over me in the trees, reminiscence of the hospital's institutional humming. I always thought it was electricity in the background.

Tribal Forces

At a wide open space between country roads, people paraded in a grassy field. It was an elimination drive. They marched toward me, with tennis balls fixed to ropes and clotheslines on the ends of large sticks. As they went they pounded the ground in rhythm. More people held garden implements than sticks. A man clothed in blue and yellow was in front of them. This fellow shouted commands; he called the people fine names.

"You are all my children," he cheered. "Come on now, eliminate. You're all my offspring; come on now, eliminate." Nearer the edge of the space, they moved more tightly and imitated the leader's words. "Well are all his children now. Oooooh yes. We're all his children now. Oooooooooh yes."

Helicopters appeared overhead. Four...six of them, and the group stiffened. Motors churned up dust as they passed in pairs, duplicating their whiplash sound. Once, the helicopters swept too close; their blades slashed and tore a few robes thrown into the air. These long clothes were similar to the Leader's. But while the headman had perfect blue and yellow stripes, the peoples' material was either mended with colored patches or left at loose ends. One woman near me probably dyed her cloak, but in her zeal she reversed the pattern, the stripes being perpendicular. A second person, bald and fatly misshapen, looked as though he was named Threat. Fatly Misshapen's yellow stripes also circled his gown, a combination of rain, wind and sun causing the dye to run: blue turned green and yellow was grey. This gave Fatly an aura of prestige that none of the others seemed to appreciate or rebuke. In this group of about 50 people, the garment of a third person also sported unusual stripes on his gown. Apparently, he too mistook the horizontal stripe pattern on the leader's gown for a vertical one. Perhaps they are dissenters who fail to appreciate the light their Leader shines on them, for on that day the stripes on Third's gown ran up and around the back and across the front, seeming to pursue one another in the wind. Third marched on the earth a slight distance from the others, ostensibly content to be included in the group, if only on its fringe. Helicopters chopped, batted and aerated the clouded air, leaving me with a churning in my raw stomach. Intense light from steady eyes in the bowing machines lit up the figures below, as if they were attack helicopters returning from the war with a vengeance. Group motion slowed in sully shafts and veins of twilight and dust. However, when the helicopters rose, people were animated again. Tennis balls hummed and flew wildly into the clattery commotion overhead, where sounds hung as though space was filled with dissolved fireworks. The peoples' joy reverberated right through their clotheslines, which shook as their sticks conveyed their tense exuberance. Leader made an oval with his arms and held this sign above his head. The people turned in a semicircle and as the procession headed back to the center of open space, the leader ran ahead. The group exerted little gasp noises, similar to a hymn when the after-tones and foot beats are recognized. They lined up, raising implements overhead, and strolled shoulder to shoulder. Their long knotted and coiled hair tangled in the wind.

My face relaxed, sensing a purpose in the horizontal stripes. This was an ideal day for imitation — opening yourself to another person's interpretation of life, allowing questionable layers of selfhood to be stripped away to the untainted universal core. The quantity of dust was perfect, rearing and blowing about the crowd. Occasionally the yellow stripes were visible. Once in a while everyone took rank, the blue stripes rushed like a river current. I was with them now and relieved that the helicopters were not after me. The machines reported to their leader, who wore a walkie-talkie radio at his side. A few people still gasped from the dust and exertion. Even I was short of breath, only witnessing an elimination drive. A few yards away, the leader passed me without so much as a glance. Leader clutched the radio and his eyes widened. His gasps were separate from the others. What appeared from a distance to be tension, on closer scrutiny, was carefree poise, more like self-discipline. This posture appeared to hold Leader together under the impact of ceremony. Otherwise, would he feel in danger of being chopped into the space he evolved from? There was a pull of strength about the person who led these people and seemed to give them purpose — this man who allowed people the will to act and to face themselves in their seminal hours. They linked arms. The Leader shouted: "Leeyah. Leeyah." I ogled at them as they eliminated in unison. Bodies and spirits curled into a huge eye which fixed on the celebration, emptying and then filling at the climax.

Leader administered a ceremonial cleansing. The group relaxed. Afterwards, he blew a whistle and unplugged a radio cord, making an oblique motion with the other arm over his head. Then the helicopters landed. Crewman leapt out while the rotors whirled in dust. When the last copter was shut off, the whole group stayed together and talked.

"Yeah, but wasn't the first half mile hell?" "Oh, of course it was. Aren't first half miles always hell?" "Yes." There was general laughter. The leader addressed his people, speaking softly. They dropped their frivolity and listened in earnest. Leader cocked his head to one side and said something. Hockers gossiped, and he conferred with a flight crew. Many in the robed group approached the leader, a few at a time. Quarrelers went to him for arbitration.

"He gave them hell," asserted a voice behind me. "He sure did. Leader gave 'em hell. They weren't paying attention today and it's the third time."

"The third time."

"Sure, third time. You don't think that show was the best we could do, do you?"

"How will it matter if there are better?" I wondered, finding a neutral ground, avoiding an impression which would pre-judge the person who faced me. The fellow, in his mid-20s, looked physically fit. He wore a flight suit.

"There are few better than this group when we get together. I've been one of us several times, returning from groups that are less disciplined and with less effort. I tell you we're the best in the most collectable of all the corridors of flowers in this region.

Shall I show you around?"

"I accept, thank you. Please tell me about your leader. Is he a good leader? Where do these people come from? Who are they? The Statue of Liberty's children?"

"These are good people," he replied, laughing, "You are too egocentric, that's all."

At this juncture, an elder walked up to me and the talking mechanic. "Well-come. Our group wishes you well-come."

"Why are you so well-coming? Who do you think I am?"

"We're not concerned with who you are, young man, or even what you are, for that matter. But we are concerned with how you are. How are you?"

"Fine, more or less, relatively so."

"Have you trouble?"

"I've seen trouble. Everyone has — nobody wants trouble but everyone has problems once in a while."

"Why are you hostile?"

"Me? Am I like someone troubled?"

"Or is it only natural behavior for those of you who don't share our view."

"Must be," I allowed, as if an uninvited witness to my own autopsy.

"Or does your arrogance mistake my modesty for antagonism," the elder suggested.

That did it. I felt like hitting back. After all, I wasn't just standing in a back garden of chitchat with a twopenny sparkler. I was part of their dynamo now, with the option to ease the elder away from his prefrontal controls, turning the conversation from imbalance, rather than a giant mobile dam sweeping the countryside and spurring me with the elder's genuine advantage.

"Yes...the first thing I noticed about this group was your leader's modesty and the mimicking of most who follow him," I said, thoughtlessly, overcooking it.

The elder took a big step backwards. "What did you say?"

"He can't..." the mechanic blurted. "He can't say that about our leader..."

The wise elder interjected: "No, not our leader does he find fault with. He insults himself. On what is this observation based?"

"What is before me," I replied, "the way you're proud to have your leader tend you through the ceremony."

"Of course, why shouldn't we be proud? He's a fine leader — the best. It's an honor to have him tend us."

"But the ceremony isn't intended," I surmised, pausing to let an effect sink in, "for your honor, or is it?" I filled my veins, more aware now of his susceptibility to my jousting emergence from incarceration, and the mechanic's deference to his elder in matters of their theology, their faith, and also his confidence. With the same shameful thrust, leaving myself, in his eyes, a dialectical ruin: "Or, are you leaping through yourself toward a new way of living to replace the I-complex, me-for-me and I-for-I?"

"I will tell you what you need to do," the elder said. "I want you to meet the leader. And while you may think you have a momentary advantage by clever use of language, you can never shake our essential faith. You can't deter us from our goal, serving a leader who is a vessel for all our personal needs to benefit everyone. You have not seen the miracles, which cannot be solved or put asunder by trick phrases...miracles which Leader does for our well-being."

"Kindly show me," I replied, wishing to regain a sense of lost dignity.

The headman faced away from the approaching trio and talked with two others. "Leader," the elder beckoned, "this young man wishes to be acquainted with you." He was as one remembered him: less than tall but with the same ferocity of eye.

"Yes. You watched us. Have you had a long journey?"

"Well, yes. Yes, I have," I said, thinking this answer an insult by its lack of detail.

"Of course. Yet you have borne your journey well. I assume that, from your dress and the way you stand and move. You're welcome to stay with us and rest in preparation for what's still ahead of you."

I was at odds with myself in an indefinable manner, no longer wondering what lay ahead because the journey is something more than wandering, writing, proceeding from sleep to food to energy and through shuffling ideas to being a guest; it's more like finding — however wobbly in perpetual flux the world around me is — that version of myself which is not a surrogate narrative driving me mad, retrospecting without wanting to piece together versions of myself that could never have cured me — rather, discovering a new version through new eyes, other peoples' eyes. Now, it's meeting these strangers and making a habit of asking myself how I am, each day. "Thanks. I'd like that," I said in a soft tone.

"Good. Come with me and we'll talk." We went off to the side and sat. Leader tore bread from his loaf and gave it with cheese. Then he signaled for drink. "Now, young man, tell me about your travels."

"I'm not finished traveling yet."

"I can tell. I've traveled quite a bit, too. I haven't been with these people all my life."

"I know."

"You do? How did you know?"

"I can tell by your clothes and the way you act and by your accent — by how you are with these people."

"I live. I live for them. Not only do I live with them, but the fact that they allow me to do it gives me strength and thus fulfilment in my daily life. It's a very able arrangement."

"I'll bet."

"We don't bet. You won't be able to take a risk here. And if you go into the town proper, the authorities will pick you up for it."

"I'm aware of that. They tried. They put me away."

"Yes, me too," Leader said through a broad smile. At the start, I was much the same as you: a troubled romantic with a naive understanding of the world — yet seeing people attach themselves to greed and power — they push their own buttons and other peoples' buttons for their own sake. And there's probably no difference in what touches our hearts: sadness for the suffering of others, people who have happiness to share, and our own reflections if they're kindly."

"That may well be," I chuckled. "But tell me, these stripes on the clothes of your followers, are you going to tell me that the up and down ones are for the people who've converted to this, well, tribalism? And those with stripes running around or across their robes, have they failed to eliminate their personal ambitions, are they still craving to be independent people, free of the paranoia in towns? Are the horizontal stripes (for elimination) well suited to their motives? How does this work in elimination drives?"

"Maybe that didn't occur to me before."

"I don't want to lead any tribe," I said. "I would've thought people should be united by their inner, vertical, authority, not the horizontal stripes of emulation, not eliminating themselves in imitation of a folkster with tall tales."

"Well, you never tried. You don't realize what it's like..."

"I remember my own helplessness under the fist of a man who was as one-dimensional as the horizontal strips of his tribe — me as a youngster...with a sorrowful father who boiled over from time to time. Is it worthwhile to be with people and feel what they're experiencing? I tried lots of ways, as much as a kid could, as an ill-equipped person to fend off the instinct to hit back. The only way to win in that state, at that age, is to adapt. So you run the risk. Like me, you live a broken life of adaptation, a kid without fulfilment that comes conditionally from others. You become what you resisted and feared — not brutal, not intentionally, but integral with how they acted. Your lack of thoughtfulness reduces you from a vain but potentially brave person to a creature barracked in an institution, stealing from garbage cans. But this life suits you when you realize the reforming power inherent in being debased. In my case, my father's patriotic conversion to unquestioning reprisals against foreign encroachments within and beyond his boundaries was hell-bent on me. Bring it on, get it out, that's all I could do. I guess there is that instinctive vulnerable take it on the chin effect when as a kid you're dead scared. So you trust that as long as you evade being cornered you eventually find the opportunity of growing a strong hand of reason; families fear anarchy and try to pacify their own base dissatisfaction with themselves by submitting to bloodshed."

Leader tightened, screwing up his face. "It's not an easy thing to be with people who want to be free when they are at war with themselves, wounded by overdosing on their quest for emulating their self-satisfying, self-defeating, bleating pleasures and merciless pranks.

"Let me tell you that this is a fragment of the original group that I joined, because we were engaged in a battle which scarred us forever. The young, of course, made the best fighters. And the best fighters are always killed first, leaving war to be fought by white-collar amateurs with poor coordination. When we realized we were hopelessly outnumbered, we appealed to the reason of our antagonists. That nearly cost me my life. We had set a trap and so had they. By matter of luck, the enemy sprang their trap before ours was ready. During a peace conference, a thrown bomb exploded in our motor repair unit. Most of our tools were destroyed and two top mechanics wounded.

"The peace conference took place in a large, open field — ploughed but not sown, and we met there in the afternoon. This day dawned clear and the winter sun was hot when we met. But as the sky cleared up, I noticed that some of the aggressors started to spread in a semicircle. These were ugly face-painted men, not like ours. The Philistines were mal-formed, because they'd lived on nothing but corn all their lives, since they fled the towns and cities. While the sun was bright they wore sun shade masks made of corn husks. These combatants were grimy and had ragged clothing. But there was something coarser about the devils. While our people adapted to battle conditions, they were never as relaxed as our adversary. Another thing about the enemy that afternoon... they had hundreds of children: scanning from a hill with binoculars; kids swarmed at their encampment. The little'uns crawled and got in the way; our oppressors' offspring played on cold, cracked ground — growing into ominous children if left in reflections of their sinister looking parents.

"The men approaching us had the group's mark: wide shoulders and the same as their chief. He didn't look at his lieutenants but sat smiling as we advanced. I left the main body of our group behind to guard our elders and motors. My peace squad included our constable's eldest son and a blowtorch expert. The opposition leader was with three other people. None of them wore a sun shield. Their eyes seemed strangely white that afternoon. The only exception to the quiet was wind and a few snowflakes. After a radio check with our motor group and a warning about the converging sneakers, I emerged from the car and waited. But nothing happened. They sat in their vehicle — a pickup truck with its chrome taken off — and they waited. Our trap called for close personal contact with their chief. It was simple: I would shoot him dead and commandeer the truck while our raiders diverted his thugs. I walked alone toward their vehicle, not without difficulty on the roughly ploughed ground. One distracting thought hammered in my head: we both left our motors idling. I put my knuckles on the vibrating fender of the pickup and spoke: 'Does the intruder fear us?' There was no reply. Suddenly the vehicle lurched. I leapt aside and opened fire with my pistol.

One of the uglies buckled. Two others aimed rifles out the windows while a forth — the driver — pursued me. I twisted and turned and struggled to keep balance on some turf, firing and ducking away, and they sped past sliding...only to halt, reverse, swerve around and charge. I noticed our car from the corner of my eye; tiny, grey puffs popped in front of it. We fired at the enemy, who were making another pass. Attempting to jump aside, I slipped and fell. The bastards backed up, grinding my arm into the clods. I switched hands with my pistol, fired four times into the truck's underbelly and shoved a new magazine of bullets into the weapon. As the crank shaft and rotaries whizzed past, back and forth over my head, the wheels of our car came into view along with a bright, blue sky, as the clouds cleared for a moment. The foemen stopped, their stubby legs heavy on the ground. A rifle cracked twice and dirt stung my face. A slug ripped through my leg and smashed into the truck's rear wheel rim. I fired at the legs but, in my panic, missed. Whoever shot at me hopped up on the running board: I grabbed the axle when the pickup jerked forward in spurts and let it drag me. Something clicked against the vehicle and I recognised the sharp smack from the pistol of the constable's son. A body tumbled out the driver's side of the truck. There was some doubt as to whether he killed a second ugly or whether the enemy just dumped the one I shot. The carrier lunged, forcing my grip to unlock. I was in the open, on my stomach, firing wildly. A shot plunged into the ground next to me; another pistol fired several times. Our station wagon sped toward the truck and showed no intention of stopping. The blowtorch man drove; he was our best driver. He had a single strategy: if a mild flame won't peel paint, try a hotter one. The truck crawled ahead and then sped up. Our car screeched to a stop, practically burying me in clods. Two men helped me onto the tailgate of our wagon and we raced for our lines. Halfway to safety, a flash lit the pallor blue-gray sky, which seemed to lose its blue with the sound of a leisurely boom. A wheel was on fire — it flew into the air from our motor group area. That's where the crucial fighting was. We arrived surrounding about eight of the opponents and systematically shot at them using a simple tactic: threat of concentrated firepower. When certain of the adversary's position, we fired until the enemy was silenced. This our noble fighters were now doing with fine discipline and from 12 yards distance, taking certain steps towards the aggressors after firing. At least one ugly threw down his weapon and ran away. 'There, stop him,' cried the constable's son, as he aimed his pistol, but the blasted thing was spent.

"Later, I heard that the blowtorch man remained parked in the car, where I was in distress with bullet and dragging wounds. At the urging of the others, he hesitated to join the attack for fear he would jeopardize our safety. This was a strategy demanding respect — the blowtorch man was very cool under fire. But when the pickup truck fired at our people, he threw a blanket over me and proceeded to execute some captives. He ordered the constable's son to kill one and killed another himself. The rest were herded off, out of sight. Proof of the executions never materialized and in confused moments like that it's easy to miscalculate.

"Tortured screams jabbed holes in the night as people of

both camps bled with fear while pursuers howled hideously. The next day was born in angry heat. Running ahead of shouts, surrounded by rifle fire, bodies were scattered across the gentle countryside; the trophy hunters' chase had been relentless. Finally, the loud lust-drunken warriors seemed satisfied they had us beaten. We were left alone. I saw two people trot along a hillside at dawn the day after the hunt stopped. I didn't dare call out for fear a stranger would call back. What I saw may have been deer or cattle or shadows or people I came to love. I can't say for sure."

Leader was silent — his head in his lap. He wept. I sat with him on the edge of the campsite until we stood, facing the sun. The day star, blood colored and purple striped, laid down and went flat at the other side of the world, setting red, like hyenas laughing, but more sedate. We slept there in the sleeping lion's posture, as background talk dissolved and other bodies found places to spend the night.

Klaus, Goliath, and the Soldiers

As we finished a meal, Leader signaled for a drink. "Now, tell me about your travels," he said.

"A friend and I moved around before striking out on my own. There was an altercation with a man who knifed his dog. I was bundled into jail — overall, a zigzaggedy journey from zero to now, sideways stripes I'd guess you'd say."

"I see what you mean," Leader chuckled. "There's no predetermined storyline, because everything is turned inside out when you realize you aren't governed by what you see and hear but by being free of mental habits spawned in the past...but enough of this," he tailed off, passing apple juice, "you're supposed to make a start."

"Okay...well, one day I found myself working on the buttholes of sparkplugs with plastic and a punch press, looking up to notice winter. The worst blizzard in 29 years laid bare the plains. I set plug holes to the right size for that day, watching the blizzard skirt my job, blowing along the town's milk-empty streets. Edges of sidewalks fell to the snow and drowned in it. The name of my first boss was Klaus," I hurried on, seeing that Leader was attentive. "Amidst the noise of the shop, during what you might call a quiet pause, Klaus said: 'Oh, well, men need a woman to care for them, to keep the kids from being another notch on my belt. Some of us can't make it on our own and find no strength except what she gives.' He pointed his sandwich at me and asked, 'What have you got to go home to after you finish your sandwich?' His sandwich was a multi-level monster, reminiscent of a warm home built of gingerbread by the witch who wasn't a screwball after all — just eccentric. The sandwich moved at its own speed, like a giant turtle, sensual and caressing Klaus' child-grinding jaw, a mighty mouth that would be useful to a turtle, even a small one. Outside, snow fell on the streets, surging and cascading, rushing from spot to open spot.

"Work on sparkplugs is a simple routine, possessing its own sustenance in restoring my sparking gap when I'm distracted by my misgivings about leaving the people I love. The routine was like my thoughts — wind blowing in space; yet, the incongruities of plugs worked on me like thunderous pistons which grew closer and colder and more bruising until my mind was at risk of being conditioned to a cycle of plugging gaps instead of how I want to be.

"Once, as my eyes took me out of myself, across the belt of town houses into familiar bricked spaces and over the prairie, I tried to lure a pigeon in — not an Antwerp, just the common garden variety. 'I'll seduce you with crackers and the finest milk off the rich old pan-handled udder of the morning star and full-faced flying cow,' I chirped at one. This pigeon sat on a window sill in spite of my comment, biding her time. If there was a pure white egg, I might have struck a deal with her.

"The pigeon — bored from her rounds of chimneys and enticed by the window sill droppings of kin — zoomed like a pear from a frantic quarterback and returned to the sill. She sat cultivating her pigeon thoughts. 'Here pigei, here pigei,' I cooed. 'Have a piece of bread; it's good for the complexion and keeps your bones from clogging.' The pigeon took a couple of uncertain steps up and then sideling along the sill. 'No strings attached. Just take the bread,' I urged, leaving a piece on the sill, an unpromising piece. The bird developed a crouch (which is just what pigeons do when they intend to fly), hung back and lost the urge. Then I added a bit of grape jelly to the bread. The local vagabond meandered over and pecked at the jelly, which spread on her face. A marked pigeon. A marred pigeon. The next piece of jellied bread lay on the workbench only a hop away, but this was a hop across shadows into the place of hunters: one of the poisoners, cat keepers and eaves painters. The bird crouched, as if to say to hell with race and tradition. This pigeon fancied jelly. She aimed at the bread. Wind entered, flapping a paper; she cocked and re-cocked her motley colored head with the intention of strutting. This fowl of the air fell off the inner ledge and half way to the ground before sensing that she'd been cheated and tricked. With pigeon grace she regained balance, lulled by her sweet smelling kin and pigeon time, swooped up to avoid a crash and, by chance, flew out the window: a delicate beauty, now graced by sun and sill. Suddenly, as if sensing a terror still waiting on the sill: a spread-eagled pigeon swoosh-scrambling to gain wing and flee an awful baseball bat's blow — all the spaces amid a community of feathers and erector set of bones, full set of veins and tiny motor of a heart, derailed and smashed beyond reach of spare parts by a sparkplug mechanic. She needn't have worried because I couldn't have done it anyway, no matter how many gaps I breached.

"A day later, after the night snows stopped, the weather

warmed. Snow became water and lay in small pools. Cars left other noises in the air now as they passed. Melted snow spray hung over curbs and curled into sewers. Through the shop window beyond matching racket on the road, mistresses took to their pets, which answered in snappy calico voices."

"Hear, hear," Leader said in a distracting, ambivalent tone.

"One afternoon, I noticed a credulous robin mottled by too many worms hopping circularly in the lawn. Normally, this wouldn't have broken my concentration. But at the same moment, a tabby cat prowled along a railroad track. Stopping and licking its flank in a single move — left rear leg jutted in the sky — the animal yawned and stood in sections, hind parts first; the belly, hung from a straight back, swayed a little, while paws under the head led legs as the tail balanced it all. The cat crept with ancestral confidence, its fluid eyes studying the bird. The robin hopped. One malignant eye stared over a rail. The rest of the cat wasn't visible. He watched, everything. (Would I protect the bird? Could I savor her pilfering worm-hunt?) Finally, the cat put a paw on the rail, testing as if he was treading on thin ice, eyes holding the Robin. Like spaghetti plopped over the rail, puss disappeared into yellow grass on the bank of built-up snow beside the tracks. Each grass blade appeared to trail the bird on behalf of the cat as he flowed beneath the surface. Then an eye — the same eye — emerged. The only eye? The other punched out by his itinerant father? Was this a budget cat, a small-time free enterpriser, operating at a minimum because he's too proud to take a government loan for another eye? Or too proud to accept the county agent's advice and learn to use electronic devices. The sneaky

eye looked at me. I grinned and the cat grinned. The Robin
continued a jig of uneventful hops, sought worms and defied
evolution. Wind's wheeziness eased, leaving a lone Whippoor-
will's cries. Near the edge of lawn where it met undergrowth
at a shoe by railroad tracks, the Robin discovered a worm,
which struggled as though it was the mightiest most proud
worm in the world — a worm to go to the Louvre, a Mr. Atlas-
sized worm. The best. Only the best, for this was King Robin.
How could this stealthy bird evade the large quick focus eyes
with big ears behind and below them? And the keen smeller?
The wildcat sprang: cat and Robin bounced apart in midair
while the worm snapped back in its hole, and the bird escaped,
sitting on a power line, nursing a shredded wing and gawking
at the flank-licking cat as if the incident was a personal grudge.
My affection for the creatures poured through the windows
and between the unpaid bills and stringent notices — the
sharp, sharper, sharpest notices. Affection that floated past
unanswered telephone calls and around notes from one or two
personal appearances by the finer debt collectors.

"Lemonade swirled in a beaker and cast reflections of the
grass-moving cat, going toward a distant Woodchuck's sound.
Before my toast to honor the hunter, a knock at the door of the
cabin that Klaus built: I was suspicious because bill collectors
knock first, like unfaithful fathers, on the edges. This was an
oblong knock — a predator's knock. This wasn't the knock of
an apologetic bill collector grown fierce from volumes on legal
rights and embarrassed by immoral experience. Curious and
half-deciding to deny my identity, I peeked through a window.
Two white-haired people stood in the light of day. Wedged in

behind them was a huge blond-haired Nordic, brandishing a flag that topped a spear. Its banner was spangled with red-tipped stars on a deep blue background and fringed with gold tassels. The flag seemed to be the brains of the bunch, flapping at the door, directing the collectors to knock again. Both women knocked while Hercules planted his feet as if he was fruit going to seed. 'Go away,' I greeted through the wall. 'Oh, my,' the others said to each other. They wrote the greeting in a notebook. 'You are under arrest, mister,' said one of them. 'Come now or forever hold your peace.' 'Peace is just,' I offered, and a Robin flittered in the spring yard and flew from the grass with only half a worm in its beak (an exciting afternoon for Robins.) 'Abraham,' the older woman said, gesturing to the giant. 'Fetch!' Lifting the brilliant steel tipped trident to his waist, he drove it through the cement porch, waiting for it to collapse. Then he crashed through the door and threw a Cyclopean fist. Plaster and dust showered me as the wall-marred fist was unplunged. I scooted for the back door, leaving a trail of tipped over chairs and obstacles to confront the Goliath. He stepped over the couch and crushed other furniture with his hooves. Holding my weapons — a light bulb and a potato — I paused at the door, heaving the bulb first and grabbing my backpack, prepared for such contingencies. The bulb popped harmlessly against a wall behind the behemoth while my potato smashed in his pitted face. He roared and stomped; his kick missed me but disabled the refrigerator as I fled.

"Within an hour, troops surrounded the house, along with two tanks and an armored vehicle. National Guard soldiers, sent to replicate best practice, and dressed in green, wore pictures of avocados on their sleeves. The armored vehicle dug canals in the lawn, leaving a flower garden of an enterprising neighbor half submerged. A quarter hour later, military technicians erected barbed wire sculptures around the house. Seven wire barriers were taken inside; the bathroom was blocked off. Two warning flares shot up and six persons in an official car across the road watched them. People I'd never seen arrived, pointing gaily at the flares, while several eager military advisors and lawnmower drivers talked with the lean boys and girls in uniform. 'Biddle…Lloyd Biddle. Come out of there. You're surrounded! Now come on out,' commanded a Korean War major in the wrong place at the wrong time.

"On the other side of my observation point on a hillcrest, children played and fired a bush with discarded cigarettes. Three juveniles threw rocks at deer grazing in a meadow. A couple of boys with a Bible dug a hole to put their sister in, just for kicks, while she weaved a net of pine needles and burlap. That night passed without a bad dream or a burp. The wood cooled near the river, where clouds hung without images, refusing to be defined except as beyond control and very mysterious and mostly darkest green, inter-reliant with me in our mutual source of vitality. Morning came after dawn. Soldiers' sounds owned the streets, by the looks of things; neighbors were recruited to support the surrounding forces, for mopping-up duties. At least the military in charge of training cannot engineer the sunset, and they had no influence on the sequence of dawn and morning. That was something. Up off the damp ground and apparently unnoticed by their night patrols, I felt the edges of my limbs, a presence as indistinguishable as the misted earth floor. I scanned brush near a railroad trestle in search of fruit, but the view was restricted at ground level. So I accepted the incongruities of hunger and the improbability of seeing myself as separate from nature, and I made my way toward the cabin a way off from Klaus' workshop. The rent collectors, if that's what they were, clearly thought I owed a debt to society or I wouldn't have been in jail. I had to oppose them because they would put electrodes on my head and recondition my mind. The soldiers probably ate my rolls and if they were still there, I'd need to plan action on a large scale. A plan of plans to unseat the military objective. Although the military is composed of many separate parts, there is a single army will: propagate and terminate, rah-rah. In the end, do we not wish all of us, to be free of enmity? Perhaps two wills conceding to be on one side is equivalent to peace? Due to my ignorance about their parts and the facts of their career patches, without victory ribbons, can they be opposed — reasoned with — opposed and reasoned with — united to a less violent cause?"

Leader twisted his eyes as if in contempt, or glibness, but his head was lunged in concentration, sensing a battle.

"Above the railroad tracks, from a rise, expansive operations appeared below. Kneeling, then moving down for a closer look, the cabin was there alright, just well hidden under an enormous web, camouflaged and ringed with trucks full of tense combatants, who sat hunched over rifles with fixed bayonets between their legs. One fresh-faced soldier glanced at the sun, his face white. He was afraid, waiting for an assault. How long had they waited there? Hours. Probably, they got up extra early to face a debtor, or criminal. Would even a majority stand and fight?

"The convolutions of my jailed brain unrolled, wishing for exit maps with directions. Then, a dog with a smile trotted by, catching like a ram between my ears. 'Nice dog.' A bold plan (The Dandy Plan) evolved from my sense of the under-dog. He was a dandy. 'Here fella,' I coaxed, petting his flexible and functional head. You respected this process whereby the ears tried to spring off his head at every sound and also the co-ordination between his smile and tail. 'Nice dog.' The mongrel followed me to a spot near the troops. We crept through the same bush as the tabby cat had. With old newspapers from my pack and bush branch, I made a pair of twisted torches and watched the fire flow, eat and flow again. As the second torch was fired we darted back and forth in the bushes to spread flames with paper balls in the grass — both of us tail-wagging and barking like foxes the whole time. Smiling and patting my agent provocateur, and with a fireball at the end of a rope fas-tened to my waist and another to his tail, we ran off in circles to spread the fire, collapsing in the brook, to douse ourselves, then returning to the tune of their frustrated screaming.

"Shouts and commands belched under the camouflage. Outside, a driver started a truck engine. Guards fired sporadic rifle shots at the dog and at soldiers sprinting over to secure the net, while reservists with arms folded in clipboards kept score. A troop load drove after my comrade. At first nobody was able to follow the dog because he scampered in patterns contrary to military policy. As the decibel count of diversion-ary yelps and rifle fire increased, the army stayed in formation.

Three troopers poured scorn on the creature; their freshly shaved faces bleeding. Noises multiplied in proportion to their disgrace at killing a dumb animal rather than a human. In keeping with their patriotic motivation, their indiscriminate violence expanded, and I slipped onto the back porch. One coil of barbed wire about five feet wide was pushed right across the kitchen floor, against the door. So I punched in a pantry window to gain access. While eating a roll overlooked by soldiers, I packed a fresh lunch. Anything else was unthinkable, since crisscrossed razor wire coils filled the hallway and probably fingered every room or other sanctuary in the house. Soldiers sensed danger from the automatic outbursts and in their own rifle sights (through vertical and horizontal crosshairs), against any man, woman, child, or animal, who bucks whichever system is offended by lack of payment. The debt collection force fired blindly to scare selected onlookers and to gee up the attack.

"Whatever the internal landscape of the boys and girls in green, they shot to kill with a vengeance through protruding barrel eyes. I shuffled from the house on all fours, eyes tracing their bullets, feet unprepared to race their swift helicopters. The attack raged to such an extent that I couldn't reach the bush at the meadow's end, by the railroad tracks. A squirrel engulfed by a flamethrowing gun fell into a mined patch of a neighboring property. Flying fire leaped hissing through the camouflage net, collapsing the hole I cut to gain access and the cabin blew apart from everywhere. 'Put out those fires, you idiots,' I ordered. Those troops who heard, hesitated, lowering weapons and lifting their helmets, which in some cases fell over their eyes. Gradually, as firefighting equipment arrived, I slid into the smoke, and away. That was a trying day. And a dandy plan.

"(The dwindling food supply of a person deemed to be extraneous, who is content with practicalities while shedding his own discursive maladies, is a phenomenal cosmological account of how any animate being strives to be free of hostility and hunger.)

"As the days passed, my stomach's impassioned plea, the lion-eyed and star-punctuated belly-itch for food, was fulfilled by nature. One afternoon, the soldiers began easily enough; they finished the last of the rolls, left in a bird feeder near the house. The army wouldn't fall again for such a divisive ruse. The collectors' agents will reimpose military willpower.

"I was unnerved that night, hanging off the earth in twisted positions, cluttering in the sky and clutching a rock or fallen tree. Yet during the days, there wasn't much lacking that a house offered — the main thing was a stove. The presence of bugs and other wildlife was compensation, seeing instinctive burgeoning life wonderfully active and skilled in activity. The bean bag of companionship rattled round my neck. The bugs rattled in their own way, genuinely for all sentient species, but unlike the enmity between citizens and militia across the country. So many living beings, replicating themselves. Nature's energies are full of life: even the energy of a brook or a flower. A clump of wild mustard waved from its bright yellow side and grew like a vine — a plant containing more shades of gray than I'd ever seen in one spot. I circled the clump from angle to angle, stooping to focus on the subtle differences in shade, and then sat to study the most beautiful part. Sunlight rolled gently off the vine; behind it the mustard glowed.

"A shadow crossed, behind, and machines crescendoing, baying, and tools twisted fingers smashing. Then a break sound repeated itself within the original cluster. Agents of the bill collectors shot at me from a helicopter! A yellow skull insignia on the copter's fuselage read STATE MILITIA. Their bullets missed and swept the water 15-20 yards to my left as if a third or so of the guns were aimed under the influence of air sickness. 'Over here,' I shouted, giving an unfriendly gesture, and darted toward a wood. Suddenly, bullets laced a rock pile nearby, leaving the air bursting with jagged scrapings, splinters and granite dust. The helicopter, having deposited its volley of bowels, followed, hovering over the wood.

"I took refuge in a cave with windswept silver rock and absent bats. Years ago, white floor sand was used to make glass. Natives staged beer parties, with bonfires and shadows leaping on these walls. Small children discovered they were unafraid of deep cave trails while adults gathered food. The cave opening was several feet high and wide. Inside, along an avenue, the interior was four times my height. Deep pits darkened as the cave bent the light of its mouth. Even the wind dissolved. (Sound belongs with light; there should be a QUIET PLEASE sign on every closet door of our memory, to expose the obstructions and opened windows jammed shut by parents imparting their trauma on life's learning curveball.)

"Touches and soundings bounced off stark walls and plunging holes without depths. My feet found a pocket of powdery bat guano, sending me backwards with earsplitting sneezes.

In the pungent stench and dust, little of what we call color decorated the cave — barely discernible noises to solidify it — dimly refracting light to reveal it; then, the breathtaking smell of bat pleasures and tasting my breath.

"Later, five more helicopters and a light plane flew over the cave, dropping puny bombs and flaming gases on the rock pile, in the lake and across patches of wood. Dead juniper trees stood like black punctuation on a white background, void of fragrance and even cedar cones vanished. One copter flying in a circle started to chug. (Or do helicopters whirr and whistle, and only Volkswagens chug?) Chug-hurg...chugg chug che che che...plp...ki kissssss wheeeeeeee!! The aircraft coasted in a rough descending manner. Tree tops scraped the fuselaged belly and flattened a runner as the copter careened into an open grass patch which graced the shores of Lake Bracken. As its rotor chopped water, the helicopter slid into a quag-mire — the propeller blades catching and flinging water weed jewelry in an envelope of rich brown fluff. The swamp-strained rotor hit once more, jerked, and the machine started to list. Screeches and smoke emerged from a shaft over the chopper's flame; its motors stopped, as did the bombing. Only insects defined this silence, whizzing around the cave mouth and exploring the helicopter dome. Other copters hovered in place while their occupants blinked with the metronome timing of the rotors cutting through space. Below, the flames stopped, leaving the wreck smoldering. A foot in a steel-shanked boot stepped through a door and yanked backwards. Sallies of whispers rushed from within the copter; a questioning rifle snout poked the air. A sun gleam on the dome veiled my view of the inside. Another foot appeared. A mate of that last foot emerged, then a leg, and finally a head. After momentary pauses between each body, they squirted through muck into the brush, one after another.

"Meanwhile, the national guardsmen waited until dark. After much discussion someone took a side; their vote was unanimous. But whoever directed traffic in the sky was unaware of the democracy below. Four copters strafed while two landed, collecting crash-wounded soldiers. The last person aboard wore a captain's uniform and sported a ponytail with a butterfly barrette; she paid out wire from the downed copter to a rescue unit. Two survivors accepted the hint and offered covering fire in a vague area to my left. Bullets splashed tree leaves, knocking down acorns, and made small rocks leapfrog. Three strafe units caught the gist, hovered over the two shooters, and roared off toward the rifle fire. Sitting cross-legged in my cave mouth, the action seemed filmic as copters dropped gas, bombs, grenades and rubbish onto a clearing. Great walls of flame shot up and licked one copter's belly. The aircraft reared, then popped, burst into flame and whizz-bang-whizz-banged apart as though it was a culmination of all Catherine wheels and candle bombs spent at once. The four others stopped hovering and flew away. A thread of flame crept from the dead machine through brush to a larger fire's flames, like water running from a puddle — but in reverse. Nobody survived this second crash. The wreckage sat, a skull in rubble and broken limbs like exclamation points twisted by a brittle shock, eliminating breath and foreign words plopped in blood and oil. Approaching the copter, I caught a smell similar to raw soybeans. Crumpled black cardboard figures: two fused together forming an abstract found-object, or sculpture. One's black landscape face fanned into the knee of another. A third prone figure gave me the sensation of not seeing whether I faced the corpse or whether the body laid face-down. Gradually and by single inches, you see on this third fallen leaf...not buttons, holes in the figure, holes left by melted buttons, much the same as snow melts under a rock, buttons fastened on uniform sides. The canny soldier fooled me even in death and lay on his side. Leaving, I felt sorry for them and now they were dead. They sufficiently changed form to be innocu-ous, a mere matter of valley floor regeneration. There was the smell. They were forgiven. Everybody must have a smell.

"Smoke bothered me that night, sweeping along the hill and funnelling into the still batless cave, waking, coughing, flush-ing tiny creatures off my eyes, spending most of the following day sneezing. What made sneezing common was this business of spending a lot of time in dusty places. So, I open my lungs on rocks between sneezes and reflect, sometimes on the fireworks dog with eyes given to sparks: about the eager way a lonely hound greets a pure stranger, bounding up to love anybody...or at least warms to you despite the lousy railroad track where he grew and nourished. This mongrel waited and wept and kept its paws clean for a stranger. The animal and I were free from their rage; otherwise, we'd be dog meat, raw or on a spit. We cared for each other, only wishing to serve, without any expec-tations back, and so we were released to serve.

"The cave was, oh, I'd say 160 yards from me. A whole day and I'd gone 160 yards; it was a curvy swervey journey. This was a day of amnesty. For the first time in weeks, I noticed

trees hanging over their brown river reflections, really noticing, absorbing myself in them, utterly relaxed. Sitting now
on a high resting-during-evening-forage rock, a different perspective lit the sky and trees, a view working like windshield
wipers clearing grit from a window."

Leader lay beside an empty apple juice bottle, his eyes half
shut in the waning light of day. "How did this incredible day
finish?" he murmured.

"A fire or lantern moved by jerks and I stepped behind a tree.
As the glow advanced, a chorus of mumbles penetrated the
faint wind. The mumbles grew louder. A gang of Mumbledy
Legs carried out a ritual. I shrunk closer to a tree, obscuring
my pretentious vision with guessing judgments!

"An object, resembling an eye, appeared to ooze from its
socket; perhaps a dribble or a monstrous tear? I dared not
move, for this was an apparition or aberration in my dazed
head from the realities of the day. At the height of the Mumbledy Leg romp, their light fell to the ground and kicked from
shape to shape, as if disowning the group's cohesion. The glow
exposed them in angles and cracks, showing the Mumbledy
Legs as semivertical planes or pyramids, and I laughed at the
purity of sounds and thoughts passing with the fanciful daydream from my mind. What remained was me being bound
together with the entire realm around me, just breathing the
whimsy away.

"Dawn mist rolled off the lake, similar to the copters' smoke
but palatable, and the onyx shining water underneath a still
current rippled as song birds began to sing. Leaves and broken
wood stuck out of my clothes, and my joints felt full of crumbs."

Each Day Is a Brand New Gain

Light shone red against my eye lids, which were stuck shut, and I felt constipated from head to toe. Leader pounded on a pan and shouted: "Let's up, let's up. Everybody up! It's a new day and let's up. Come on, let's up! He walked among the sleepy forms, even kicking a few. Most of them performed a blanketed jigging about rigmarole and quieted into a foetus position. One double lump shed their bedcovers and the couple bloomed in a salute to the sun. Sitting up, my lids flapping open, the twin girls rose from white ground as if folded together flush with the earth. The day felt so warm I thought that corn in a nearby field might pop off its cobs. Somewhere beyond a green-bleached Chevrolet pickup truck, a Bluejay hopped and swung on invisible ropes. People started their chores. The twins chased a small animal. An elder looked under the Chevy's hood. Two people hung robes to use as a sun shield while they bathed in the percolating stream. Traipsing from form to form, Leader attended each one, focusing his light, illuminating every new riser for a few seconds. Then the animated twilight of day resumed. The group sat at picnic tables and ate their spread of food. I listened to their talk, awake to peculiar and similar features in it. The twins argued already and now chased the phantom in each other. The elder tracked a lady friend, who said as he grabbed her: "But you know that sort of thing can't happen." He nodded grimly and nudged her, insisting it could. They both giggled and went off.

The group seemed unconcerned about Leader eating breakfast alone. Or me either. I sat cross-legged, gulping the food,
practically inhaling it. Summer's sky pulsed, so different to
winter's ashen hood and the autumn sky which changed character with its leaves. As dishes were piled for a later wash, the
people chatted over coffee and tea. A few glanced at Leader.
One man approached him, only to be rebuffed and return
with a sour face. The twins were silent. Elder hung from the
truck's entrails. A trio of teenagers sat, smirky-mouthed. The
sun inched across the forehead of another day to bring autumn
closer and winter, too. Leader mopped his shiny cheeks and
strode over to me.

"Well, I want to say goodbye; I suppose you'll wind up back
with your family, eh?" he declared, then belched.

"No relatives."

"Pardon?"

"Oh, a wise mother who dislodged an extreme husband.
That was years ago and nobody very much cared about war veterans going berserk or alcoholic grandfathers and so on. The
family split; relatives were shy or mostly absent or ashamed."

"You mean people change, sure; I guess you must have a
sense of home," he insisted.

"Home is probably a time when fathers are pals. Time is what
makes a home — spending peaceful time together surely gives
a home dignity and mutual respect. Home is a place behind
adventure, where if you're lucky you uncover genuine energy
and confidence and it's a revelation to be with pals, or especially
with your mother, at least for awhile. Even now that first house
is like all houses, with mementos, memories of an actual past,

reenacted in opinions, where kids grow into a crazy jumble of wanting to cover up unwanted feelings and not cover up...and the circumstances, Saturday movie nights, where from outside our houses we were surrounded and penetrated by TV assassination events and sports spectacles, Pentagon radio features about the latest most lethal bomber...is it any wonder us kids retreated with books to find out if imaginary people can be free from the disjointing lifeline between what is and what is not. Friday night's The Big Fight, names forgotten, landscape changing, a Caterpillar tractor pushing earth over our fallen tree, cars whizzing past the house-box at night, more half-truths pumped through airwaves to keep the home safely inflated — so many tempers and instincts circumnavigate throughout that eventually you leave and realize that home is how you are in yourself. What were you doing during all that and how did you get along? You say change; did your home change from a time of baby's affection to a memories compost heap, fuming hot inside the weight of reconstituting what happened? Is home a place where what might have happened doesn't happen because you're blunted and in qualm stew and foreboding? How shall we ever touch in the light, free of the menacing helter-skelter paternal unease? Our own? No never or ever? When every day is full to the cocks of any comb: an increasingly intricate web of maps, changing faces who want you and don't want you, unlike those times on the lake when we were pure group — no ritual — we drank pop in fire light we didn't need. Some wanted fire. Others built it. We mingled, webbed in the moon's gleam. Crops, wind, water, and trees all around. Someone went to swim. There was hesitancy. Another left for the water; the group converged when moonlight was less direct. No idiotic pretensions about security. It was wholesome and shared. No gimmick, no authority, no home in house as such: just group, with the willpower to abandon our hang-ups."

"Each day is a brand new gain. You've gained something important in your losses. That pain is surely reconciled by what we have now, even as strangers; rejoice with me in that and we'll say goodbye. Good luck in Frisco and watch out for maniacs on the Golden Gate."

Leader walked away, silent. He picked up a basin and scrubbed at it. Most of his group looked as if just being together was awesome, a high regard for each other which presented them with time for thoughtfulness and the practice of heartfelt devotion, allowing them to reveal to each other their happies and sads — like a collection of x-rays in a dark closet — their mutual fidelity visible by the glow that people emit, as if when a light switches on, a door opens, a vivid new being is born with the benefit of the parents' best intentions — the prior bads being dissolved in the light of good deeds and the new human forms emerging, forever like that, reborn.

Persistent murmurs chopped now, sounding much the same as the first water of spring. The people grew restive; some even snapped in anticipation, or stared briefly, at Leader, with inquiring gazes. One twin's nosebleed came to a head; she sulked and tensed. The piqued twin stood, bunched her fist and flicked the other twin's ear. They shouted and squabbled. A helicopter pilot crushed his cigarette in the ground and tugged at the twin on top. Two mechanics helped. With fierce grunts and sharp jerks, they separated the pair. The bloodied twin stamped and glared at Leader. The chubbier other sat in a whimper, the breath gone out of her. Elder, hood-peeping Tom, who again nodded warmly at the opposite sex who he fancied, circled Leader. Everybody watched. The elder-bodied fellow seemed to derive courage from the witness and as he spoke put his hand on Leader's shoulder. The patriarch dropped his jaw. Tom relaxed his grip, spoke quickly and meandered towards the group, which stepped back, away from him. A few moments later, Leader approached, stopping at the fringe to speak with a youngster. Another person joined them along with a pilot. Soon, they laughed and the rest gathered. The twins cut in last with expectant smiles. "Now, since it's such a fine day, we're all going to practice," Leader said. "Good," said Tom, from behind. Others echoed some of the fervor. "Get your things," Leader shouted. "I'll prepare myself." They robed with restless talk and seconding shouts. In good time, Leader asked them to line up at the edge of a clearing. The keen group shifted their feet and exchanged remarks until he led them in song. I heard only bits of chorus, from a distance. Copters left, whirling above the group, scattering dust on leftover breakfast. Lines of people swayed to ceremonial habits.

A mile into the wood, I threw up my arms and shouted. The echo seemed to shout. With a fallen branch, I ran in circles, swatting around trees, plants, and shrubs, swatting and chopping air. "Hey. Hey. Hey," I yelled again, chuckling cordially, lying, and rollicking as if it was no one else's precedent to be cordial.

With all the bright stars crashing into each other every nine minutes — even in daytime — microorganisms regenerate during the tests of time, moving across the misty earth like drawn figures on the lake's surface as if living profiles etched in rock and reborn an age later.

Ray Needle's Zero

A chill tingled in crusty, warm eyes as the blinking wipers washed across the sleepy corners. Arms were locked stiff in a careless position between my belly and the ground. Rolling the body, including eyes, to one side, the right arm jutted out from my chest like a tree, while the left was rumpled beneath. Rich, dark, formless colors — greens, yellows, browns, greys, reds — pressed against the eyes. Straining over a blue lump, groping with toes to note that it was my sleeping bag-covered feet, the bleary eyes converged on other particular colors, following contour to define form until objects were recognizable. Sentinel trees posed in the moon lode, full to the tops of searches, wailing on the edge, viewing, and the moon grew long. As bodily sensations began the transition from welcoming light to their key positions, my body felt slain by course roads and steep paths.

Even walking, the arms were reluctant to swing alongside — to reach on the swing as far as they were supposed to. My hands worked roughly, forcing twigs between fingers until they broke into rice size pieces. A train whirled below, metal clover in windblown moon glint: freight cars chasing each other, barking at a waning moon and back again at hazy morning, while roads silently waited. Eating scrambled eggs and fried potatoes, I thought of traveling for the first time in a couple of days.

Behind eyes, the comedy and tragedy, claiming rich minds as their own, absorbing more juxtaposed lullaby than the Lilliputians casting ropes that rivet Gulliver's individuality to ground. Last night's lullaby merged into trees along the road, which stood as though they were grim barbers, or talked with wind like the eyes of a fisherman. That was a modestly quiet night with most goings-on ended. A few people probably slept hard, their labor of the day moving with the mist, free from viewing and viewed. Only shapes remained to impregnate the earth while fleeting images fertilized the unthinking sleep.

Clean clothes dried on a rock by the fire, I set off—all around golden grass, its wealthy looks ignored by goats whose trail took a turn for the worse: setting off, my oak staff fell to the wayside as I clung to small footholds and grabbed at granite pimples, toes burning and the dry swollen tongue shooting-out between my teeth. Jag, rejag, steeper, jag, rejag, steeper. Hawk-holed space tugging at my pack occupied several hundred feet to the valley floor. Breathing ahead of my lungs, saffron-faced summer rolled with ribald laughter. Body numbness overcame an impending peril, allowing me to negotiate a rockfall. "Gifted goats," I mused, warming to the chill on my tear ducts that morning, rather than plotting a course.

The decline from the heights where I camped urged stiff limbs into motion, into dancing and dodging the glare of morning sun and cool shade. At a place along a logging road, my ear detected two voices—a campsite, with food. Creeping up an embankment and peering over, a middle-aged man and his companion were in a fray beside a pink car with astronomical designs on it. Nearer the river bank they'd pitched a deluxe tent, including window frames and a small refrigerator on a dolly in the porch.

"I don't care," the heftier one said. "If you want to get out on the left side of the bed, just do it. Don't make a big scene about it and don't — I repeat — are you listening, you crotchety grouch?...I repeat — don't try to drag me into it. And do not give me any more of your gyp."

"I couldn't drag you with a ten-foot pole if you were bagged in a net," the disgruntled skinny one answered.

"And don't try to be funny. There isn't any canned laughter here. You're the sole laughable thing out here."

"You, an expert on cans? You think the only kind of cans are made of tin."

"So what? They're the only kind you'll ever get close to, you little squirrel-pecker."

"Eat it, you witch. You always start the goddamned bitch-youments whenever we go anywhere. I try to take you some place and get you to relax and what happens every damn time? You..."

"Place? Anywhere? Where in hell do you think we are, Ray Needle? The middle of the goddamned mountains, that's where. They don't even have bears up here. It's so damned miserable...they don't have rats or weasels or any a those neat little types of animals, or even people. Do you call these rock formations and lichens people?"

They argued about some damn thing. I stuffed a gunnysack in my belt and left the pack. Sneaking across the campsite fringe to the back of the tent, I edged along a veranda to the porch, pulled back the netting and crawled behind deck chairs to the inside door. Through an aluminum shade I saw they were still at it. The hefty one appeared to have an upper hand, talking most while the skinny one sat, watching the ground. Porcelain gewgaws littered the tent. In the middle, a large bouquet of yellow, red and green synthetic flowers crowned a Sears icebox. The squat, bronzed, thin man looked like he acquired time on his hands: weenie but lean gold-fingered hands held the potbelly, which grew like a tumor welling out beneath his medallioned chest and knees as he slouched. He looked at his partner and his face bloomed in crimson, through a sunbed tan. I tossed three firm pears and crusty bread in the sack and stepped behind a shower curtain as the short-winded man marched stiff-legged toward the tent, with time in his step, and anger feeding his conflicted face. Ignoring my sack left on a table, he picked up a single-bit wedge axe, testing its weight, wobbling his wrist, squeezing the handle in his hand and slapping his left palm with the axe head. Then he smiled and went outside. From the freezer, I bagged a package of pasta, a head of lettuce, quart of milk and green beans. His companion approached as I was opening a metal canister in search of matches. Duckwalking backwards towards the shower, my gunny sack snagged on a handle and stuck there hanging on a chest of drawers. She searched through a suitcase on the bed. Behind thick glasses with tweedy rims, her eyes sloshed tears like black and blue paint when she turned her headdress of brown plastic hair curlers.

"You witch, what's the matter? You start a quarrel and run away. Haw," he snorted in triumph. "Or have you gone to get your gold-plated pistol again. Huh? Afraid of me?" There was no docile husband, if that's what he was, in his voice now. The man with seared and yellow edges was enraged. Toting a shiny pistol over her head, the wide-shouldered woman snapped-up my sack, straightened and left. Her shower-clog shoes clip-clopped on the tent's ratproof floor and then slid in a coat of pine needles on the ground.

"You screwball. You puny whelp. You are zero. So you think you can frighten me with that axe, huh. Well, who gives a damn? Who's afraid of you? Nobody! There isn't a pine cone in this forest that couldn't make you back up...that couldn't frighten you...even if you had an axe and a fireman's outfit. You, a fireman? Hahahahahahahahahahahahahahaha-haha...hahahahahahahahahahahahaha. Of course, nobody would fancy you. After all, most orangutans are kept in zoos." They watched for an effect on each other, sneering as if half-disbelieving their own words.

"Can this couple be fertile ground for mediation?" I whispered, trying to rationalize their contempt, resentment, and hatred.

"You're pinched up," he shouted, "Not from shrinkage, but to stop leaks!"

"That's odd; we're usually pinched up from drying out. Your battles mister are long past. You prefer teevee to sex or walking."

"Ha! The only bang anybody could get from you is from that pistol," the man declared. She jumped off her stump scream-ing at him and threw a pine cone at his shouting.

They'll need their food to survive this row, I thought, col-lecting a few matches from one of the waterproof film cases. Screams and shouts outside progressed into a crescendo.

They stood face to face, yelling unintelligible words. The axe-wielding fellow shifted hands with his weapon and she pointed at the ground with her pistol. I crawled through the tent door and the porch, tracing my path along the veranda to the embankment.

The futile battle between the couple burned up their potential for positive energy and willpower on both sides with the reckless intensity of zero affection. Where to find goodwill in the absence of expressing care and in the presence of being mistreated?

There are zero enemies, just conditions and circumstances which cause the grouch with gyp and this lady to differ. To think these two are a link in a chain of being, all created by the same light, a perfect ray needle piercing their zero to liberate the discord between them, ultimately to cherish a shared zero.

Farmers Joy

Relaxing in the crotch of a weepy willow tree, quiet in her night skirt, arms stretched along a trim branch to cushion my head. Bronze-windowed houses showed their proud edges in the jagged moonlight. Nobody stirred. Gas pumps across the street looked like sleeping hobos upright. Empty porch chairs sagged weightless.

Dogs muted their bark signals as I walked past the cool athletics ground, glancing into parked cars. Most of the white-washed homes were two storeys high, in night vision unsoiled, pristine. Houses existed above the land like a shoal of identical fish, breathing and watching and resting. "Children may be the same," I said to myself, "fining along, darting from place to place — abdomens puffy with mothers' food and, if like me, backs barbed from fathers' belts, eyes closed, lidless to the real ancient currents of this place...until wham, we're caught. That is the real tragedy, trying to own and master the instant, yet caught in that impossibility."

Humming while searching for keys in a parking lot for impounded vehicles, a sharp eye peeled over my shoulder, sensing the moon-cratered shadows of jailbird drivers enraged at the wheel by a tumultuous sea of agitation pricking their mind's eye. "Little money passes hands when there is little money. The criterion is circumstance, more than price. Like this one." The doors of the clunker were unlocked. Chanting *Johnny B. Goode,* entering the circumstanced car, eyes drawn wide, a quiver hanging across my back, a quiver of kind words to haunted fanatics who drive until their mental wheels fall off and to my recalcitrant father, who disobeyed my mother's plaintive defense: 'Joshua, don't, stop it, leave him alone.'

"Go Johnny go, I dub you Naught the Chariot. And now, sturdy charger, let's off!" Powerful sputtering and choking from its solitude, the Buick lunged from its weedy placement, with troublesome steering. It tended to overdrive, turning 90-degree corners with enough force for a circle. Soon it lynched itself out and we had ourselves under thumb, so to speak. Off and away, silent in the ghosted countryside, free from streetlamps glare, above the chewed town air, beyond the end of a dog bark. Vegetation along the road spun like a busy turnstile in the car's wake. Daisy-meadowed armies marched in soft wind; the moon coasted white through tousled clouds and glided in whirly seas of unspoken sound. Cruising by pastures on an asphalt road, leaning out the window to swirl in fresh air, sending the glee I felt to all those who hit out at anyone who didn't fit the bill, that they might use glee instead of cruelty and relieve the burden of callous instincts. "Only cattle are safe on the streets at night. Their butchers sleep and dream of meat. But the meat breathes."

At the top of a bluff, easing off the road, the moon blazed from huge catacombs, as though full of meaning. Then I saw the temple — a brick structure that stretched across acres of parking lot. "When it's awake, its priests shuffle from the tin-can, cellophane, plastic and popcorn bowels of the temple, to carry out bags of groceries, new garbage cans, lawnmowers, appliances, toys and clothes to the town's remaining licensed cars."

Next to this hygienic property, battalions of green blades were swollen in their own silence, waiting for the next trampler. Near the bluff bottom, a soil-hardened farmer and his duplicate, a child, ploughed and ploughed and ploughed, as if their hearts were parts on their tractors. Farmers in their conscience may resent the temple, its demand for overseas products to suit people wasting for want, not need, farmers pinched for their costs on their own goods by the temple's profit margins, its need, not theirs. Yet, the resentment dissolves in a devoted and informed feel for what they do, leaving them among the very few with a straight posture and unfettered mind, without designs on the sky. Farm machines creep along parallel to imaginary boundaries: official lines drawn on paper, miles away at the courthouse, but the boundary is expressed in one farmer's corn and a neighbor's alfalfa. They provide for each other and for anyone who winks at mankind in general, in good years.

"Farmers go on as though their blessings come from within. This is in the nature of the community they form — their necessity and enthusiasm. From farmers acceptance a joy evolves which starts in the utility of land, everything making up and adding value to their effort. With their contentment comes a respect that they reserve for one another and the crops. I, for one, admire them. They're joined at the loins to each other, to the crops, and to their tractors. They smile because they have tractors instead of horses. A hundred years ago they were just as content with horses and before that with entering into collective harvesting. So they must always have been joined at the loin to everything — must always have given up everything in return for their timeless connections."

Others, from towns and cities, are bargainers, with the smiles of bargainers, having yet to discover farmers' glee. Owls might flutter around their heads, the dirt secrets wash away while they exchange goods, while farmers first thoughts are rooted in the space where they are at any given moment. The light of a farmer farming is washed and unspoiled and colorful.

I pushed the accelerator to the floorboard. The 2½ ton machine lumbered into a school of potholes. Tires punched the undercarriage. The car skidded broadside for a few yards, caroming into a gully, elbowing me in the ribs with its gear lever, throwing me onto the gearbox bulge with a thud that snapped my heels together. The poundings caught me with lungs full of air and a giddy head. My legs were tangled in pedals, my back beneath the steering column. A thingamajig under the dashboard stuck into my elbow. Blood trickled from my forehead and left arm, dripping off some fingers. Straining to locate the thing, it cracked the air, then: "...Five." All the joints in my body jumped at once.

"Check 18. Twenty-five, I said 300 North Farnham for one." I hit every knob in the cockpit's intestine.

"Chet? Eighteen!"

"Eighteen."

"Chet, you seen Pinkney? I give 'im North Farnham and Ruby's on the phone sez he ain't there."

"Saw 'im in the Santa Fe Depot takin' a leak."

"Twenty."

"Yeah, 20."

"I seen his cab parked down on the square at the Eagles Nest."

"Okay, Andree, you get yer butt in the joint and tell 'im to get here to the office. Ruby's already calt yella."

Whimpering and reaching to turn it off, my feet lay like dirty socks, arms stiff over the bulge. I hit the armrest with my hand-heel, opening the door a few feet — the impact seeped from the right side of my body and hammered my feet.

The cab was without decoration; no signs of it. It used to be One: the number One cab that tells errant taxis to avoid steep driveways so exhaust pipes won't be damaged. To determine that cabs in front of the Eagles Nest were for leaks, not drinks.

Most hurt parts worked as I pulled through the door. The right arm was idle to protect an injured rib. The Buick, almost concealed from passersby, was near a buzzing swamp — a brown-green quagmire with contented ducks. Pressing against the engine hood, heat nudged the joints and my head cooled, while aching feet and legs soaked in swamp water.

Fog in shifty folds coasted among leafed trees, touching its own layers. Soft fog filtered over my bones. Sometimes the folds crisscrossed and seemed to restrict the play of muscles. Warm air dried the wounds — blood in shrunken knitted doily patterns — making me stiff but together. Pulling a wine-skin bag and a fistful of fried soybeans from my backpack, I filled the good lung through the working nostril, swirling on feet lined with new blood, to catch as much wind as possible. My circuitry dimmed; judgments and all the rest of it flickered out, leaving one primitive reality — the breath of air in and out — sitting cross-legged in tall grass, wind wrapped in patterns of light shadowed with leaves. Millions of new leaves, parts, speckles of molecules, oxygen in spots, ragged doll pieces, lizards playing around with limbs tightly held as faces in nature, close together. A dynastic sense of presence walked inside me to the tune of kinship and the land.

Circling a town, a copper ray shone above the busy horizon. Moseying inwards, gold metallic trim gleamed on the sun side of the Mormon steeple, where light flowed like milk on the sky-silhouetted bell. Jagged branches split dawn from day in irregular triangles and unseen shapes. In a pasture, a bright column cloaked a statuesque tree. The mottle-barked branches were stained white by crows. One large branch was broken, touching the ground as though it was a road sign pointing to a hole. The clear, fluty sound of a yellow-throated Meadowlark sparkled, similar to a rainbow across air. An adult and a child walked to town across rabbit burrows and growth-green ditches. Town, for a child, was bright with unbought store things, treasures behind unexplored bushes and rare jewels which glittered on rain-shiny fire hydrants.

I flipped up my jacket collar against the cool rain — an ooze with the sound of a motorcycle's hacking. The blue and emerald curtains of rain were mostly to one side, passing in grey sheets, columns really. Raindrops patted dusty welts of nude earth ready to be healed. Little puffs spat back from the drops. The play of savage wind flurries on crystal light and sky blue dark dangled between thunderclouds. Sidewalks and curbs bordered brick streets which shined in the ooze together with flat-faced storefronts. I hopscotched, dodging bits of rubbish flying with the force of child-propelled corn husks. Streetlamps blackjacked against their stands, lights whirring and clicking. Lyric traffic coughed in an unreal fog veil which thickened from an industrial works across the river from Cherry Street. The wind hushed and nesting places emptied. Buildings were vague beneath a cloud of birds.

"The sun is yellow! No, it's red," I called out to a flyer-by, laughing. My heels burned, still and slow, darting into a boulevard. "Police! Cops, cops." Three pairs of patrol cars in successive waves, each larger until I was dwarfed with surprise, jamming my left arm into the free pack strap and jogging across the boulevard, through a sales lot of used cars, then sprinting to the right, and safe, but my body was a rack hung with pain. "Amen. Amen. Amen," I said, with the sincerity of a chorus of evangelical angels set to civil rights.

In an alley lined with barred windows and the mockery of boys, a Robin — chest full of pellets — lay breaking down under a board. Bricks were stacked on the board so the bird's last supper propped open its beak. A sick dog probably ate poison or choked on marbles. The animal sported crude stitches in its neck and a kerosene smell. He might just as easily have been set afire or had his nostrils and mouth stuffed with yeast. A croquet ball rested on a refrigerator top, which was under a boarded up fire door of an apartment building. Obscene phrases and initials sprayed onto garage backs. Potatoes rotted near a swing set that separated two garages. Foot ruts carved in tarmac under swing seats. Bags of decomposing garbage gained strength in a stove. Automobile parts filled a decayed rowboat. Cardboard boxes were stacked to the beginnings of clotheslines. Past oil smells and mutilated toys; flat blunt light appeared to seal the alley at both ends. Areas of smell rose and shifted like Skunk fume.

I wore an expression of straightening the decreasingly painful rack of body, as school kids occupied the streets like a Lemming migration en masse from the tundra, on lawns, around trees, poles and homes, at their leisure. "Retract your trigger finger," I cautioned, in the direction of an elementary school. "You knew my preferences, freedom from bruises and their origins. This echoed a message from my foot to my hand. What kind of aptitude would the school principal think is attached to that language? I shall tell them my brain was reaped off a cotton candy excess sale. Ding. Ding! Recess. Recess! Scratch phooey-wax. This echoed a message to my brain from my ear. Get along little doggie, get along. This echoed a message to my brain from my arm." And so on, until silly distractions were excuses and the body was at ease again.

I keep an eye on myself now, these days, and even sense an urge coming before I act, cautious and somewhat more thoughtful; that must be progress. Hearing the rustle of rashness, a thought wave coming from inside, sounding like a hum — from a multitude of throats comes the sound like the droning of thousands of bees.

The swollen river steamed along at parkside, accompanying it to a bridge where park and river separated. A down-and-out wrote on a log that a girl was kidnapped by boat and the etching said, "Leave 1,000 bucks here, beneath the bridge." Ancient trees in their foggy grave yard watched and contained the down-and-out's best wishes. Young trees flexed their arms after another day's striving for sun. The river chopped into green-blue pieces, the reflected roundness of rocks floating on top. Fog shadows floated on it anyway or just above it: stationary momentarily, sticking in air as if something from nothing. Fog moves along the river, a translucent herd. Fog animals are alert, beforehand, to a vehicle splashing out of darkness and roaring over the river. The fog leaves a path through itself, and then resumes its migration.

Cleaning mud from my boots and blood from the wounds, transcribing notes and writing in my journal that I lay like a damp L against a tree trunk, using poetics in a world full of hurly-burly trains and people clinging to flaming brooms who chase youngsters and ship-lashed flags. The elm and river birch evade the night earth and sleep in the mornings. The whisper of wind across a green bastion answers a call from its forebearers. Stretching limbs, pulling out the twilight breath and storing up their rumors, the trees stand, embracing the night in their palms.

Passing Through a City

Empty freight cars sounded their steady stroke of cymbals. Mostly though, bumpety-bumpety-bumpety-bumpety-bumpety. Sometimes a pull and a poke, pull-poke-pull, and once in a while a lunge, but mostly bumpety-bumpety-bumpety-bumpety-bumpety. Much the same as riding in a convertible on a spring day, racing the clouds and corralling the hiss and thunder in the wind's belly, steaming along straight hard roads, listening to a clear inch of lark in a blurred mile, stacking the T-Poles and ripping them off two-by-one, and then pierced by the sun's egg yoke. The westward train into the city, to penetrate its hide with pencils and study habits that beat against its brain like the song of a divine angel, on a good day.

Going here and there bumpety-bumpety, the land passing bumpety-bumpety wrapping T-Poles as one and being present with the one, answers lying in the cool rustle of wind which blows over groves, around cedar fence posts, across a narrow dirt road and through my prairie bush proud hair, a shelter for debris that the ancient sea left behind — wind blowing through blackbirds eyes and filtering the milk-smell breath of a nursed child. Water and earth and fire and air and space, uniting all time and lodged in all breasts, protected by the goddess of sopranos.

The cemetery slipped by in a mixture of peace, longing and eternity. Some stones cracked, a few fallen. Does death stop human existence from renewing each person? People under the stones came, occupied the earth, were slaves in many lives, to their preoccupations and desires, and had gone, to relive various stages of decay and development all over again? Each person, living in one form or another again and again, followed the same path as those before them, to the same end and beyond. Is this life-on-life motion like traveling, like strangers who bring new gist, transversing old habits, going forward? Wind and other elements remain free of misleading dreams. Does it matter to the stones-people whether they loved a few individuals only, or whether they loved everyone in the world equally? If they disagreed with people they knew, were they still averse to hurting them? Above the stones, do we inherit their conciliations, how they acted to get what they wanted?

The train's slow screech almost pulled the flesh off my head. I jumped from the boxcar. A first milk-tender's truck dallied past, tasting all the juice of dawn. Then an interval occurred, when the sun was up just so far — a comma in the day: a place for bright rays to shine on the bellies of branches, to flare over river waves, catch unseen night tree hollows and shoot exclamations of wonder into squirrels' eyes, setting them alight with the color of fire. The interval passed with early roars from beneath a smokescreen on the concrete horizon. Buildings tall in the sky bounced out of the pavement. These were silver buildings that formed in the distance a crawling crust over the sky. A firm-footed road led to factories in the midst of the smokescreen where people waited for light to be switched on, and motors lubricated.

Honk. Hononnnnnnnnnnnnk. "You S-Oh-Bee!" "Hurry

the hell up!" Honk, honk-honk, hononnnnnnnnnnnnnk.
"There she goes, now!" Hononnnk, hononnnk...resembles a
host of geese and dish-throwing seals gone berserk.

Sun crossed between buildings, changing shadows in a
car park where five kids played with a soccer ball on a tarmac
playground, where a pig-tailed girl rode a tricycle and uttered
nude noises to herself. Two dogs barked and scratched on a
paw-rutted screen door. A man with dirty trousers and a pregnant woman pounded a parking meter with a book. In front
of a school that waited for children to throng, an ice cream
peddler counted popsicles in a pink and white van.

"The flowers of your time are straight lines," shouted a man
in a group. "Take your museums of straight lines, build a
ladder to Mars with them and notice your hard, pale excess
corpses lying on rocks as if dung-splotched by birds. Did you
ever see anything so delicate as a straight line? Try to make
one while you perspire!"

Neon trees and trucks brought shade to a side street. At
a school playground, early-bird-gets-the-worm youngsters
buzzed around each other, their scarlet faces extended into
each other, their shrill voices jubilant in the absence of parents.
A huge hotel grew on its side, while a fading bird's song paused
on the edge of its sound. Ashes blew in the wind, through the
offal of rusted air. Sky floated away time-dried, like a proph-
et's spirit. People hurried to places they knew on weekdays,
through coffee or small change.

"...hectic," a voice blurted. "And we're rushed at the factory
and didn't have time to complete it." "Oh, God!" A fellow
slashed Xs in his face. He lay down and blood trickled back

and forth. A baby in a car cried to unhearing upholstery, to the smell of a vinyl dummy with acetate silk hair and button eyes, while a hustler alongside peddled unmarked packets for $100 each.

Every so often I tugged at my beard, more fluff-like than pullable. Traffic passed in a mournful parade of hearses. Streetlights changed. Traffic seemed to hold its breath. Crowd flowed across the street, not in a semblance of order, but in a tide. If the beard meets with the crowd's disapproval, the whiskers might grow inward. Will anyone notice? If the pressure of city life is too great, everyone's whiskers may grow inward, to be bitten off first, and then spat out by people in bus backs and at the ends of aisles. Always in the background, the city's roar, or a machine grinding yellow flowers? Part of the roar belonged to people who took meat from machines and held their health in equations.

I sighted a lake and inhaled the smell of wood preservative added to hay, manure and sweat from my creosote smelling boxcar. At the unoccupied end of beach, sitting with my boots unlaced, a fisherman stood by the shore a dozen or so yards away. The wave engine made a new sound as old as the sun; nude trees stood grasping at the sky. Along the shore, little piles of used bricks littered here and there. A dog chewing debris-studded breath went by with a hollow-eyed boy. The fisherman reeled in his line and raised the rod, which followed up and back and with the flick of his wrist the forward-bending rod spat the plug over the lake. Parts of his shooting line flashed in the sun. When the plug was about four feet off the water, he pulled on the rod handle and the plug settled easily, almost floating onto the surface and with practically no splash. He had accuracy, too, skipping the plug alongside some stumps. Other times, the fisherman dropped the plug at the edge of lily pads, making it appear to be a small frog jumping into the lake. Usually once each cast, he coughed. Not a real cough, just a small "uh" from the bottom of his throat.

Past shallows and far out on the waves, where life on land was a shout blown away or a bird that coasted to another side of the park, I dove deep, then surfaced for air, breathing with the waves, diving again, swimming down until I thought my ears near-popped, until my sight blurred from lack of air. Light on top hissed through the water in translucent columns. From my eye-corners green shadows stretched as far as I could see.

Then the wind was right, and children's shouts were audible as they ran on shore. The city blended in a high-pitched rumble. Then a gull squawked and the squawk rose, laminated above the other sounds. Sky and lake teased the trees. In response, both moved as though they knew their roots: floating on my back, listening to waves gurgle, hum and splash. Tree cheeks filled with wind, a backdrop to the other sound. Always, there was the hum of aversives — wrapped in headphones plugged into water-resistant radios. How strange people move, each making sounds as do their things. The only sound I heard was blended and hung isolated behind them like a giant quilt, as if sound was there first.

When people move and need sound, they shop for it and pluck it from the quilt. Or does the sound pick them? All our lives, the quilt hangs and waits for us to make the exact movement in the exact situation which requires, elicits, a particular sound. When the moment passes, the resonance deserts us and passes back into the quilt, to hang in suspended animation until another occasion calls for it. A sound is in use once and affects the next sound. Afterwards a new one is created, from the result of its preceding cause, waiting for new circumstances to choose from. So the process continues, an unbroken quilted mat, built on its own preceding and succeeding remnants.

The quilt opens many possibilities, unending in its potential. A man dies, his sounds fade, body goes off, and weeds grow around his house. His partner moves to green pastures. Long after death, a child finds a picture of him and asks her mother who the man in the bottom drawer was. She remembers. So his sound has a presence. His merits pass to those he touched in whatever form they inhabit. Or a fellow plays an exceptional tennis shot. Just for a second he hears the ball's echo, or his laugh-salute for the shot, or any of his life's other echoes, and they mount up, diluting less worthy habits.

Even though my youthful brainwork in-progress view of death is limitless, it is without bleak overtones — the end of life expressed by previous lives embedded in sounds of another time and among natural elements, sun and wind, earth and fire, water and air. The outlook appears to be lives after lives lit in a way which also runs under sea and over sky, with people wrapped within and around their illuminated landscapes, minus popcorn boxes, tin cans, or light blue haze hanging over natural gold light. In this perspective, colors coalesce, blending into a vacuum color — an intermingled translucent filter, rinsing me of ingratitude and childhood obstinacy.

A gull flew buoyantly, tern-like, quacking and flapping

wing tips; another gull met her and they fenced. A breeze dimpled water and the chill sprinted across my chest, kicking the nipples as it went. Back at the shore, a few people were on the edge with mottled sand, rocks, my clothes, and more stones than sand in the shallows. The fisherman changed plugs. "How's fishing?" "Oh-uh-pretty good; coupla bass since you went in."

Scattering the birds, a man with a toy came to the lake. He jerked the toy's fuse several times. It exploded and glowed with black smoke. It was a boat. He set its teeth in the water, and it bit its way in circles under the fleeing birds, barking at them with puny pistons. "Each circle gets the man further from himself," I said to the fisherman. "This man flees with the boat, flees in its yellow circles, flees and eases his bleeding under the sky, in yellow circles." Stepping into the water, amid summer wind and waves, he turned his boat faster and faster. "Is he — uh — sitting on it?" the fisherman wondered. "Yeah, rolling on it, now snarling, biting its back, steering it across the rim of his world, bouncing on jolly waves." The man spat, as if he left someone behind, and purred with the old garage boat. Such a boat. He left someone way back from shore, behind a street and locked, or framed in a door, or like myself as a boy, frozen against a wall by a giant. A person who seals himself in envelopes and escapes his son for good, with a boat. Then the harvest is an unthankful one, on national holidays, which leaves no alternative but to give thanks even if there is no thanks to give. The man stood and pulled the boat's fuse again. He pulled harder and the handle on the end of the fuse came off in his stuttering hand. The boat choked smoke for a while and stopped under spinning gulls. Vapor blew the boat a bit and left it bare in the sun, falling in and out of waves, silent staring, torpid, drifting to the sand beneath his feet.

Through a park, past pigeons' short, flappy applause, I entered the cathedral of sound, streets putrid from exhaust fumes oiling the air until the sun was green. Traffic wore and polished each intersection of streets into webs, which gleamed. Buildings swayed high above to block cloud paths. Traffic inched. Something with one foot, pounded. There was a noise like antlers shredding clouds. People carried parcels and parcels carried by people; the cathedral is a threatening form of exclusion, more dangerous than the forest.

People walked along bumping into each other. If they knocked someone down — tough luck — and if they were knocked down, that seemed to excite them. Still, it was a clumsy way to travel — knocking people down. To get to or on a bus meant crowding to the point where nobody wanted anyone else, including the driver, to gain entry, and where all the comfort was what they carried — the bus, a refuge from sidewalk fanatics.

Store windows bulged: glassy eyes reflecting merchandise inside and an occasional hurried shopper. A matted jungle threatened my hearing and sight; rain made their madness obvious. Hair fell round the ears curly and shaggy on the neck: it tangled hearing, contorted sound, and reached for my eyes. Probably, it was too many months of hospital coffee, which was blue, or so it seemed in that light; it stank. Being conditioned to it, any other coffee was preferable.

"How to meet anyone in all this mess? If there is somebody to be friendly with we will discover each other. Someone will make us aware of each other. Or an echo will find both of us apart and offer each to the other. What will they be like? Will their hands fit their fingers? Will their fingers fit their arms? Will their ears be too large?" Thinking about the city's uncertainties, I leaned on a window and caused its glass to be oblique, producing a double-distorted image of the street. "Will they have ears? If not, I'll communicate in sign language. How can I tell them that they are the only sane one in all the pandemonium of fighters and knockers and whirling store windows and foul-backed buses?"

"Hey, you. Hey. Hey."

Somewhere among the masses, a human found its voice and, like an insect, buzzed at me.

"Yeah?" I looked up, searchingly. The voice belonged to a teenager, odds-on a girl one, dressed as a garbage collector, in coveralls, with an inscribed sailor's hat.

"What you doin' leanin' on that window?" she queried. "Yer from outta town, aren't ya."

"How can you tell?" I asked, frowning at her and at the same time admiring her adolescent impudence.

"It's as plain as yer face."

"Who are you?" But she was gone. Well, she was not deaf and had ears — at least one because I saw it. Her eyes and ear followed my movements, with some train of reasoning. Was the ear pointed on top? It did have a point on top, above the advancing opaque and brown eyes, unblinking.

An elder stopped, stared at me a second and hurried past. This left room for a lady with a fox on her shoulder to brush past, between a pair of boys who listened to a portable device which piped music through tin, straight into their rebellious, unfinished brains. Many street people wore heavy robes on their summer-coated shoulders, adorning themselves with rich colors, glancing at patches of sky visible between their buildings, as they hurried. City people appeared to derive a strange exuberance from their anticipation of fall's flying fingers. They knew from experience that the after-fall was harsh in the mountains, where winter ended in swollen rivers. These people tingled with natural anticipation, having felt a future presence in summer's balm. Something drew them to a reassuring certainty of after-fall and after that. The seasons were there. That was something. Whatever, they acted like moths attracted to a bright-colored fan.

Could their science reach the point of catastrophe forecasting, when a smug pride attends initial minor catastrophes? Will their predictions antedate sports — ball game betting becoming less of an obsession? The thrill then will be to bet on a catastrophe. After several forecasts prove correct, predictive science will proclaim its success: science finally tames or at least throws light on the inner mechanism of chance. Organizations and things of the city grow a sense of worry if any profitable options are left unexploited, irrespective of damage to the gullible, the poor, and the sick. News media will call the prediction a hoax, evangelists claiming that it's based on their proof.

Walking along, there were shouts on windy intersections:

silk-bearded ramblers sewed a ragged ghost-coat of Whitman-singing danger, if not doom. "Here me my fellows," one corner songster whimpered. A lady next to him hurried across the street, under stop-and-go lights which danced on strings.

"A million vengeful pennies fall on them," another croaked. "A million pennies sharpened to darts that prick them, blot out the light and flash red eyes, day and night. A million pennies bleed them dry as feathers and then bury them deep in the warmth of winter, deeper than a soul!"

Turning into a café, a flat counter represented a serving trough, from which short-skirted waitresses scurried to tables with plates of steamy food. Shuffling through the crowded and clangy room, I took a place next to a middle-aged man with a question-mark face. "Nice waitress you have."

"Oh, she's not my waitress; she belongs to the ages. She's common property," the man said, putting his face behind a newspaper.

"Really? How do you *know*?"

"Everybody knows."

"Oh. Why?"

"What are you sitting at my table for?" the man sighed.

"I fancy your waitress."

"Do you know her?"

"*Know.*"

As though offended by this pun, the man sat stiffly and returned to his paper.

"Yes sir," said a waitress who zoomed up to the table. "May I help you?"

"He doesn't appreciate puns."

"Ah, I *know*," she shrieked gleefully.

"Will you two stop that, you'll ruin my digestion," the man croaked, rattling his newspaper.

"What's in the *knews* today that could make such a noise?" I asked the waitress. We both giggled. She blushed.

"Please!" the man demanded.

"Please? What does he mean — will you *please* tell me?" I chanted.

"Oh God!" The man stood, giving us a look to boil a lobster. "You two can have the table. Take it; it's worn out anyway and there's nothing but teenagers' bubblegum holding it up."

"Sit down."

"Thanks. You smell like a lake."

"I was born in the sea. What brings you here?"

"I was born here."

"Right here?" I gestured at the table.

"In this city, silly."

"Where?"

"Oh, about ten blocks away."

"Show me."

"In an hour."

"Okay."

For an hour I watched her. She brought tea while balancing food in each hand. Her arms synchronized with amazing steps, gingerly pouring her between tables. Requests for orders were inserted without notice into conversations. She knew what she was doing alright, and she was only ten blocks from where she was born.

By the time we went outside, the traffic rush died. Air cleared and most of the sidewalks emptied.

"Do you like the city?"

"I've never been here before."

"Why?"

"I've been on the move a lot."

"Oh. Where?"

"Everywhere."

"It's not so bad now the people've gone."

"What do you think cities are for? Now that the people are shoppers it's not a city anymore."

"What is it then?"

"An anti-city, I guess."

"You're funny and…"

"I like you," she professed.

"So do I. Me do you, too, I mean."

"More than I like you?"

"We'll have to see; how much do you like me?" she asked.

"Not very much."

"Why not, what's wrong with me?"

"Nothing I fully understand. I just don't like full-scale right away."

"Oh. Okay."

Inside one store, fretful-faced people served mannequins supper and brought them slippers, newspapers and polished appliances. Outside, the sky's bottom turned purple. A soft-colored robe of royalty lay directly above the city. The haze made clouds even more pearl-glazed as it spread up toward them. On a ledge, half a dozen pigeons reddened as the last beams of sun stroked them.

"Look," I whispered.

She clasped my arm, burrowing into my side. "I never saw that before."

"They're pretty."

"Yes, when the sun is setting. Otherwise, they're opportunists who drop their jewels on peoples' heads. It's not very far from here."

"What kind of place is it? Were you born in a hospital or a house, or on a card table under a streetlight?"

"It's a hospital, but it's more than just mothers. It has every walk of life and all the epidemics."

Suddenly looming, the hospital cars were parked on three sides. In a corner lot, two men took engine parts off a vehicle with foreign license plates. The car hood was raised and a piece of canvas for tools spread over a fender.

"I got the distributor; I think that's the crux of our little problem," said one of the men.

"Yeah," grunted the other, "the crux."

"Or anyway, a big part of it. It's probably why the damned thing won't start."

"If it isn't the distributor, what do you suppose it could be?"

"Damned if I can make it out; maybe the distributor; that's about all I can fix on these buggies."

"Well, I hope it's the distributor, because if it's not we're never going to get this buggy moving except to light a fire under it."

"Well, we can worry about that later."

"You were born here?" I asked again.

"Right here. I believe it was on the seventh floor."

"Awfully high."

"Hey, I think those two men were here then, too. Only if I remember correctly, it wasn't the distributor, it was the generator causing all the fuss, and a female was calling the shots."

"I bet they never got the generator fixed. Did you notice how old the car was?"

"Yeah. Why don't they get another?"

"Guess they're too modest."

"Here's the entrance. Hasn't changed a bit since I came out."

"You mean you can remember all that stuff from when you were just a baby?"

"No, not exactly. But I remember most of it. The rest I imagine."

"Is it true if you imagine it?"

"I look at it this way...by the way, what's your name?"

"Paul, just Paul."

"Well, Paul, if my recall isn't true, I wouldn't be able to imagine those days. Remembering must have been there when I was born with a certain fixed way — a kid with questions. Memorable questions, and as a hyperactive kid, this manner was momentous in opening my imagination. Isn't yours? I can tell you were a handful. In fact, searching questions established the scope for my memory and draws its boundaries. So, I'm in fact not literally imagining things, but imagining that I'm remembering them. So, there's no knowing past from present because of the fiction that we make of it now, the mistaken beliefs, unjust opinions. Meaning, there's little difference between an imagined memory and an imagined reality.

They distort our ability to help anyone, so we need to be free of distortions."

"You learned all that as a waitress?"

"No, not exactly. I have a lot of time to think and just made it up. But sometimes it's harder to recognize whether you're really in this life or just imagining it."

Fourteen storeys high, the place lit up on every floor; it stood even with larger city buildings. "Here it is, Beulah Hospital. The first three floors are devoted to keeping books and records. The next four are for emergencies and immediate cases, such as train wrecks and births. The eighth through tenth are long-term care. The last floors are for terminal cases and geriatrics. Staff call the top floor the vegetable garden because that's where they keep everyone who is uncontrolled, or after they work their way up floor by floor they fall over the edge of the roof."

"You're a quixotic girl."

"This is where I learned to be quixotic. We're going to the 12th floor."

"Why there? I want to look round," I said, as the elevator doors opened.

"The 12th floor will keep us busy for a while," she said, smiling. At the fourth floor, two men dressed in white rolled a wheel-cart onto the elevator. On the cart was a writhing human form.

"Hold it down," a masked man said, gesturing to me.

"Okay, begin," said the other, who sighed, switched on a music player and put several knives against the form.

"All set, chief."

"All set, begin."

I loosened my grip on the limb. The waitress lowered her purse to the floor and stood against my back, hands touching my shoulders. Tiny puffs of her breath tickled my ear, but I couldn't concentrate on her breathing.

"Lucky you happened along," the understudy said. "One of our interns developed a criminal hernia, and we've got to take immediate steps. Does the young lady mind blood?"

"Heavens, no," she answered before I could say anything.

"Are you sure about this? I mean do you usually operate in elevators?" I asked.

"No, only during holidays. You see, our regular anaesthetists took the day off and there was an emergency at one of the workhouses, so we're a bit cramped today."

"It's night," I declared.

The chief looked at his watch. "Oh. Of course it is. It's been about nine hours since I've had a rest from these damn elevators. This is about the only elevator clean enough to operate in anymore."

"Yes. Yes, of course we do," the understudy replied. "We're not in the Dark Ages. It's just that we have our standards to meet and, as happens, there is law which forbids an operating room without a functioning anaesthetist. But the law says nothing about elevator operations. So this is what we're forced to do — nobody's fault really; it's just a lucky break for us that elevators are legal as operating rooms or we'd have to leave most poor devils out on the street. I think you'd better get on with the operation, doctor."

"Yeaup. Yes, of course. We'll begin immediately."

The intern came from the cart's feet-end to the head. His chief selected a scalpel from the row of tools and, humming in tune with the piped in music, started to slice. As the form writhed and kicked under the sheet, I nearly lost my grip on the patient's limb. The waitress offered to wipe the forehead.

"Are you sure you gave this person an anaesthetic?" she said as she mopped gingerly beneath the sheet-hidden brow.

"Sure."

"Then why all the kicking?"

"Just nerves and reflexes."

"That sounds awfully fishy to me."

"Well, are you a doctor, young lady?"

"No. No, I'm not a medic."

"Then I guess you're sort of ignorant about this sort of thing."

"More or less."

"Well, I guess that settles it. I will repeat: I gave a potent local anaesthetic which renders the patient completely numb in the area where I applied it."

"Oh."

He cut further, making an S-shaped incision in the mid-section and lower abdomen. My bellows pounded my air pipe raw. Elevator music covered heaving commotions and scalpel scrapes; doctor's work was quick. In the distance, a large motor noised. The patient's struggle weakened. I loosened to stretch my hands and rub my wrist, resuming the grip an instant before the patient kicked, arched her back, jerked from side to side, and bucked much like an objection. From between the pale green sheets came backbreaking coughs and sucks, and she punched a hole in the top sheet. Then the patient was still.

The intern grabbed the upper limbs; the rest lost form. The elevator stopped and descended. Doctor sighed, throwing his knife into a bucket fixed on the cart. "Well, that's the worst of it," he announced, timing the wrist pulse with his watch: "Getting pretty weak."

"Stopped struggling at least," I said sincerely.

The waitress leaned with both shoulders against the elevator wall. "It wasn't that bad when I was growing up. Nobody bled at all."

Both of us wept while the chief sewed his incision, making neat small double reinforced stitches. A gurgle escaped beneath the sheet — then a terrific belching as the long lump-form arched and bounced, arched and bounced on its fluid-soaked cart. Doctor stuck a needle in its stomach, much as a seamstress would use a pincushion. He listened for the pulse again.

"That's what I thought, we've lost her."

"Well, I usually can tell when we lose one, even without a pulse," said the degloved intern. "There's sort of an expertise which seeps through you when you've seen death as often as I have. Too bad, it was a good job. This is where we get off," the assistant said, pressing a button. "Will she be okay?" he asked, motioning to the waitress.

"I think so; we're just a little pale," I said.

"I'm really surprised we lost her; the doctor's done thousands of these — it's a simple operation."

"Wait, are you sure he gave her an anaesthetic?"

"Positive, I saw him. Here. Look at the larynx; you can still see the needle mark."

"The larynx?"

"Yeah. Some people refer to it as a voice box. Goodbye," he called over his shoulder, wheeling the cart off.

I sat on the floor, in disbelief, stunned by the silence, touching our heads together as the elevator rose again. "Damn, can you comprehend what they did?"

"Yes," she said in a weak voice.

"Could she have died for some reasonable principle?" I wondered out loud. "Did she concede to die long before death, before birth, believing that any way of dying was part and parcel of a better way of being? Perhaps the elevator patient struck her initial bargain long ago — a summer night when she gave absolute love to her first boy. Could the end have been less bitter since, secretly, she lived on eagerly generous and unselfish moments? Perhaps she didn't worry about submerging herself in a houseful of indulgences, wishing rather to have happiness with others than be plundered by a Viking doctor, her home sacked and her body carried off to a distant land where she'd be fitted to a communal bed, and with social overdetermination, stretched and mutilated while being continually spoiled in order to adapt her to foreign ways."

The elevator patient must have died for something. When the end came why was pain forced? For the many bargains planned to generate a summative bargaining place? Or, at the bitter end was it intended to convert a listless spirit in life into a living one in death? Did the hospital want the preposterous exhilaration of deciding fate? Or was this a directive from City Hall to free the expensive rabid ones from sexual predation.

"Did doctors think that the lifeblood of the elevator patient was sucked from her heart by school teachers who exploit the why and devour the wow? No, they wanted to prevent the elevator patient being back in the hoped-for healthy market place, where she could catch them pinching goodies and allowing corrupt politicians to build detention centers for misfits who avoided the hospital. So, the doctors would have her faith healer, or butcher or candlestick maker, die in place of them."

"Whole damn thing makes me sick," the waitress muttered.

"That was a crazy trick. Where are we stopped?"

"Oh, this is the garden."

"Oh. This is it. Nobody here to care?"

"The patients are all stuck in bed. They get sedatives, so the diapers aren't changed as often."

"Diapers?"

"Yes. Well, not actually diapers, but similar. Changing diapers is only a matter of form in most cases. Unfortunately, most of the vegetables sense whether they've been changed or not, and visitors are absent for fear of their lives. Worse, too, for these bedridden, they aren't even aware where they are. Here, this room?"

Inside, at the foot of two beds with human forms, a television set played. A cowboy show flickered back and forth: horses ran...gunshots...men fell...cattle stampeded into a commercial break in the story. Cattle continued along with gunshots and a fistfight...saloon with dancing women...poker game...gunshots...another fistfight...another advert. Men and women kissing men...solo love scene...commercial break. Another wild west show: cattle grazed on the prairie when gunshots interrupted...men fell from running horses — most of those that fell had feathered heads...a fistfight, arrested by a deodorant commercial. After that advert, a cattle stampede...somebody kissed a female gunfighter...then, a fistfight and a horse galloped into the saloon. The forms were still. A mischievous gleam rose in her eyes as she led me into the room. "Help me," she said, lifting one of the spaced-out straight-jacketed patients, all of whom wrapped as if they were humanoids from alien planets. "No, never mind, he's soiled. Unwrap him and try the other. We'll clean up after." She was as audacious as Nancy. She lifted his feet and looked under the sheet. "Okay, let's prop him up in that chair to get the blood flowing and we'll see to his exercise later. There. Now, let's squat in the en suite seclusion room." In a flash she was on the seclusion bed, shoes plopped on the floor, the zipper of her dress melting. "Well," she hinted.

Yes. I decided to join her. Before my body responded, she pulled me down — a hand on my thigh, the other floating on my chest. We kissed unsteadily but heavily with half-roll motions. Would-be words evaporated like feathers on our lips. Only murmurs remained.

The waitress slid under bedcovers while I stood to strip, joining her, with eyes wide and wandering — she with eyes open to her senses. Lifting the sheet, I examined her lean body, caressing the short flat belly with the heat of my palm, kissing her loose, unassuming breasts. Powerful thighs and muscles hidden in her neck lay still and silent. We swept over each other, sensing the warmth and then damp in our bodies. She rose to caress my smooth, firm flanks with the back of her hands, widening her eyes to the vigor that lurked inside of us, stroking — first more of a push stroke and a squeeze followed by a light tease stroke — pulling, rubbing my calf with her toes and scratching my nape with fingernails. I smiled, moving one leg between hers, and rolled on top.

Her size was frightening, transforming from a single room less its fourth wall to a whole infinite refuge. From oblivion outside she brought me this — where would I be, and how, when she returned to that hectic table service, if she did. She was both door and threshold to an unlimited unrestrictive timeless journey, which revealed no interior organs, as if to teach me what to replicate without genital stimulation, because once we started I felt that tranquillity and peace can only be for sharing and independent of all distractions and constraints. Inside, were vast reaches of unstructured years ahead of her time. "I am inseparable in your beginningless time of repetitive echos." She just looked into me and pulled. Inner walls touched my legs, then squeezed as air rocked back and forth; womb fingers held me where she chose, wiping away my trumped-up mentality.

Despite puppy flab, she was eager and quick, soft as a head-spun dustweb filled with motion. Hot blood steamed the windows of our sheltering, not containing but yielding a strange confident new assurance. Rolling me by the arm pits, she then sat with hands clasped behind her neck, long auburn hair hanging in a child's laugh between my knees. Her face was a bright ball bouncing to the ceiling. She collapsed into a hug, rolling us over again — suddenly the rocking: waves eddied around the sky which felt part of me: I was attended by a sense of ultimate being, beyond all doubt and uncertainty or scepticism about her engulfing me and existing for eternal truths. Flower-arms and fur-strokes later she began: short grunts far down in the thighs pulsated to her throat and she gasped in my ear: "Your heartless mercy." I swallowed noisily. Then the reaching, as motion became smoother. She rolled from side to side, legs clasping behind my back. The strain, the jerking together of all fall leaves and pinpoints of light which ate us in passing. Her body passed now, filmicly, as I did, as we immersed, radiant. Our rapid-flowing, spring-swollen brook increased, and the nervous play of immobile peripheral comic parts cut in: a big hand stuck in the corner of a smile, the lower half of her face like sunlight broken on water, splashed in a village duck pond, bulls before and after a stockyard. Every human concept became uninvented as strips of gentle waves covered us: all attitudes merged, layer upon soft diamond bright layer — an all-encompassing stillness deeper than motion. Climax began in a rush of heartbeats and sweepy deep breath, continuing a most undespondent fall, as nature remained organic and inter-twined to our universal film, leaving us without a rhythm or unwholesome context. Plumbed now for counterpoint, we smiled at some unthinkable, indescribable primitive meaning, tuned by the passing interplay of toneless sound that clinched the final clash. Another oratorio, picking a new will in the bowels of my being, wishing to not want as long as possible. She sucked me in and locked her muscles tight, swaying us with a choral unity to stillness, exploding in a peace with abstract signals going on around us and passing in oceans deep with motifs: action expressing our appreciation and wishes to flood the world with rejoicing at the diffuse speechless exchanges between people. Deep and above us, a river flowed.

All this remained as we rolled off. We curled, wiping sweat from our faces and backs, pulling up the covers. The depths were crystal clear and currents flowed on and around. We lay in this place with our angles of light.

We dressed clumsily, returning to unbind the bonds of the human beings, exercising and cleaning to release these persons from the indignity of their wraps, injecting, or with that intention, our pleasure for their pain, and taking our leave via the stairs to the ground floor. Outside, the light flew at buildings like flack made to caress instead of kill. After the dark-light show, sun speared shadowy buildings. Sunlight put us in irregular water-edged patterns across the city. It made sky a blue-white glow built to return to earth a nun's mother's omniscient eyes and kindly expressions.

"Are you asleep?" she asked, giggling, rubbing her soft chin on my chest as we lay on a park bench.

"How could anyone sleep after that? Why, are you?"

"No, we are a retreat, and each other's healer," she moaned, biting my biceps, and laughed. "You are an ocean, I'm your current...Say, I'm due back at work. We'd better get out of here."

"I'll just stay for breakfast."

"No you won't go back inside that place; everyone has an antipsychotic enema at eight o'clock."

She massaged my neck as we sat up and stretched.

"Oh well, I'll walk you to the restaurant," I said, stroking her forehead.

"It's okay. Come any time and I'll feed you."

We fulfilled each other all right. One priceless thing—she is a happy embodiment of a pioneering disposition. Her motto: make the most of every situation for someone else; give yourself without anything expected in return. Her great charm is based on that postulate. There is another step: choosing the right actions for your benefit, and her's. This is a practical philosophy, which is gentler than it appears, and it is deeply charming. Never-ending time will pass before I forget how deeply charming.

The Soiled City

Office buildings hung from the sky in a white-shirted blizzard, down and down and down to an earth entombed by the liveliness of its residents. People scattered on sidewalks like Mexican jumping beans dumped from barrels; then a new batch fills the bald. Similar faces, outlines of the basic form, face shapes swathed in vein. What appears, with everyone trotting to their own discord, must be a mystery. The light misled me, or vice versa, and there were smiles or tears, programe notes or applause. Stranded on a safety island, buses almost ricocheted off boot laces. Puffy faced reflections dripping on bus windows, faces dwarfed in their crowded presence, wariness which hovered around — eyes and shiny cloth bottom buttocks stuck in a vast shimmering boulevard. A rescue must be imminent. Right.

Traffic stopped. Island people swarmed to the next concrete safety and halted. Or, they hustled somewhere to form a new bunch, some staggering off like lint while others bumped-in. Brown hats, green hats, cigars, protruding right jowls, the glare of sunglasses, a cop hat, a hand behind a bus lady's legs in square wooden feet demurely camouflaged with alligator flesh. How do they all agree?

Traffic stopped. Rescue imminent again. Bracing my body on a semaphore pole, swarms of bodies shot round — meteors searching for their equal parts. Or, was it all rehearsed? Suddenly a sweaty acrobat put on a moment's show for the high geared, flaming-face people who burned the ground. A new crowd burning brighter when the flame of one becomes the torch of another, a stranded one rekindling for an instant, then gone, and the crowd reborn with an afterglow. A left wooden cane...odors of cheese...whiskers on the face of a man with only a left side...a person's large oval face joined to a handsome physique...a chested-breasted married to a Lester or a Louise.

Traffic stopped. Rescue again imminent. Five to 20 storeys high and more...swarms on carpets instead of concrete: people at every level. "Where are they all going?" One hand larger...a bus wheel with cracked rubber...glass faces with streaks and hard knocks...a feminine hop to another foot...lean-waisted shopping girls with toric hips and butter-colored lips.

Traffic stopped. Rescue imminent. Watch out! Bus engines frantic...store windows in bus gaps...a fierce sweating nomad with a nest of crackers in his hair...the dog lady's dirty fingernails...toe groping sounds inside millions of cowhide shoes scuff-sculpted in polish...Pharaohs' pigeons flying sideways in motor fumes...three men on a scaffold splashing windowed walls with vinegar and urine. "Where? Where? Where?" Sweat rivulets froze in a glass cage. The obelisk, shadowing a pawn shop, where men pray separate from women and wear good will in their pockets, sends pithy blessings to all beings and their things. People moved less quickly now, through the mud-soaked soppy-heated evening in all its corners, putting off each in breath as long as possible. Car roofs and windows opened to the air as I hiked, wincing at my memory of the writhing elevator surgery, with gratitude for the waitress, who gave me a sense of, yes, agonising with the patients care, but also the wider picture of how the surgeons hardened, shutting off their feelings, unleashing a homicidal cycle, a genocide resonating globally, entrapping people everywhere in a self-preoccupying zero.

The passing of the elevator surgery lay burning in my belly, absorbing my fellows' barbarism deeper than ever. Why do they suffer from the aberrant desires that drive them? Unlike an isolated act, the cutters knives opened her to view a world-wide sore, confronting us with vast unseen horrors, society's limitless crude dimensions. The ease with which they duped themselves, as adults, myopic Jack-the-Lad scalpers, now in the form of a hospital's lackadaisical, serially murderous attitude toward elevator patients' pain, their dignity, their life. Imagination filled with screams which their anaesthetic muzzled. The incessant writhing translated into postures and gestures of countless people from metropolis to desert, who echo her pain in their turn with indiscriminate howls, leaving a sedulous fear in the city's pantomime.

Nobody seemed to notice me, sauntering along gesturing and seeing them not notice, disinterested. The more they didn't notice, the more I noticed. Why don't they even suspect that each person's choice is cut to pieces, enduring operations that cause inordinate pain of all kinds, homicide on highways, in family homes, on battlefields? Must we survive by possessing only one thing in common, suffering? Is there a futile sense of being a THE END kind of bookend life, compared to a waitress, or a Becky, who possess a NO END kind of being. People legging it all round for the luxury of store-bought life, forming hip clubs, as imitation celebrities summon THE END according to cosmetic needs? What negative power this gives them, this simple backward motion. Is this how, in a reversing forward motion, they free themselves of the long-term pain in their heads? Can it be that between their remarkable controlling resilience and THE END, only a well-moisturized life matters, and in the end they contrive, directly, their own incendiary fortune?

The waitress' restaurant appeared as a lantern at the base of a mountain. Above and alongside were offices lined with identical steel desks in rows, machines with plastic caps, grey shredding machines in sub-rows by each desk and no smell. Silhouettes at dusk more animated than in day. Latticed shadows seep and splash light on the sides of buildings, like gigantic birds, roosting on the city's walls. She spotted me and crossed the avenue.

"You've been thinking haven't you, Paul," she prodded.

"Yes."

"What about? The way we made love?"

"Ah, yes, more than thinking. I've been considering the elevator, too"

"What about it?"

"Oh, I'm not sure — just seems that, well, growing up...was I averse to being sceptical, to investigating, or just an idle being, if you can call me that? I'm disappointed by my lack of foresight and courage, and surprised. But, the beaten-up emotion of a pint-sized kid is no excuse for being entangled now by self-recrimination."

"Paul, you're not on the cards to enter this urban life for all its stresses and body strains, just go on and no silly business. Here are your sandwiches. Look after yourself and drop me a line when you're settled in Frisco...bye!"

She returned to the restaurant, disappearing in the wild quirks of traffic and goofy building blocks.

Here Was a Bus

A white-eyed, empty bus was parked by a sidewalk filled with people. There were people in animal outfits, and sun-colored skin. Some inhabitants wore pieces of painted glass on their bodies, with faces behind makeup or pipes or basket-size hats, sunglasses, and smiles. Traffic piled the length and width of the road. Other buses, full, lunged from stop to stop with every vinyl seat seam stretched to the limit, sagging under the inert weight and bulk of banter.

"With all the full buses and full sidewalks, one must consider the vast amount of excreta being carried," hollered a soapbox radical. "Much the same as a credit card or war club (the latter to repel an indigestible personality). This is practical democracy: we adapt and carry our habits with us."

Posters on the bus ceiling beamed at vacant seats. No human shadows fell on the floor, no driver's head to stare at the back of. In their flight, people hurried past, blithering like bits of tinfoil blown by a wind with few other visible effects. The overarching atmosphere was a giant orange screen thrown over the sky.

"Only a maverick wind will punch through this dim air and show itself in a place where trees mightn't grow for years," observed the street-crier.

Humankind in the bleachers and byways either failed to notice this bus, or if they did, they preferred to pay attention elsewhere. The still-empty bus bore close examination for some kind of sign: OUT OF ORDER or QUARANTINE or KEEP OFF or APRIL FOOLS' or NONE OF YOUR BUSINESS, HURRY ALONG. Here was a bus the authorities were ignorant of, a complete jewelled bus all by itself, shuttled off and forgotten. I stretched out on the rear seat, unpacked salad and cheese sandwiches the waitress bagged for me. There was also milk, coleslaw, an apple, and pecan pie. Two weeks or a month might pass before, in the hurry and bustle and turmoil, a Martin Luther or Rene Descartes will rise to say: 'Hey, what happened to that bus we shuttled off on the side street and so carefully parked two weeks or a month ago?'

Should I report the whereabouts of the bus? First, keys were in the ignition. Second, there will be denials that such a bus existed. Denials saying, if it does exist, it will be parked elsewhere. Or, if it is parked there, a reply is unavailable. Probably, any report will be shelved for another day or transferred or sent to the sanitary department or laughed at. The bus might remain merely an institutional artefact for old advertisements.

Thoughts rolled around, turning and flashing like bones in the dark. An automobile was parked in front of the bus. A yellow curb lay dog-faithful at the side of the vehicles. Stop useless conjecture; this bus waited for a mission. The auto's windshield was decorated with traffic court summonses for improper parking.

Either police failed to spot the bus, or — or, buses were immune from traffic violations. This prospect made more sense to my lateral eye. I heard about bus drivers being waved through busy intersections by purple-pocketed police, while cars were jammed two storeys high and a mile long, never to receive privileged consideration. If buses were special, to give free rides to people deprived of money, why not make one available?

Here was a bus, fine and empty, a typical bus, made to serve. Here was I, full belly and restful feet, without plans for the morning, sauntering to the front. No visible objection. No protest from the hurried crowd. I plopped into the cushy driver's seat, surveying the instrument panel and the weight of street traffic.

Three boys with firecrackers exploding in their joints jumped on and raced to the rear. "If they want to play ball on the bus, I'll let them," I muttered, cranking gizmos. "And I won't bark at paupers." Someone with prosaic skin and an artificial limb climbed aboard carrying a dictionary and asked me for an instruction manual which was not beneath the seat or in the lost and found cracks alongside. A man boarded, dressed like a bombardier, with little more to him than that appearance. I sensed the fellow when he beckoned for a token from the farebox, without noticing his face, if he had one under his oxygen mask. Probably, he only showed it on demand by military authorities or kept a picture of it in his wallet. This man could be sitting on a porch across the street when the mean neighbor's garage burned. There was a bland yet sinister sense of him, as though he hoped the mean neighbor was asleep in a pile of old tires while he snored in his air mask. I went to work on the switches, trying combinations in concert with gadgets which pulled out, buttons that pushed in, trying the ignition and pedals. A still-as-dawn teenager entered the bus. Blood veins arched in her neck like the skeletons of waves. The boys shot off their cap pistols at her and she stumbled. A salesman, who followed, picked her up with one hand. His other hand held the salesman's laughter valise which cannot be let go of. "Well, I can't get the beast to work," I said. "Damn national genius for specialization."

Walking from the rhombic shapes of the city center, I trod steps and back steps, sidesteps and double-decker-dodge steps. "I see the way now. Follow the pigeon flight, skirt the city's day until the right time and until I'm cleared of all misgivings. I'll share their giggles in a rainbow flowering glass, down gilded throats to heal cantankerous bellies and out plaster tubes, through porcelain pots to iron-rimmed infinity. Good on them!" Exchanging smiles now, as strangers we crossed paths, with an effect of forming one path. The spirit of taking part was reflected in our varying paces and our myriad adventuresome gaits. Dallying along their edges and meandering towards the front, flowing along with lighted commands and official whistles — sounds of traffic delays blocks away.

An elderly fellow used a golf putter as a cane, and he walked alongside. A dude with gravy on his trousers trailed us. Then another person joined — a stranger who appeared curious about our smiles and curiosity. Three ladies rejoicing shopped for livers. An off duty policeman, his jaw revolving from directing relatively stagnant traffic, chased a man with a belt full of keys: one person fell and couldn't get up. An empty-eared grenade thrower walked on his hands. A belly dancer waved his belly like a flag and mopped the tubas on his chest in a fountain, while his navel spoke the old language. Five tall, bespectacled girls with black and white THE HUDDLE uniforms, giggled at a dog eating bread. A reporter who knew the off duty policeman, reported. One shy foreigner drove her car at walking speed, causing dozens of horns to join this cortege; some horn blowers decided to take part in the hike — others faded away. The foreigner spoke a language other than English and evidently thought that the horns were a sign of formal procession. A pair of lovers smiled, while a minister with a tic said he wanted a Baptist toilet. People wearing flashbulbs in ammunition belts and flamingo plumage bonnets, made the man with keys listen to their pantomime. One of them told shoppers who carried him that his brain sounded like oars striking water. A pickpocket, who yelped every few steps, sewed many pockets together. Dope addicts were absent.

To complicate matters, pedestrians in the reverent group's path lost patience. Three husky youngsters veered into a stallholder and commandeered him. The crowd swept round its muggers: the brief swirling battle hinged on the smallest youngster of the three, submerged by interested dozens of perfumed voices, greased armpits and sticky feet. Lunging forward into traffic, the knot gained momentum. Fistfights broke out on its periphery, but those who remained centered on our path grew more in tune with each others' hiking ability. Around a fruit cart and into a bookstore, the crowd curled behind, breaking its progress on the cart and storefront; the proprietor fled to a back room, telephoned police and locked himself in a washroom. We emerged from the store with a volume on insect repellents. Twenty minutes after the crowd left, according to a news flash, the store owner was arrested and charged with disorderly conduct: lady in the washroom.

"Now is the end of all our wishing," the fellow with a putter told a reporter. The law officer drew his gun and blew a whistle. The crowd whistled. More horns piled onto layers of frenetic sound. A wino caught a shoplifter in the farmers' market, but he fell, breaking several bottles of wine which tipped out of his cardboard box. From a second storey apartment balcony, a prankster showered the throng with coins. The march continued. One or two people bled from the impact of coins. A few fled. The coin thrower joined in, riding with the foreigner. Assorted teenage boys browbeat the pickpocket and threatened to take his haul if he didn't share it with them. A city council official in a purple and white check dress sat alone on a curb, head in her hands, crying.

Picket signs appeared. Two proclaimed: WE WILL NEVER SURRENDER. A third pleaded for sanity. The off duty officer, joined by four colleagues, arrested pickets. A photographer paired with the reporter. Two Greek priests, searching for a confessional, entered the trek and bumped into the minister, who discussed evolution with them. Members of a canasta club jumped onto the bandwagon, flapping their cards. Counter pickets infiltrated and protested police brutality. The reporter started a fistfight with a television cameraman. Police intervened and one shot off his lower lip. An ambulance roared in; the host flowed around it. The priests, who stayed to help the police, asked for an ambulance ride to the nearest public convenience.

Stores closed for the day. Shoppers looking for an auction merged with the tide. Traffic increased. Horns screamed. Constant motion felt necessary. Someone handed out coupons.

The shy foreigner spit up in the minister's ball cap. Emergency vehicles wailed their sirens. We skipped, taking light steps along a concrete sidewalk. Those in the coterie who were so inclined followed the fashion. A golf pro danced a version of the Lindy, while four cross-dressing people responded with what they said was a Frug.

By dusk few originals were left. Most left to ramble on elsewhere; others joined along the way, and the procession was about the size it had been in the morning. The least populated hours were just after the stores opened and before the commuter rush. Even then, scores of people joined in, to reach a destination, still without stripes and no robes. Someone wearing a sign that said MAYOR'S OFFICE shouted: "I will lead you gaily across the city's bank, slide mud-goblins into the river and float hanging edgewise in glorious rejuvenating blue currents," spurring the minister into an oratory, of sorts: "Whiskey toil and muck-leaving, dinosaur odes to hymnal racks belong, behind us and alone, to book-burning fathers and to bird-feathering non-do-wells. These all along have owned their properties and we leave them at their temporary launching pads. Set our course after the stars and hand-milked cows. Bright wheels of morning begin to roll. Sun proves the worth of day, the birth of night. Growth of trees and houses... birds and fodder malingerers wait for a word, and extracting that, the illusions proceed without us.

"Let's return to our origins, leaving behind gossip and vice-versa and long sounds about things. But we — we miss none of that, for that noise is a poor relative of virtue — we offer these junctures every day, free from frost. We travel to the end of return and repetition, beyond concepts to prayer. To this end we nurture our means, for the benefit of soiled city and country folk everywhere, thus ending our need and furthering, for a while, their reflection on this day. But we...express a secret, to be free of their pandemic virus, and we can share our experience, if only they listen. Are you now free from bad memories?"

First distinct voice: "No."

"Well, neither am I. How far must we go to be free? How far have we come?

A second voice, distant but clear: "Three blocks."

Third voice: "No, no, six blocks, a mile."

A fourth voice, over a host of mumbles, "Nonsense, you knucklehead; we've been walking for hours; even at your pace, that is three miles..."

"What?" the minister asked. "We've been on this journey since birth: at least 4,445 miles and more! You mean," he proclaimed, "that none of us were with each other at the start? Does anyone remember the heroic origin of this march? No, because it's with us since the beginning of time!"

My face lit simply, with glee: "Had this happened ages ago, maybe it would be only a gesture rather than seeing a steady path ahead." A pilgrimage with a sense of unity, without grasping to conform, and the fact that many of us now see ourselves in each other, that realization is a breakthrough, something released. Providence shared, destiny tailored equally inside each person, even the originals from home towns can claim any part of it; so to go on, each on our own, it was right to carry this glee forward from that moment onwards.

Hot Pursuit

Not a tall fellow or short either, all pretty ordinary, the height occupying anyone's varying postures, and lean legs which belong to this vessel as do brief emphatic arms. Any head is fine: mine is on the wide side, high brow, deep set brown eyes, a reddish face stretched over prominent cheekbones, framed by auburn hair that benefits from stream water luster and flops across to the ear tips. My forehead isn't of significance either, bearing as it does a few wrinkles, easily mistaken for casting ominous looks, caused by squinting under the sun's flat-handed glare. The face is sufficient for taking in pain or smiles. The hands are relatively unnoticeable. Waking to clamorous bird-ringing bells on tree backs, heavy dew and grey skylights splice the river in steamy silver colors. Above, the sun sits like a coiled snake, while birds sing their warning songs and little bud things float around tree tops. Behind one tree trunk, pre-dawn greyness remains. Perhaps my trouble was in rescuing that dog, or in our defense stabbing her owner, or generally being recognized as an impostor to someone's cause, unmarked by their tastes, habits, or rituals.

Across the park a child in white and blue costume enters the zoo. Queer animals — probably striped gophers — take residence in a hallowed parish well pump. Elders walk with a breath of Sunday on dewy lawn, crushing dry spaces in the grass. Like a bombshell, a battered key on the sidewalk stopped me; its shiny eye smirked. Its long, jagged and irregular beard bore the initials QR. The key pointed to a small, green egg-shaped vehicle. I squinted and snarled at the key. Then I leapt on it, as if a tragedy of hammers, wrestled with it and grimaced. A false move: it locked me.

The key lived in my psyche while swimming and studying the river and eating corn left for bears on Bear Island. What key? The key to humility? The key to unlock inflamed living? Is this the key? Or *the* key? Is this the key which unlocks doors to the city's dissonant enclaves, or the happy key which joins people in harmony?

Sure enough, it was a key, still pointing to the foreign car, wedged between two others — a brown Nash with chrome bumpers and the stern front grille of another. My naked eye appraised the fine motor car. Its quiet music played to the tune of being just reasonable. There's no more denying, no more criticizing the big heartless country out there that is striving into itself. Haphazard, nomadic traveling is an exercise in flushing out my imaginings of one thing or another: let other people do their always longing for the next best moment, person, dwelling place, but circling headstrong in the roller-skating rink above their shoulders. Their endeavors only want an imaginary rail to hang on to; let them avoid imploding there, devolving, or dissolving in that blinding space at the top of the guest house they're inhabiting.

The car was discarded, judging from debris blown round the tires. Keys were in it, too. Inside, the car felt mature, gauges behind its brain alert to mechanical digestion and speeds. It sat there like a victim of history, the result of an industrial tantrum, a facade of human dignity: the motor car as a face slap. The souped-up egg, and the enclosure that it demands, denied its owners a swift path to redress the poverty and greed that religions failed to alleviate. Too much to ask, and unnecessary to procrastinate about what's beyond my control. The green egg car drove like pretzel eating: cracked, snapped and jerked through its kick-starting gears. Rapid-transit-gutter tornadoes below the wheels tightened my grip on the steering. Birds drifted off as if to escape a hold by pistons fury. Wind gathered its parts from places known only to wind and also left ice along shoreline bits of a lake. Trout instinctively boarded an eastbound train to a steam heated hotel, avoiding their spiteful spear-armed predators, gawking through holes in winter's ice. Pretty far up a near-mountain, a lady appeared on her roof, pulling leaves from a rain trough. EAT signs hung beneath her in two bay windows.

"The smell of bacon and all those things frying...they're just poetry for you, proposing events that have to be, so you can have a place to be, because when I first saw you I knew you were no ordinary person, no ma'am, not any ordinary place suits you. This is a special place as I watch you now, on the roof this morning and you are...well, a wonderful person gazing over the mountain. Perhaps someone very dear is down there, like your sister. But if it's your husband you miss, I can give you a ride down there and we'll search for him. I'll give him a belt in the head and dust him off with a few odes, except that he's probably just a casino junkie if he left someone like you."

Her hands looked as if she danced alone, such long expressive fingers, arms a fine white flavor, firm and strong. Her shoulders stuck straight out, spine straight as a stack of silver dollars. Her belly—from the front—was negligible—her wide shoulders, powerful.

"Oh, you're nice to say those things, but I get so lonely up here. Well, you didn't come here just to hear a forlorn person mope around."

"No, no, you're not any forlorn. You're a fine young citizen to inspire a traveler's writing and…"

"Now there's no one for me up here. I can't think why I stay. I guess it's just the place and the hope, but I reckon he'll never come back—not to me anyway. Probably, he's with an adulterating feminist, down there right at this instant and they're… laughing at me because I'm passing time. I'll wait constantly as long as I can…see how that goes," she said, peering down my upturned nostrils.

"Sure, uh—say, what can I call you?"

"Oh—Doreen—just call me Doreen."

"Okay, Doreen, just call me Paul. A similar thing happened to me. Yep, left alone with a cousin, I guess, while her father fetched groceries, or went bowling. But he never came back and left me with the kid, who flourished."

"Oh, you poor man; I'm so sad for you."

"Yeah—uh, me for you, too."

She cried softly into the trough. I retracted my head and shoulders from the window and climbed out of the egg car. "Hey," I said, brightening, "that rhymes: "Me for you, too. Consider that the first of many odes for you. The whole area is an ode for you. And so is this place here and the warm nights to take its place."

She sat and stared, chin on knees and hands at her ankles. "How are things in town?"

"Warm nights and lots of commerce in the beds. It's pretty crazy out there; people have driven themselves to extremes."

"How many people stayed after their immune thingies buckled?"

"Oh, probably just a few property owners. And doubtful clergy, who regard parishioners as pillars of ebbing salt, staying on course to keep watch over their buildings, make repairs, seek donations."

"I mean, do you suppose someone who wasn't native would like it in the town? I mean if he were sort of there but thinkin' of movin' on?"

"I think he'd move on. If he was found to be a carrier, that is. Anyway, the government rations food. And everybody has to maintain a certain bodyweight. Officials come from the city on inspections and examine everything, according to my journal. They offer treatment but people are reluctant to accept it, and afraid, thinking it will make matters worse or that it will do little good. So the town's dispensed with charter functions and adopted a policy of live and let live. They attend to their own business and meet in each other's arms."

"God, I bet he's there."

"No, it's not science fiction and the bizarre impression is that nobody is likely to object to fornicating on the streets since few people use them in the small burgs, whereas in the city the streets are virulently with desire. Choirs voices perversely heard as sexual demands and lurid chat show laughter

is accepted in lieu of greenhouse gases. Folks of the world
live in sweet craving epidemics, disintegrating mentally and
physically."

"I can see in your face you're trying to cheer me up," she said.
"You're one of those writers who pass through and I wish you
well, Paul."

I turned toward the town with an open palm at the end
of my outstretched arm. The sun was rising in the best basic
sunrise tradition, rays slashed in shafts through cracks and
passed across the distant city to the southeast, so parts of it
quivered in silvery sparklings, while elsewhere corridors
glowed in red and blue light. Since the sun only touched hill
tops at this hour, it left a luminous band across the cement
tract. A road stretched down into this band, resuming in one
of the city's bright spots. From a distance, there seemed to
be little movement. As the sun grew parts of the metropolis
that were dim, or buildings of just a few disconnected lines,
swung around or fitted together and made sense. Among the
landmarks: off to the left, hit by a corridor band, stood a high
building for that part of the city — a school where kids learned
that right and wrong were one in the same thing because they
were so many different points of view that you couldn't separate white from black.

"Say, you okay?" I said, as she gazed behind a frown.

"Yes, I suppose so."

"Naw, I don't think you do. Why are you staring out there?"

"Just lookin' at the sights."

"Where is your husband?" I asked, coming to a point with a
not unnoticed flair.

"Oh, he went down to town a long time ago. But he never came back, either."

I flapped my arms and galloped into the eating house, thinking she might at least be agreeable enough to come down off her roof. Inside, a man on a stool revealed his official character — a claw of shielded things — a deputy sheriff: his features reflected huge institutional buildings and serious crime forms to be completed. Besides, he wore a club. "Looks like rain," I said to a coffee urn.

"Yup, sure does," said the lawman, whose bandaged hand held up a coffee mug.

"I'll just take my leave then," I said, with that feeling of, 'Oh no, not again.' The deputy rose off his stool and said: "You'll do in the name of mistaken identity. We got plenty of law round here, just no justice."

I slipped away to the egg. Doreen stared. Deputy blew dirt out of his nose and headed for his patrol car, with long glares intended to freeze suspects in the irony of his brown-stained fingers. We left just a few seconds apart.

The lawman searched for my head, his pistons pounding, eyes buldging their red nests, roaming over and along his dashboard. Keeping a nervous eye on my rearview mirror, anti-bandit markings and the bubblegum light on top came into view first. Saw it coming after me and nearly alongside in the other lane. Then, sight of the driver: the chrome-plated, four-barrel-chested deputy looked furiously elated. I stepped on the gas and he whizzed past. The deputy's brake lights pierced the egg's chrome. Deputy waited for the egg to stop or pass, goosed his machine and was in pursuit. Hot pursuit.

I leaned on the engine, coaxing it to top speed. The deputy was behind and gaining on the long road, while his quarry prayed for curves. The egg was outmatched by the official vehicle. Deputy's eyes expanded in a vast spaceless void he edited with lead and stale electricity. "Deadly business," I said, "deadly." Searching for a curve now; if the road stayed straight, capture was a mathematical certainty. Deputy would obliterate me with fire-gas, helping to fulfill his delusion that any stranger was potential vermin and that absurdity recommended crime. "Yes, Deputy is alive, like me, swallowed in the attempted depersonalization of upbringing, digested by duty, and excreted by our habits. We are as enchanting just now as a KEEP RIGHT SIGN. I'm at the end of a taking and pilfering living, in the monkey business of poisonous self-interest."

Deputy was within 100 yards. The first shot whistled past. A second and what may have been a third flashed past. A piece of gravel or a bullet burrowed into the egg's side. I hunched over the wheel. "Deadly, deadly, deadly." Deputy was closer. The alien license plate loomed larger behind. A bullet pierced rear glass and smashed solidly, sending me into the steering wheel. While I was down, I pulled a kindling knife from my backpack. Checked the unsheathed blade — what was I supposed to do? Speed: 70 or so from the gasping egg — the needle bounced to the rhythm of mill-racing sounds. Pistons cracked, and gas shot through the car's lines, but Deputy was closer. Closer. Closer. I saw a country road, a county line, beyond his jurisdiction, if he had any! A car waited on this dirt road to enter the highway. A second of thought: too late; the road was past. Behind, the car began to pull out, and then stopped.

Deputy swerved and kept coming, even closer now. I switched on the radio and lowered the window. Deputy set off his siren. "Yes," I said, jamming my wheel hard to the left, hearing my wrist cartilage pop. The car tail snapped around, swayed and was off-road on a shoulder, swinging wildly and finally under control, heading straight back at Deputy like one of his bullets. I thrust my knife through the window and flashed it three times. His blasts were late, likely blinded by the blade's sunlit edges, thundering instead into the Deputy's fender. He grappled with uncontrollable steering, a bullet somehow puncturing one tire; his last bullet sprayed the egg's plastic parking light into a woodside culvert. I gunned it, looking in my rearview mirror to spot Deputy perform a perfect power turn. The pursuer's car wobbled side-to-side and fell back. When out of the Deputy's sight, I took the next road, raced along until reaching a highway, headed south a few miles, switching to a zigzaggedy dirt track.

Meanwhile, I expect that Deputy bled through his bandage and changed the tire. So much the better; the chance of a pathetic personal appearance was avoided. Surrender was a consideration. Refusing to show a license, take a breath test, give a specimen, and get out of the car. Deputy would no doubt preclude such points in deciding to cuff and assault an itinerant who was ignorant about the ways of his domain. The quantity of his experience would have been qualified.

A wind worn farm shell appeared in a meadow. I drove through high grass matted here and there, under a fir tree to a wood-rotting barn. The steel shoulder-jaws of the egg decimated the barn back. Splintered wood's crusted curse and brittle mouth-sore metal screams rode roughshod in the explosion of idle chicken roosts, milking stools and cattle pens. "Enough of this stupid itinerary that only entices entrapment," I insisted.

Nearby, the walls of a wood frame house were papered with 1926 Minnesota and Oregon newspapers; a cinema advertisement offered '*THE FIGHTING MARINE, with GENE TUNNEY, for 10 CENTS.*' Wind hovered over the crop, nearby, and moved it. The oats, like grass. Even the rye is unprepared. Soon fish will spawn, bluegills still, above their fanned out brown and shallow nests. Then food would be in the fields, mediated by spring. At a corner where the oat field joined barley, I climbed a hickory tree. There was clear distance on the land, and warmth. The earth wasn't limited to short fog paths of men's breath from colder days. Wind gusts crested over the rye, through a dotty fence, rippling a creek, passing back to the clouds and through the world.

A crow landed on the uppermost branch of a craggy tree. Below the crow, a hawk napped. Clouds shifted, consolidated, trading their moist light-pockets and sky-shavings, silent locomotives in a switch yard, rasping clean the sky. Beyond, the city's striving was outweighed by purchasing. Overhead, a rustic veil evolved into a purple pyramid which sat on the horizon like a howl in vast silence, where green, crawling land met the city. At the bottom of a creek pool, bronze weeds and grasses were prostrate in current. A fox drank, watching with its ears. Near the stream, cows carefully planted roundish, black flowers. A half mile distant a white house with a blue roof and matching gutters — plus two red barns, one with a copper weathervane, lots of machines, and chickens. And chickens!

I sneaked along the deep-ditched road. A dog barked — at its length, or from boredom or for a reason exclusive to dogs. Probably it smelled and felt the heat from a rabbit burrow. Or because it remembered a summer's night spent in dewed fields. A few chickens pecked among small roadside stones. These were far from the patrolling ears of farm dogs, languishing on a magnificent porch, across the front of the sheriff's house (judging from the shooting range and gallery of wanted poster targets). As I grabbed a small one by the feet and neck and pulled it to my chest, the other chickens flinched and moved a few pecks away. The bird was firm and warm; it shifted nervously without making a noise as I withdrew via the ditch. Considering the bird's impending agony, eggs from the henhouse was a better option. After lunch, I doused the campfire, even though my stomach called for more eggs.

Leaning towards a new forest, my ears started to vibrate. So soft were the tones, they may have been smells. I stopped and slowly turned. A red-faced sheriff with dilated nostrils and pointy boots glared at me. I bowed and glided away.

"Hold it you!" the sheriff ordered. "You there with straw in your hair. I see you."

"Who, me?" I asked, just to be certain.

"That's right, you. Come here."

"OK, okay, I'm coming...This true nature that exists with us is always the same. I'll be grateful in future when we're convinced to travel in a unified pattern, to go where we want to go and to do what we think we should. We are each part of the night, you and me; it dissects, chopping us each into what at first seems like our separate pieces and then makes a single harlequin animal. Night rearranges us into a pattern which fits its design. Look at us now, swimming in near-night, free to move anywhere and even into the light of understanding each other. We're fused with the forms of the day. Look how trees change after light. It's their concession: to survive trees cooperate with all their causes and conditions and give rest to weary birds and caress bat teats with breeze they stir in a seamless night."

"Hold on, now. What are you walking backwards for?"

"There's quicksand here and lots of dirty newspapers. I can't walk in this stuff. Anyway, I'm shy of the light. It's a reminder — a prod to get going during the day. We're responsible for light after darkness, don't you think?"

"Okay, you just put yer hands up and don't talk shit to me."

"Okay, here." I put my hands in the air and took another step backwards. "We only admit to being man because it's so obvious we can't lie, so why not be friends."

"No more of that backward stepping! You come out of there... Arnie! Chet. Here you guys." Two stocky, efficient looking deputies marched over the road shoulder and reported.

"That's the kind of guy who would do it to a nice lady's car," said the one with a handle on his head. He bent closer to check my size and strength. "Yup," the other responded, flexing his forefinger menacingly, like an army barber with scissors. "Go get him, men, and don't take no for an answer," the sheriff commanded.

Dropping my hands and skipping through brush, the two deputies leapt after me, blasting open channels in a meadow with their bodies. Youthfulness, and fear of their fatherly clubs, I evaded them. Emitting stiff yells and accusations as they fought the bush, the lawmen left a trail of ballpoint pens, an address book, hat, one club, an aerosol can, and the arm of a shirt.

Leaves threw shadows on their faces. The skin cut into hundreds of parts by the arboreal presence, and I noted the same on my body, slashing into too many pieces to count, yet indivisibly floating in an irregular pattern, lost forever to clothes, shimmering like figures drawn on water.

Am I the opposite of what I see, somehow separate and regular? No, I too live in the same circle of patterned reflexes, in machines' shadows and crimson-deep, deeper and deepest cavernous spaces. Still, shades of longing are there and lead to trouble, when in fact I yearn now to be in Frisco and work and just be enveloped in my nearness to loved ones, and no extremes.

John X

A road slanted under the trail and into a crossroads town, the first sun a warm shoulder mantle, arms relaxed and swinging, despite a weighty backpack. Dog violets, Watercress and Meadow Parsnip graced my button holes and pockets. Eating flowers, my belly still nagged for food, searching. Foraging is, therefore, a deliberate process, compared to the nonchalant but preservative act, for now, of eating. The other basics are appreciatively simple, too: breathing, drinking, taking rest to reflect, writing, and the occasional bowel and bladder break, sleep, responding to unfavorable circumstances with an even-handed attitude and without fear or favor.

The western landscape posed with large old hardwood trees, ruins of the occasional small cooperative farm, white houses grown faceless from long years of wind, and green hayfields hummed. Farm people with faces like maps: each aspect a mirror of the land. Farmers who traveled never forgot to tell about the journey.

SELBY. POP. 256 — RADAR PATROLLED. A benevolent intersection semaphore controlled a waiting pickup truck, headlights radiating its beam across the dawn-mixed countryside. A child spoke: "Hey mister."

Startled, head turreting in search mode, I found it down around my hips. "Oh," I said, taking advantage of the word's lack of linguistic bounds.

"Hey mister, you one a them painters?"

"No — no, I don't paint."

"Whadda ya do?"

"Oh, well, I travel a lot."

"Where?"

"Lots of places."

"Uhhuh, you ever seen Montana?"

"Once, at the movies, and the other week or so."

"Hey, what did..."

"*Billy*! Oh, Lord! Billy, come here!" A woman rushed at the boy, calling on her god and someone named Harry. "Billy, didn't I tell you never to talk to strangers? You come here right now."

The woman gritted her teeth and folded her jewelled claws. She ushered the child back to the porch of their home, giving me hostile glances, then, bawled about gypsies who roast small boys and feed them to dogs six feet tall. The child stared with his mother's resplendent awe. They seemed convinced of the truth of her proclamations and withdrew into the house. A shave cream-bearded man appeared in the doorway, expressionless. "You're their minister and she's inspired a sermon," I said, walking away.

HAMBURGERS — BY APPOINTMENT ONLY. The blue plywood, circus gloss sign with circus fancy letters, hung in a window. Next door, an elderly man polished brass on a ladder and hose truck, parked in the driveway of a garage with a FIREHOUSE sign. The red fire engine, probably brassless when new, looked as though it improved with age. Little brass was bought in these farm towns, in those days.

Being unusually hungry, I entered the restaurant, which

didn't seem to be the kind you'd have a reservation for. Several
people were in the place. Empty flowerpots on white paper decorated each table. I went to the rear; the MEN door opened an
inch and caught on its hook-lock. The toilet flushed and then:
"I've got it!" A hearty voice rang loud and clear through the
restaurant. The noise backed me into the LADIES; nobody
inside, so free to use. The toilet gurgle across the narrow hall
ended, and the voice left in silence. Up off the black polythene
lip of the stool, and undressing to wash, the tone of talk from
a person who walked around the eating room belonged to
the toilet voice. Poking my head out the door, a weary look
of relief fell from the fellow's face, fell from his erect posture,
leaving him with a cheerful readiness. First of all he started
to grin, widening it into a full-fledged 100 per cent smile that
would take in anyone.

At a table in the center, the fellow stopped and sat with intention, opposite me. "Howdy. I'd like to welcome you on behalf
of the town here. I'm the poet, sheriff and mayor, in that order."
A waiter appeared in something resembling pyjamas and slippers. "You, my five sisters, yours' are smiles that keep a roof over
our heads and bring commerce to dream-filled beds." I clung
to the table with both hands as the roaring fellow banged it,
squirting ketchup from between hamburger buns in his right
hand. The flowerpot bounced and rolled across the room to
the pinball machine. "That's where I get my poetry," he confided, pointing at the waiter, wheezing with laughter, pressing
a napkin over his face: "blow." The stoic young man handed
me his pad and pencil: Soup, bowl of fresh lettuce, chilli with
crackers, six raw carrots, and coffee — white, I wrote.

"Name's X, John X."

"Oh, yeah," I said, seriously.

"No. That's what it is, John X. I had a last name once, before responsibility, when I didn't have a leadership role in the community. X not only represents my say-so but gives me the protection of anonymity. A letter came months ago or so, said anyone whose relatives have the plague of the Anthrax madness must report to those camps. So, X!" A disparity, which left the fellow, crept into my face. "And I sent for one of these new loyalty machines, too. It can measure loyalty by the tone of your voice. We've been havin' so many arguments round here. And me being the responsible person, initiatives rest with me." The waiter reappeared with my order. I leaned over the chilli and took a deep breath. "I get it from the army — leadership..."

"Say, sure is a nice fire truck you got down Main Street," I said, entering the spirit of the place, and keen to eat. "So, another leader in the outback, and lawman, rolled into one."

"Yeah," the fellow said quickly, tumid eyes ahead of his speech. "Truck's got brass on it, too." "Brass. That's class," I joined in, dunking a buttered cracker into the chilli, munching carrots and lettuce, to the crisp and snappy sound.

"We got it for him 'bout...Oh, I forget. But we had a drive — for funds — and bought a real brass plate for the right side of the engine. And ol' Nate, he should miss nothing. He's the fire chief. He polishes that thing twice a day...in public. No, ol' Nate hasn't put out a fire in three years..."

"Three years?"

"Yeah, well we had fires, but Nate never made it. I mean he's o-l-d," said John X, enunciating each letter. "And part a my job is maturity. A lot of things got to work for ol' Nate...but he keeps the engine runnin' and puts a shine on her pretty chassis. You're gunna' say I got to do something. But I appointed him fire chief, so I can't fire him, can I?"

"Well, why don't you convene a meeting, offer him retirement, for instance," I suggested. "There must be a dozen people in your restaurant..."

"We need to have a meeting," X shouted at the waiter, who nodded. The poet, sheriff and mayor climbed onto his chair. "This here is a free country...well, right here anyway...and anyone who has a permit can meet with other people. Now, as grantor of permits in this here, I'm callin' the meetin', without Doc. Anyway, I'm sure," he added, scowling at the waiter, "that nobody here is a carrier. Now, our five fair sisters at the counter to take seats behind this guest and his meal," X ordered. "Bosalinski, you and the rest be seated back of the ladies. And you," he said to the waiter, "you and the cook behind the men." X stepped to the floor, hands in hip pockets, hamburger buns crumpled on the table. I finished my meal without so much as a glance at the group. A napkin to my mouth, I said as an aside, feeling uneasy about being X's muse, "John, what happened to your doctor?" The poet-sheriff-mayor reddened: "They took him to work in the city, where the real trouble is, the scum. By the way, that's privileged information.

"Bosalinski, you go get more people," X shouted, turning to me with bated breath. "I tell you, about the biggest happening here is when ol' Nate revs the fire engine most Saturdays.

Sometimes, he even drives it round the block. But when we really need him, he clutches; he just can't put it all together under pressure."

"No stranger's been on our streets since the plague," X said to the audience, "just this." He moped and pointed at me.

"Can we have refreshments?" a sister asked.

X pounded the table and I grabbed my dishes. "Yes, we'll have refreshments. You fetch them!

"Bosalinski, the shoe man, he talks to ol' Nate a lot. But it doesn't help. It's a ritual. And ol' men are only comforted by ritual. But nothing else affects folks nowadays, except talk about ol' times."

The sister served coffee and doughnuts. Bosalinski returned, reporting that Nate sprained his back cleaning a fire hose. Several others filtered in and took seats behind the waiter and the cook. X brooded over his hamburger buns. The crowd drooped. "I...I....could..." X whispered, "...I could..." He swallowed his treason and blurted out: "There's only one way out." He raised both fists in the air and shouted and pounded: "I could break the goddamned law!" The sisters gasped. Bosalinski gasped. X gasped and stood down. I cleared their table, putting the debris beneath it.

The smile of X returned slow but sure and grew to 100 per cent, ready to be broken into his laugh-roar. "Well, I certainly want to welcome each of you. Your poet, sheriff and mayor is glad the prominent citizens are present and accounted for." X surveyed the proceedings; a couple dozen people were attentive. "Now, as you are all aware, things aren't quite what they should be round here...around here. We've had no urban developments here or real interest from the outside world for three years, or thereabouts, or five. Furthermore, nothing has happened here. You! — Charlie," X summoned, as if the man hadn't been called by his first name in so long he'd forgotten it. "How long since there were any real good fires?"

"Well, uh — 'bout two years, I guess; ten for a real hot one."

"Uhhuh," X moaned smugly, directing attention to Bosalinski. "How is your business?"

"Everyone says it's bad."

"Exactly!" he snorted and pounded the table for emphasis. "And even Melba's beauty shop is closed. Things are dead round here; is *this* the kind of place you want your children to grow up in?" A murmured agreement rose from the audience.

"What children?" I asked.

"Well, there are a few. We could do *something* for them, don't ya think?"

"Fire your people with passion and commitment to providing for the town's welfare," I suggested, sombrely. "Like a library with a big kids' section or a health center — a project that's a hell of a lot of fun to involve everyone; ignite the wick inside them that shines light from the inside out — a coming together on behalf of their well-being and civic spirit."

The audience looked puzzled and X gathered in air. "I've watched these poor five sisters try everything to save their boutique. Nothing has bought them business...well, almost nothing. Why? Because there *is* no business." He waited a few seconds; then he pounded. It was out in the open. Still, a few perplexed faces, as if to say, 'Where is this going, the line of thinking?' "But it's so simple: there's no business because there is no business," X chanted helpfully. "A good slogan."

Like most jargon posing as universal truth, the revelation was so evident at first blush that most of those listening appeared to wonder why the problem passed unnoticed. Several people ventured toward the head table to touch his shoulder.

I looked sternly at X, tightening my cheeks and fists, immediately tasting with regret my lackluster suggestion, wanting to have it back to regurgitate as a heady principle, to spit it out and envelop it in an open discussion, without X's lurid judgments, so even he could recognize the game he was playing here.

"Please, please — I'm not through," X said, foreclosing background chatter. "Now, I'm sure you all wonder what's next. Clearly, *something* must be done, today. Do we want our business back?" Yet, stupidly, I joined an approving peal of applause, the audience banging their feet with enthusiasm. "So, it *will* be done," X insisted. "Now, the question is what? Are there any suggestions from the gallery?" More audience chinwagging. X leaned across the table: "What the hell?"

"You're doing what you think is best, but where is it going?" I asked. "Go to the tables; find out what the talk is about. Try to unite people, search out if there's a common cause among them, hopefully to celebrate Nate rather than run him down. Test whether your ideas are going over their heads; seek out cooperative responsibility if you want people involved, like sharing the fire duties. This is going to take sacrifice on your part to be of benefit to these folks."

There were no suggestions from the gallery. "Well, then my people, let me tell you the idea I have. This occurred to me, ah, four days ago. It's obvious we must sacrifice something which will get the undivided attention of those on the outside. This is for a good cause," X promised, furthering the process that would convince him of his truthfulness and finally drive him. "This action will show the world we mean *business*." X looked around the room truculently, removed his hands from his hip pockets, expanding his chest, and planting one foot in front of the other. When the restaurant was saturated with curiosity which X mistook for consensus, he resumed: "Now then, because of the nature of our problem, there is no alternative solution except drastic and if needs be violent action." The audience shuddered. "What is our most valued possession? Sit down, George. This will take some sacrifice on our part because *everyone* has to appreciate that you can't accomplish anything without a sacrifice or two. And I'm sure future generations of those whose folks brought business to this soon-to-be-popular town of Selby...those grown-up kids will look back on this time of judgment as a heroic age — an age which will set the pattern for future human conduct." I shifted, anxious for the point when John X thought what he was going to say would sound plausible. "I have decided," he said, folding his arms on his chest, "that the only thing we can do..." On his chair again, he raised the planted foot onto the table. "...is to burn the fire station to the ground...with ol' Nate in it! I think this will be more than adequate," X hurried on through audience jaw-dropping gasps. "But it's hard to say and I cannot make any promises. *However*, I *can* guarantee this will get the attention of the outside world, sick as it is in its own house without windows. That was your poet speaking. This sacrifice of one of our values will show them we mean *business*. And," he added quickly, "from the practical side, we can use new business to rebuild a more prized fire station with a new wagon *and*...guess who as chief, George?"

George stood. "But where will I park the fire engine?" he asked.

"First things first, details later," X shouted, throwing his left-fisted arm into the air. The audience jumped up and ran outside, its initial energy spent on noise.

I pressed the sides of the Styrofoam coffee cup between my palms until it smashed, then backpack in hand, strode through the back door to find speechless Nate and escort him up the hill to the church.

Hullabaloo filled the town, but the appetite for firing the station died down.

Faces in the Jigsaw

From the dense wood above the town, a smell of smoke lingered in the air. How rich the wood, awesome by its light fluctuations, and dampening. Shade casts alleys of light with a palate of colors for its favorites. How this is like having sun on the end of a faucet.

Why must farmers who live in the valley spirit their trade away from local crossroads? There was a general store in Selby, or at least a sign for one. Farmers are well-intended towards each other, with too easy a tolerance of conniving speculators in the city, even conceding their losses that the city seeds to the valley.

Farmers are people able without a groan to rise early in the morning every day. A coffee pot in a lone kitchen can be the only flower for miles. The pot will not burgeon until — across frozen ground, along singing power lines with unseen spectacles of snow, ice, and unslain rabbit tracks — a farmer lives. Little else lives vibrantly alone, without the faces of farm life and those who sit in dawn kitchens, behind a map, drinking coffee and planning their day.

How is it for those who dwell in Selby, facing recurrent fires, able to confront the diminishing number of trees no longer shod in winter's shoulder pads? Can they see past summer branches to the rich sky and still be part of the booming and graceful growth on the land? How can they live independently and yet coalesce with each other, to save the ecology dear to farmers, against genetic evolution, intensive animal farming, new machines, superstore profiteering, and X? By compromise? Just as they are? Engineering the weather and geography, or feeling all the quirks of each encroachment and then cultivating the habits of lifetimes? So many faces. Are their expressions all that different, or the same cob core surrounded with eccentric kernels? Like the rest of us, perhaps each face makes the bargains that we all live and die by, conciliations eventually become the protagonist, cheerful countenance or otherwise, according to the resolve of strong hearts and the irreversibility of farming life.

I was in this land, no doubt about it. The ground grew. Farmers without time or the wish to sleep. In fields where no man planted, subtle raspberries grew beside wild flowers: Pasture Rose and Sundrops. Birds and animals flittered and toyed with each other. Nature caused this harmonious rural process with gay abandon to any favorites, a cycle which grows until eventually, if you're receptive, circumstances occur with a protected joy. Farmers are immune from losing their color in autumn. Their husbandry is like the earth: it gives them strength, sharing their winter-slackened muscles and pulling them straight in posture. The faces of people are, on the one hand, unique, yet, on the other hand, a convergent expression evoked by a rich green parcel of earth. Townspeople prowl and scratch at their leaders' foresight in wishful attempts to add the spirit of the rural domain to their possessions.

Unlike farmers, people in Selby are averse to rising even earlier than dawn to pull a stranger's car from a ditch. Farmers treasure that. If the car belongs to a friend or a neighbor, a festival might be in order. During winter, a warm jug of home-brew does the trick. In summer, cool brew lay by their protégés, at dark places in the wood. Young people sit cross-legged on their blankets with nearest and dearest, throwing songs to the wind and knocking down its chills. Machinery rusts. The ecological inevitability of all that naturally constructs and eventually deconstructs, especially during winter. Kith and kin take delight in perpetual evolutionary cycles, talking across the unspoken sense that wind passes forever and they thousands of times.

Daughters and sons are secret to farmers' commercial trials and tribulations. Townsfolk appear baffled and scared by farmers' siblings. There is a certain power inherited by the children which is gleefully possessed. Passing urbanities pretend not to notice kids playing with farmyard animals, and the earth. Tourists and officials witness the grace behind a farm child's clumsiness: style from dreams of future farmers on a blanket. Eventually, all of our faces will be reconciled from the moment-to-moment differences that, only momentarily, appear unconnected, and distinct, one from the other.

Around a bend, grainy hillside textures eroded to the creek. Another fence — the third since last night's sunset: my tracks between fences, close behind or in the distant past, disappear and reappear with each new imprint. Across the fence, I took a step and froze: an inky-eyed man threw me an appraising glance.

"Come on now fella," said a voice of authority — a mature one but not as haggard as the man staring at me. "Just tell us who you are. We want to get your car out. Don't you believe us?" A middle-aged lady belonged to the voice. She wore a uniform, badge and pistols which hung across her ribs like third and fourth pinnacles of her momentous chest. "No use, Stan, I think he's gone."

"No. I seen him, he's..."

"I mean his head — he ain't..."

"Ya think he's drunk, hey?"

"Naw, he's gone — he's strange. He's one of the pestilents."

"What about his car?"

"Uhmmmmm."

"What about his car, Stan," the sheriff demanded, remembering her exact words.

"I don't want it Marge."

"Yeah. Hey stranger, come here." She stepped forward and grabbed his arm. The captive eyed me. I slid behind a tree. "Hey, what you lookin' at?"

"What you see, the past? Hahahahahahahahha." Deputy took the fellow by his other arm and they steered him back to the car. Startled and stooped by handcuffs behind his back, the fellow jerked one arm free. As if in a fog suddenly parting, he said: "Albuquerque."

"What?" the sheriff asked, "Albuquerque what?"

"New Mexico," the man replied, as if the sheriff was a senile pestilent.

"Is that where you're from — New Mexico? How'd his car get Kansas plates, ya suppose?"

"Mabbe he stole it. Hey fella, is that where you're from?"

He was silent.

"Come on, bud," said the deputy, shaking his arm gently. "Hey...hey...Goddamit, I guess he's gone."

"Does he live in these parts?"

"I never seen him and nobody new lives round here. Somebody's been gettin' in Sillie Evans' grapes, but it was just tramps, not this guy."

"Gettin' in Sillie's grapes, you say?"

"Yeah, happens each year. He's gonna get 'em sometime."

I crept closer, inching up a weeded road shoulder, peering at their heads and the sleek roof of the car which carried this stranger into the clutches of misfit hunters. The sheriff and her deputy, after consultation, returned to the man.

"Why'd you say about New Mexico?"

"Beats me," the deputy answered for him.

"Yup...ain't this sheriff a strange job, though."

"Yeah."

"Onawa City and Dubuque."

"What?"

"What'd you say? Where are those places? I think Dubuque is in Ioway..."

"Mabbe he's too far from home."

"Yeah," the sheriff chuckled, stepping away.

The suspect squatted. As he rose, a long, deep whistle came from the base of his throat.

"Crazy."

"He's gone...yep, he's sure a gone one."

Working his jaws, he laid the foundation of any statuesque pose, planting his heels far apart, flexing his thighs, and he built it right up to fix a courageous gaze. "El Centre, LeCenter, Centre, Centerville, Centerritte, Centennial and all regular stops." He gathered his breath, gulped and plunged on: "Centralia, LeCenter, El Centro...Centervilllllllle, LeCenterrrrr, Centrallllllllliiiiiiaaaa."

When a truck whooshed past, the stranger showed his crimson empty mouth, which closed like a three part instrument. He sat while the sheriff and deputy deliberated, deciding to draw him out with small talk. "Nice enough day," she said and sat real easy. "Could be a lot worse, I suppose."

No response.

The deputy examined his overshoes. "You from a farm?"

Nothing.

More tactful than brave, the sheriff chose a different approach: "Say, you sure say lots of towns. How'd you learn 'em."

"I'll bet they're hard to remember," he answered without so much as a quiver.

"*Sure are — say*, how can a person remember all them towns, eh?"

"I'll *bet* they're hard," the fellow said, grinning. "You and I'll *bet* they're hard to remember."

Struck by something funnier, he flowed into a cataract of laughter. The sheriff didn't share his joke. "Well, where'd you learn 'em. Did you go to college?"

"Yup."

"I thought so. Say, where'd you go? Bet you didn't go in these parts. You don't look like one of those college kids from around here."

"Nope."

"Nope, huh. Yeah? Say, where'd you go to college?" the interrogator asked. Then the sheriff grinned as if the two shared a secret.

"Tell you where I went."

"Hey, okay, could my boy go there?"

"That your boy over there," the man said, pointing at the deputy. "Fine lookin' boy; little old to be a boy, though. Bet he ain't been to college."

"Oh, no. Nobody round here's been," the sheriff said, playing a part. "Nosirre, ain't none of us smart enough."

"Yup, bet you ain't."

"No sir. Say, where'd you go to college?"

"Tell you where."

"*Where?*" Marge and Stan shouted at once.

"Well sir, went to the college of hard knocks."

"Where was that?" the sheriff asked, set back but not down and cut.

No answer.

"Well, we're going to take you into town," she concluded. "We'll come and get your car tomorrow." She led him to her squad car: a fast maroon vehicle with arrogant headlights and a certain hefty stance. The sheriff and deputy talked in front while the stranger stared from his space, clearly not a blank space, behind.

I backed into the brush, blowing warm air into my palms, visualizing the fellow as if seeing clear jelly-like pictures of him in long stripped robes among the trees. Why did he leave his town or farm? How, and now this hell? Are his veins cracked by addictions, or abuse, or cleansed by the cycles of farming? How is he right now, with black-and-blue bruises from steel hand cuffs? How did he come this far off-track, to be dragged by Marge's henchman, kicking out the light in his face, forcing him into the patrol car?

Veins in the bark of a tree pointed to water running beneath it. At the hill's bottom, standing on the clackety teeth of creek stones, water soothed my hands and legs, bubbling around tingling toes in the brown bed. While a cloud covered the sun, restless currents gushed and swirled. When sun returned, the creek idled.

Among a clump of flowers, a few broken stems of the pendant jewels quenched my thirst with their juice. Under the bridge as the many-pieced river floated by, birds held school, riding in the air, whistling, sounding for depths of love and war. Behind sounds of water current, cows swished through grass downstream. The livestock tore up pasture in clumps and munched in unison. "Now my beauties," I said to the cattle, "come and eat. That's right, come here." Most were shy. Two who knew their appetites and were bored with weeds, ate my corn — their kernels once milky stubs on a green land. After this it was my turn.

Cows took well to the exchange. I approached one. At first touch, the cow kicked, knocking me head over heels. The blow left me on my back, momentarily concerned about my bloody scraped knee. "All I want is to...is that I...or so if anything..." When mosquitoes replaced flies, a plump Jersey face appeared above me, eyeing a pile of corn, my only food, butting me with her face and pawing. I nudged the milk sweet animal with my hand, nudged her nose, again and again and she went away, without crushing my chest after all.

The rest of the evening amounted to hopping a bit as bodily sensations returned, then bolting up the stream bank, turning and plunging, sometimes landing or just floating, turning in midair and coasting to the top of breathing again. Where the bank rose several feet, forming a drop-off on the other side, my mud twisted toes straightened with a few long hopscotch steps, leaping over the bobbity creek, glimpsing it twirling between rocks, feeling the leap from the one side to the other with circling feet, my body coming together in segments and unfolding upwards as the recoil of landing shot me out full length. There has to be a leap to appreciate the connection of one face to another — the symmetry of faces beyond all the song and dance of finding a place in the mud, or elsewhere. I sprang and rolled in a sand patch on the bank, lying sprawled and smiling while the moon licked my joints, kicking sand into the stream, which drifted with its particles and settled them to bed. Water rolled by and the moon made spots of tree branches on my eyes.

"What does the cows' milk mean to health? Everyone should have milk or a similar sustenance — there is little enough food here — some milk to keep the tarantulas away," I cautioned a family of attentive leaves. But how? Thoughts moved and merged like clouds overhead, developing into a "hum-mmmmmm" — a long collected one, neither lazy nor excited, it nevertheless felt as though it was a lean belly.

Flat-looking cows grazed among peaceful trees on a hill. They moved stiffly in pursuit of grass which roused whispering air-scapes in the breeze. This was their place; my listening and thinking camp was at a higher spot between trees without dung. At the hilltop in a circle of birch, I made a weed cushion, taking leaves and small plants to the spot, scattering them into a thick soft heap, digging out riverside rocks to pile open and downhill around the bed, packing edges with mud. Unrolling a sleeping bag, my head hung over loins now like cliff erosion from a resurgent sea. Positioning myself to sleep, hungry, the moon blossomed and gauged the pulse of fish as they broke water.

The Wreck

A breath-blowing dog trotted on a sidewalk, grinding its teeth. The animal flung some of the breath over its shoulder like a silver silk scarf. Off a residential street into the country, sun polished a water tower; the reflection reached such a pitch that, for a minute, the sun seemed to be inside a long house, which was in front of the tower. I slurped green celery scented water from a trough below the tower.

The encounters in custody convinced me of at least one thing: accept the cruel primal treatment of certified experts, the aggravation they cause, similar to parents tantrums, accept that their captivating influences incarcerate them in their own entanglements, giving them less and less wiggle-room for new ground and new strength. Those thoughts stalked me like an imaginary crane, which said, 'Keep asking, what is the state of *my* mind?'

The crane circles now as I stroll through a town at dawn. This town is situated on the south side of a broad-based hill, starting a range to the northwest, where snow-capped mountains ladder the earth and sky. I toss a garden hose in the direction of the preoccupied crane, which is the usual scenario when referring to the crane to explore my foolishness. She glares remotely as the missile falls with a feeble flop beneath her hard snout. "You the global crane? Lower the boom." Staring back at each other while the town woke with busyness, the crane sits on her haunches, keeping an eye on me and the town.

Then the bird lies down. We're both hungry. Do I spend life hobnobbing with crane imaginings? She looks away as if distracted, as if in disbelief that naval-gazing is in anybody's best interest. The crane, liberator of the world, stands for freedom. It was easier than I expected, mitigating mental projections and petty blather.

"Won't you come into the house and have some from a glass?" said a female voice behind me.

"Cer...sure...but..." I choked. Apparently this lady hadn't heard of Lionel C. Hartlett, poacher and threat to local folk. About 35, in a pretty floral frock, she stood in a concrete driveway curving around behind the house. "I'd like something to eat, please," I said between my teeth, tongue-tied trying to pry algae from my palate. She looked as if she didn't hear. I approached the drive. "Do you have scraps of something I could eat?"

"Oh, yes, come with me."

Past washing machines through a garage, the cool house smelled of lemonade and another untraceable odor. Inside the kitchen, she motioned me to a chair.

"Must be unpleasant walking out there." The woman scrutinized my hungry face.

"Yes, partly unpleasant indeed," I said, thinking of the posse and its dogs, deputies, guns, and sheriff — guns that tacked Lionel C. Hartlett posters on trees. Posters alleging how many chickens and pigs he poached. Guns that splattered flesh in 50 directions and allowed a poacher's blood to seep into the ground, where it turned brown and was eaten by huge marauder ants native to the region. Guns that chipped bones and left them fragmented to bleach in the sun.

"Would you like some sugar in your lemonade?"

"No thank you, this is fine." And dogs. "Ugh." Dogs that cheated buzzards of poacher flesh and ripped the finely sewn stitches of seams. Remains of dog-chewed clothes will be tied in a neat bundle, mailed to Mrs. Hartlett, in a burlap bag, with a card signed THE POSSE. The poacher's body will be sunburned, his stomach emptied by the dogs.

"May I join you?"

"Yes, please do." Deputies with clubs made of the realm's finest redwood — their gouging thumbs and high-heeled boots.

"Won't you excuse me?"

"Sure." A scowling never-give-up sheriff: three days on the rascal's trail and nary a trace; 'nough to make a blind mare grey.

"What's that? What in the world..."

"Oh, nothin', just humming." A sheriff with his posse behind him — the horses foraging under Douglas Fir trees, the men groaning. A sheriff who suddenly slapped his wide-brimmed cowboy hat against his legging, climbed on his horse, Throbber, gave the posse a steely glance and commanded: 'All right boys, let's mount up; we're on to something. I said mount up!'

"What's that, you say?"

"Oh nothin' it's just something that happened and made me think how our fascination about ourselves plays out with someone else. Would you like to hear about it? It would ease me some if you would."

"I'm easy, either way."

"Two unidentified persons died today when a vehicle they were riding in crashed and burned seven miles north of Visalia on Highway 33. Witnesses said it was going west when a deer darted in front, causing the car to swerve, hitting a clump of brush beside the road, turning over and bursting into flame, according to witnesses. An eastbound car, car two, veered out of control and crashed on the opposite side of the highway, after its passengers tried to get a quick look at the wreck."

"Holy shit. How awful for you, my dear," she whizzed, through her gin-spliced lemonade.

One witness — a man, trapper and farmer — scrutinized the crash from his pasture, 40 yards south of the scene. 'My name is Harmon Johnson and this is my pasture,' he said. 'It's a rich pasture and I'm fascinated watching from it. Sometimes we come as a family with egg mayonnaise sandwiches, and we watch the road. The watching is usually best on a tourist day.'

"A young lady said the deer, an albino, was graceful. It babbled and pirouetted with a boundless grace (don't quote me on this; it's just an observation). However, this was verified by a picador who waited in a meadow. 'Tra-la-la, tra-la-la,' he sang, standing and waving to keep the lady's waning attention. He confronted the motor spectacle with a graceful haste.

"Still another witness, with a raffish air, and her plentifully rouged shadow, said the deer was a pure albino, in the area about a week. They added that it, or one like it, was seen by them two years ago.

"The man, trapper and farmer ate scraps near his traps and fraternized among several cows. He said: 'But it often ignored them and they often seemed to ignore it.'

"Three witnesses declined to comment and several people said they'd not been forewarned of the event, so were not present at its occurrence. A group listened to a car radio. 'Now to our WTB...uhhughuk...WBCT man at large on the spot, Rod Challenger. Ah, Rod? Come in Rod, ten-four.' 'Yeap, Frank. Ah, weather in California is mild and clear this week, with little or no precipitation and some falling space debris in west central parts. Raisin drying conditions are excellent and work continues on local roads. Ah, ten-four, Frank. Frank?' 'Yes, Rod, and that's all from us for a live report from the spot. And now at...exactly...two-forty-six...more, um, in the daily crash news, but after a musical interlude.'

"Chorus. (There is always a chorus, which chimes a eulogy about traffic near the accident being damaged as much as participants in the motor vehicles, at least when death is considered the least important part of dying.)"

"Hahahahahahahahahahahahahahahaha," the floral lady laughed, staring at my stomach, as I sat down again.

"Traffic, normally a constant flash of flag colors by sleek ships plummeting along the polished roadway, was stopped by a policeman with a flashlight. There existed a crowded quietude; needles of sound scratched. Shade lifted and birds blanched. Trees crowed, flaming into sky, and grass swished in the breeze. The quiet was outside sun, a dog bark, a child's shout. The witnesses searched for it but only found a policeman at the center. They looked as though they wanted to avenge themselves like a bat on his face, as if unhappy because they couldn't find the quiet even though it was there out of respect for the dead. A truck parked near the wreckage, ready to load carnage: broken cheers and bent faces. An ambulance screamed through a shimmering heat field which stewed over the shaking cars and trucks. Crowd elements faced a single focal point. The

first boldest elements — two males and a female — emerged
from a metallic gunmetal car, paying strict attention to the
point. She was young, shapely, and dressed in a gaudy geometric mix. The effect of international orange was strong around
her. She wore the males on either side, like gloves. 'Looks to
be a real one,' the left-hand male added. The female stepped
briskly toward the crash site to observe the deceased man. He
was on his back and stretched the width of the front seat above
him, a few blood splatters on his face and on the shirt front.
(The ambulance driver slammed a door on his only thumb as
if there was only one. Judging from the ensuing obscenities,
union rules stipulate that comrades must be at each end of
any stretcher so stipulated to be under union control.) Most
of the injured woman was heaped on the cadaver's legs; under
the passenger's seat, her head rested against the door. 'Why,
he's almost as good as new,' said the girl with two men. 'If he
had a clean shirt on, we probably wouldn't even think he was
dead.' The trio laughed and another person, a man, joined
their laughter. No doubt about it now. The elements were as
plain as the paint on their faces. This was going to be a crowd
of wrecked bystanders. The fourth element quickened his step.
Those further away stopped on tiptoes, pointing their noses up
and then continued to converge. 'Well, looks like a good crash;
how'd it happen? Anybody firsthand on-scene?' the fourth
man-element said.

   "The trio confronted him. 'That's a silly question,' said one
of the males. 'Yeah,' said his mate, 'who cares how it happened? You with the insurance or something?' 'No, no. I was
just curious. You mean you're not? I'd think everybody would

want to know how it happened. So it could be, ah, prevented next time.' 'Yes, I'm curious,' said the girl with the orange effects. 'I am very curious about what happened here. I mean, we got here too late to see anything really happen. All we could see is this wheel still spinning.'

"They gazed at a wheel on top of the wreck, the focal point, as other elements assembled. The wheel, moments before, had been spinning on the road, and now the car lay on its roof, the wheel spinning in air. A badge stood out as the wire wheel spokes flashed in their spin. 'It's a Jag,' said a twerp, smacking his fist in a baseball glove and spitting from beneath the long red bill of his oversized cap. The crowd appeared spellbound, reconciled to staring at it, each revolution more slowly until it, almost without notice, stopped. They continued to stare as if one of them dared to touch the wheel, to spin it with a twitchy hand, causing the spokes to glint in the sun. A rough-neck fellow with SMITH, JR. stitched on the back of his polo shirt, was first to break the freeze it had on the crowd: 'What the...' a giggle came from the car. The crowd bent low. The wide-eyed injured woman saw them through a flurry of white deer parts, swaying road and flashy stars. 'What's so funny?' asked the young lady who wore two men. 'Do you think this is a proper time to laugh? Look at the poor man: mashed in and squatted like a pancake, his coordination nothing but an echo. And here you sit laughing, as if it were a practical joke,' she moaned."

I wrote this episode in my journal, based on a crash the other day, and began telling the story because my gut feeling on entering this house was one of being in hostile territory again—that during the telling she might forget her suspicions and not call the sheriff. I drew myself into the thick of the story.

"The wrecked woman turned, showing only half a face. Blood streamed from her neck-shoulder and permeated her white taffeta blouse. 'It's just that I kicked him, and he pumped the brake. Surely he's passed on,' she said, crying again, sideways, kind of blowing the words sideways out of her mouth. 'Why'd ya s'pose he'd do that?' asked the middle-aged son, SMITH, JR. 'Reflex action,' said the roughneck. SMITH, JR. nodded, having thought it at the same time. 'It was so nice, so laid-back,' said the lady with two men. 'Spinning there, spiral after spiral. It would probably have spun all day and far into the night if it hadn't stopped. They were careful spirals but so soft, so undulating...' she paused. The crowd eyed her, and then she concluded '...that you wanted to climb in there and feel their air stroking your body...' 'Well, I wouldn't call it simple,' the man on her right interjected. 'Actually, it was more a group action. I mean, as she kicked him, which may have been well-intended, he pumped the brake. Now, because more than one person acted in concert to achieve a desired end...that's a group thing, even if, in this case, half the group is technically dead.' 'Sounds like him alright,' said the injured woman. 'He had tremendous reflexes; he was quite a man. He was nearly 50. He loved to drive. We roamed the world. I was his accomplishment. He's taken care of me the last ten years in exchange for common services. Actually, I was utterly fond of him. He always told me he was 40. I guess the part of his brain that thought he was getting older just stopped and he picked

40 as a good age to be. He picked it because it was my age when
we met,' she went on, sliding into a silent gaze. Blood rolled
down her arm and splashed in a pool on the wreck's ceiling.
The wrecked woman rested her head on the door and breathed
deeply, but her chest didn't expand. The half face was pale and
the side of her throat tinged blue. 'Oh, Jesus, I think I see what
you mean,' the roughneck piped up,' and then burped. 'Come
on,' the young lady whispered, tugging at her men. 'Can't you
picture it; they want to be alone together? Poor dear,' she murmured, 'seems as though she's turning into a frog. The last
thing she wants is a bunch of strangers asking questions.' The
middle-aged son followed the trio, noticing for the first time
how the young lady strutted. 'Sure is a good crash,' he said,
looking back. 'A real good one.'

"The crowd changed weight from foot to foot and decided,
in the silent way that crowds decide, to tarry. The girl and
her rubber-necked pals frowned at each other as if in psychic
debate: who should reply to SMITH, JR? Finally, the right-
hand male (who wore swim trunks) grinned and said: 'I
wouldn't be disrespectful of the dead, mister, it might have
been you.' 'Oh, oh yes, well, of course, I didn't mean any disrespect; these things fascinate me. I suppose if I saw them every
day, they'd be dull, but watching them only on weekends, as I
do, well, I try to have a good sense of humor about misfortune
and wars.'

"A senior couple, more like one person than two, joined the
gallery. They wore matching homemade plaid shirts, except
the man's pocket was on his right side. They walked with arms
linked. People kicked up so much dust that the swelling crowd

was barely visible from the pasture. They become anonymous when filling in the spaces of a crowd, people whose troubles and sufferings become unified in the fragments of someone else; each of us onlookers was conflicted with the strains in coming of age, each naturally swaying to be loose from one life's mess.

"The man, trapper and farmer snapped pictures with his Polaroid camera. He showed them in such a manner it was clear he wasn't going to part with a single one. Bunched around the dead man's car, the bulk of the crowd peered at its leopard skin upholstery. The man, trapper and farmer stood by the other vehicle, across the highway. Although its occupants remained inside since the crash, there was action: the driver read a book. Two ladies next to him got dolled up. In the rear seat, two tanned men talked while a third donned a polished leather jacket, which was decorated with drawings of wheels, chains, cogs and a battery. A silver wheel was painted on each shoulder. When the man moved his shoulders the wheels appeared to turn.

"The people of the second wreck opened their roadside doors and emerged. The man, trapper and farmer took pictures of the event. They marched single file toward the death car, right past the policeman, who dropped his flashlight. As they advanced, ladies first, two men, the jacketed man and finally the driver, the crowd kept back. For these were survivors. These people felt their car screech out of control, spin across the road, and slam into a pine tree. Their car folded in on itself, metal upon metal, paint lacerated, torn and shredded like colored water drops. Yet these people were unscratched and cool as cucumber — people unbothered by the crash, and who now casually inspected the body of the man who passed on and his injured companion. These avoided being part of a crowd; they adopted a presence that others might want but couldn't assume those qualities. These were swarthy people, pockmarked, as if they spent most of their time in a hungry sun. In bright light, their skin revealed variegated features, resembling stained glass, as if many seams were soldered together by fire — people who knew the automobile only as a convenience, not as a necessity. (This complicated the crowd's reactions.)

"The young lady who wore two men and SMITH, JR. reclaimed their first element positions in the crowd. 'What the hell are they doing?' SMITH, JR. asked. 'What do they think they're doing?' No answer. 'Why are they examining him like that? Aren't they aware he's dead? Don't they have any manners?' SMITH, JR. pleaded.

"From across the highway, the senior matching couple approached the intruders. 'Say, this is a death scene,' she berated them and stilled the hand in her plaid breasted pocket. 'Don't you have any respect for the dead?'

"One of the swarthy men gave a feather to the jacketed man, who tickled the corpse's nose and then the woman's face. She smiled, wanly. The elder woman, shielding her partner — which made her the closest observer — was shocked. 'Look. Look at that,' she exclaimed, stepping back onto his sandals. 'Why those heathens are molesting the body of a dead man.' The fellow eased the woman off his toes. The left-hand male shoved the senior woman into her man and glared at the wreck. He smirked, gestured to a lady, arriving with the other male, who whispered to her. Not wanting to be outdone, the left-hand male laughed. 'Do you think it's funny? Are you with them?' the elder woman asked, pointing with a fist at the swarthies as they probed the debris. 'My Lord, I hope this dead man will forgive you. Look at that. Looky! They're disturbing his everlasting peace.'

"The injured woman strained to sit up, but she gasped and fell back into a heap. SMITH, JR., who intended no disrespect for those who passed on, gave up his crowd element position and edged towards the wreck. 'What are they doing?' he asked the young lady. 'Playing? Well, is there something wrong,' he went on to the senior woman, 'with playing?' 'Not playing,' she declared, 'but they aren't playing; can't you see? They're desecrating!' she declared. 'Oh.'

"Leaning on an escort, the young lady tied the bottom of her blouse into a bow. The adjustment showed part of her tanned belly and a few bikini hairs. 'Well, I don't guess there's much wrong with a little fun,' SMITH, JR. expostulated with a sideward glance. 'We all should have more fun.' The belly smiled at him and glowed in the sun. 'In fact, having more fun...' he continued, setting his face in the woman's eye...'would keep some of us...from dehydrating.' 'Well, I can tell what kind of fun you're thinking of,' she sparked and rotated, as if to go. The older fellow came to meet her; other crowd elements, gaining courage and now looking quizzically at the wreck, also moved forward. 'People like that spoil everybody's fun,' SMITH, JR. said, smiling at the girl. 'Oh, really?' she questioned, grinning formally.

"The strangers (though few in the crowd knew one another, the consensus was that the swarthies were the strangers) continued their antics. The jacketed man, at the wreck's steering wheel, frantically gestured in a pantomime of the dead man's efforts to miss the deer without losing control of his vehicle. Frank laughing, by the youngish swarthies, caused crowd members to emulate them, joining in, hesitantly. Meanwhile, the jacketed man's upside-down face reddened. He relinquished the steering wheel and climbed from the car. One of the young lady's men applauded with her, continuing to clap by himself, and he didn't quit until she frowned at him. The jacketed man produced a flower and tossed it to her. He circled the wreckage as if it were a friend, prizing its smooth metal, whispering. This time he mimed putting on a hat and strolling, patting the car fenders affectionately. Most of the crowd streamed after the young lady and her man as they pressed in behind the swarthies. The jacketed man crawled into the wreck and clasped the steering wheel again, pulling dashboard switches, humming as he performed driving motions, seizing it until his knuckles whitened. Suddenly he muscled the wheel, forcing it back and forth; mimicked bouncing with his shoulders, then fell and landed with a loud burst of wind from his bottom onto the expired man. The crowd, more engaged now in the swarthies' farce, tittered and laughed. Even the seniors were less upset at the atrocity. The plaid-shirted man snickered at his partner. Fresh applause began, led by the middle-aged son and emulated by the young lady and her men, growing until clap sounds spread across a meadow, where the man, trapper and farmer took pictures of the picador, and beyond, up an adjacent canyon wall.

"The injured woman still lay against the car door, her eyes half shut, listening to the celebration, aware of strawberry malt and summer's eyes, with stripped miles and spinning fruits in a basket, and the clapping. The fact that an arm was numb alarmed her, because she couldn't remember which arm, even with the applause. She grinned very, very gently and said: The unsung numb one...the unsung...numb...one...unsung ungnb... one...the...uns...gnmbb...un...th...'

"When the claps stopped, the crowd buzzed at the remains of the write-off. The jacketed swarthy tickled the injured woman's nose with his feather, examining her face for several minutes. He threw the feather away and ordered his helpers to pile wood on all sides of the ruined vehicle.

"The crowd put the albino deer on top. Who will fire it?"

The housewife lifted the receiver of a telephone mounted on the wall, dialled, aimed it at her mouth, eyed me, smiled and patted a white refrigerator watching over her. "Well, after all," I muttered to her, "it has coils, intestines, lights inside that are always on and power to retard decay, but no fenders."

"He's here again; come and pick him up, please." This person had heard of Lionel C. Hartlett, poacher!

"Rightaway," an urgent voice replied.

"Well, you'd better run. Here's the candy you wanted."

"Thanks. Which way will they come from?"

"Who cares? Aren't you a little flip?"

She stared at me as I backed out the door," chuckling and running, jogging until the water tower was out of sight. When sun passed through clouds of variant thickness, tree shadows expanded and contracted as if breathing deeply and loosening their shoulders in preparation for an athletic event.

Christmas Day

Rain, rain that longs to come. The rain in Frisco falls mainly forever. Standing beside the car, wet door handle, inhaling the divergent fall, smiling broadly. There were others like me doing similar things: beginning the car journey — fresh from the first sweet coffee-stained kiss after morning's breakfast, neat suits creased to the steering wheel, aiming for the freeway and across the bridge to the city. The bridge is like a tongue from the center of the sprawling glut of noise and obstruction, a tongue rolling out and in from its huge concrete mouth. For my part, having an incomplete education, Nancy sent me off, happily, to the clockworks. There, I write about the daily tally of road deaths, animals swabbed and suffocated in oil, mud slides, and articles about the outbursts of people outraged when their own instability touches them each day.

The bridge is a remarkable commonplace. Built many years ago with concrete and steel, it stands out of the bay like the back hair of any suspicious dog. Above beckoning water, untold animals swim beneath its surface — fish, usually unobserved, jellyfish and sharks, even a whale now and then, on special occasions. A whale, to a whale, is a natural thing. Not surprising. To me, on the bridge, there is a vague part of me wishing, even while traveling so far off the ground, to understand them. Or anything as uncertain passing on the bridge, an affinity now, even a sense of fellowship. After crossing it a hundred times, I remember the first squeezy nervousness at its height, but remember the constant flux, below and above it. Now I pay homage to being steady, even though being hyper-alert for fleeting daydreams; then, recognizing that unease again emerging, when a hand brushes my waist, checking the seat belt, feeling to verify that the emergency brake is off, then on an even keel.

At the end of suburban streets, the freeway — the first in a flashy series of eight-lane transactions. Zip-a-Dee-Doo-Dahing all along the ramp, with Louis Armstrong on the radio, pressing back into the seat, elbows semi-locked, left eye circling an area in the space ahead, an estimated place where my car will hit the freeway, right eye squirting over my chin at machines blurs racing to the same spot of freeway. Massive white and green signs clamored for obedience. Urging on the accelerator, the car winged into a merge lane, switching lanes, the momentum moving me forward in the seat as the turn signal flicked off.

Halfway around a curve, the huge arms of the bridge came to view, through the rain. I always wanted to see just the bridge, unobscured by narrative dresses, because it was beautiful. So, seeing it as it was — also feeling a sense of continuity in the rain, which appeared to give the bridge a force, a certain power.

I was at a point between Oakland and Frisco. Cities in front and behind me. Plus the inanimate bridge and toll station between. "Blinking toll station accepts thousands and thousands of coins each day from those who pass through, with ready tokens. If the money is uncollected, regularly, the toll booth is likely to sink down through pavement into marshy bogs at the bridge's foot, out of sight. By the ingenious, devised process of collection every few hours, accumulated tons of wealth is buried elsewhere, in official vaults. The blinking toll station is saved day-by-day, solving that problem, sure, but what about the balance of nature, above and below the bridge? Solve that later, now appreciate...dry feet."

I worked in a typical journalist's way at a typical wire service, Associated Press, and wrote news and feature stories, as well as collecting those daily doings from local and state government offices. The broadcast media, like TV and radio, the newspapers, and members of the public, reported 'leads' to follow-up, for news of interest around the country and abroad. We checked out the leads, interviewed, and delivered the finished article, prepared on yellow paper and sent to clients via Nick, a jocular Manilan who wore a .45 caliber automatic pistol under his arm and dispatched our reports from electronic teleprinters.

One night I had a dream. It was about the way people related to their faces. A single phrase, "As temporary as a face," kept coming at me. The meaning was open to interpretation, until the following Saturday when Neil telephoned: "You'd think, with so much available these days in cosmetics, wigs and nose jobs, and/or space travel, she'd do something," he said, as if we were still at college. "Of course, it is a scarred country, with flat highways and tool sheds all over the goddamned place. But you'd think she'd fix the front of her head, if only to reveal her true identity and a skin-colored face.

"It is getting close to New Year's, though. That is something new. There'll be a few days away from advertising then — even a housewarming party when we're a little more settled.

"Yeah, that's better; it's not good enough, us just meetin' in town. Since you two set up, I haven't seen Nancy. Anyway our office voted to send its Christmas party funds to guys doing the job across the seas. The Big Effort. National Security. Nobody knows exactly who originated the idea. But most agreed on its value. This isn't why I prefer to be absent from the party. My Felicia will be drunk again and in a way suggesting that she attend to her looks, something like strangulation!" We both chuckled, and he continued: "A voice, inside me, similar to the one that ferrets around for some personality, rather than the coffee grounds and egg shells of my genital appetite, tells me to be more constructive, or at least pleasant. I dreamt last night that my voice sounded like a parent. Which one? I couldn't tell after all those years of not having a real one. The dream is a disjointed void, or more likely it's an illusion, as you mentioned all those years ago, leaving us to live outside of ourselves...Paul, how about if I come next weekend and help decorate the bathroom, but only if Nancy chooses the color! Look, I'm going to turn the radio up. Chow."

Monday morning was a bit unnerving: wet and slick. Arriving at the midpoint of the bridge, the wind picked up and rocked the car. I paid little attention; the rocking happened most days, as we're joined with the weather. My face strained at the windshield, wiping away the blurred view to make the way ahead clear. At the sweep of rain, slowing down, looking for taillights. "Well, even if my ashes are in a wreck, with rubber-neckers searching for tragedy, crashing into my behind, probing my entrails, the ashes grafted onto a rusty tin can, I'd wish to light up the assembly line with a fresh label that reads

NOT AN INSOUCIANT DRIFTER AFTER ALL. Keep the wipers going to clear the vision, rain or no rain.

A revolving head is what's required here, and making a quiet secret wish that vehicles avoid hitting you. Then with a whoosh and vip-pipipipipip into the viaduct. The rain and the wind stopped, car jerking without sliding, and smoothing to normal again. Shiny tile and dry amber lights. The others in their cars, similar type cars, individuals into types, similar-type others, types into individuals, a comforting view of ants on the way to the hive, the same beaks, and similar foods. There is an easy and uneasy sense of belonging to them, warmth in the viaduct, going through the first island. Rain splashed at the windshield again. Outside, on the bridge, the car bucked in wind all the way to the city. All the way off the expressway, into the slow gag of traffic near the mouth. Cars closed in front, braking, faster braking, the rear swinging, starting to dance. Dancing at my expense. I spun the wheel so fast that it clocked. Then she was in control, at 40. (A ripple of wildness isn't much, ordinarily, but a disturbance in the waves of a highway baked in iron bellies causes a chorus of revolt. The ants wheezed and coughed in the debris of their consumption, threw their podgy arms and adorned themselves with desperate-to-be-there ahead-of-where-they-are faces.) Slower, easier now. On the right, a wreck: it came out of the rain at me like a horse in the road. Police cars flashed red lights. Two cars parked neatly, one in front of the other in the far right-hand lane. The sea blew past in rain gaps. Both vehicles demolished. A person with a bloody head and backwards eyes was helped into an ambulance. The wreck was past. Traffic sped up. All hopes back to near normal. Back to normal speed. Shut off the radio. The day was normal movement, if you can call speeding normal.

I drove to work several days, weeks, without incident. Except for my acceptance of their normality — that was a difference. On a clear day, there is a view of men standing on ships in the bay. Gulls sky-gallop and reign-in and coast and cruise over the sea and the bridge, following a school of fish. A picture-postcard day. Too bright for distance viewing, or to grasp at what point the scene is a mirage regulated by light. Does each single impression alter it? "Is that real because of the way I alone experience it, even though produced in a multitude of forms from all the gladiators in their speeding frames of reference."

Traffic in a ventilated smooth around me, on the even keel. Cormorants fly easy through the sky. Ships move, like magnets in the water. Below, further away, toward the horizon, they appear to be above the sea. A car zips past so fast it leaves its image behind for a second — a red car with much chrome. I glanced at it, when all the pieces came together. It passes the car in front of me, and then swerves into my lane. Brake lights glare on the car in front. Easing down on my pedal, pushing it towards the floor, checking my rearview mirror as though it's too late, and swerve into the left lane to avoid the car. The consequences of going straight might change the face of mortality, particularly if the Grim Reaper is driving. Curious about its swerving, pressing my speed foot and chin forward, pulling parallel to the red car, glancing at the driver, whipping my brows at its pilot, bleeding his eyes with the strobe of his wrath. "Too risky," I shouted. The other driver wore ski goggles, his, or her, face obscured, except for the mouth. I smiled and gassed my machine to a place of safety; it shot ahead, then fell back, stupidly as if playing and waiting, as if inviting Buck Rogers to jet off with a Lone Ranger sidekick, if there was one. Without thought, eyeing the red car, its commander, and protesting simultaneously: "You're reckless wreckage." The commander saw my lips move and laughed at my incredulous face. Next his car swerves in front of me and roars away. "Goodbye almighty," I said, wondering whether it was a he or a she. Grabbing the steering wheel fiercely, the wind bucked my car and forced a jagged finger nail through the flesh of two other fingers — essential appendages during long fluorescently-lit days in the office, typing so much that the main sensation was of stubble on the end of my hands. I like writing, for radio in particular, because it's like talking, and to convey personal circumstances about the effects of mayhem and subversion in the violent hyperactive dramas of society, how well-intended survivors find life-giving resilience to recover strength of spirit and stoutheartedness when their world turns upside-down.

One day on the bridge a police car parked itself, with a live engine, at a small level spot just above an island exit. A vague form inside the squad car resembled a state trooper's wide-brimmed hat. Checking my speed, peering into the rearview mirror several times, there was uneasiness in the bottoms of my feet, as if wheels prepared to turn under my skin, after a long nap.

Sharks glided under the bridge, in the shadows of its speed, eating their way through shoals, lying long and lively in the

warm motion of fright caused by their presence. I pulled in
at a little Italian cafe near the bridge. A small Sicilian lady
with an incomprehensible accent slipped a genuine Italian
coaster under my drink. It warmed chilly organs going down,
as the TV blurted out battle reports, fights over rice, oil, and
heroin. The speed of televised images resembled a mesmeriz-
ing electronic fantasy game. Across the bay, behind the city's
light, lay an ocean bed. All that space and then the wars, a
television screen with pixels and tracer ammunition festively
spotting heartbeats on battlefields. Next on-screen, football
teams battled in one era or another: the plastic struggle, the
recorded roar of a holiday crowd, with applause for mascots
and coaches that ruled them with tense numerical codes, swift
feet and Incredible Hulk shoulders, heavy on the day, and
empty stadium seats where the ill-disposed once cheered. The
squad car will still be on the bridge. All the time on the bridge,
leaving occasionally for a wreck, to safeguard the loading of
carnage into an ambulance which moves effortlessly away in
screams, with broken optimism and bent faces. After my third
juice, I said to the person next to me, "Some people drive as
if there was going to be a tomorrow — they wouldn't want to
be in it." "Yeah, haw-haw," he laughed, as his veins glowed different colors and his body sorted out the mixture in his drink.
The cherry made a bump on his face. "Most people these days
are damn crazy," he said. "Look how they fight all the time," I
put in. "You mean such as over there?" he asked and gestured
to the TV, which sat like an owl above the bar. "Yup, only
worse. They're just like kids over there. They don't know any
better. I'll tell you man, we're the ones who should get medals.

We're the folks in danger, here. Hell, it's World War Three on those freeways and we don't even get helmets." We both cringed at the cheap analogy.

This day on the bridge seemed excessively mediocre in dedicated mist: no sun visible even though it is there with bulges in air caused by cars' relentless pressing against one another's spaces, no actual clouds or not in recognizable form, and no wind although there is always motion.

Christmas was closer. That day, closer all the time. The day of gifts, relaxation, and angst, when there is less employment than usual for those folks with paid work and the only traffic around was round the corner. Mostly, people placed themselves in front of TVs, except for gang warfare, embattled people traffickers, emergencies, war-torn provinces everywhere, and state militias up in arms. Looking at cars in the refreshing smooth, at my steady place in the pack, the way they steamed along on this marvelous bridge, made me feel like resting in the midst of pandemonium. A single car passed others; from the rear it closed in, on me, as if taking aim. About 50 yards back, its red color evoked the image of a gargoyle, the squirrely mouth and invisible eyes behind goggles, which may be a cover for a war injury that left this genderless being visually impaired and impatient, appreciative only of speed and particularly its untainted space, unsullied by the closeness of other vehicles, but still a Gargoyle, and closing in. Now the red car was behind, driving almost grinding my tailpipe in its plated teeth, waiting for a chance to pass. Waiting, that is, to first anticipate the damage of the bullet before the trigger pulls. I slowed to let it have its right-of-way. (We're better off to have them ahead in full sight.) There it went, all the hooves pounding almost at the same time. Offset just enough, however, to make a long stutter, stampede and disperse in a canyon. The red blur had swept past around one foot away. The darkened form glanced and pointed the goggles back — trying to place me?

The red car swerves in front. I brake, hammer, and smash at the brake, as if stomping on a snake, veering right, clear of the red machine, and bouncing off a curb. It's ahead: going, going, gone.

I sat stunned, feeling the shock. "What in hell?" I asked the smooth, settling round me, from behind. In the mirror, colors merged while vehicles and freeway quivered in panting heat. What is it, primitive dirt from the past? Specially from my past? But why?" All the way across to the office I thought of the reckless red. Yes, it must be a him. Female gargoyles will be coy. I even caught myself in a daydream over coffee and writing the ten o'clock weather bulletin: "He tries to bring out the dirt and disbelief and disgust he thinks still resides in me because it resides in him."

I joined a slow multiple smooth near the spot where state police sat in waiting, where the black and white squad car crouched on the bridge. I slowed and maneuvered to the right-hand lane. Cars in the smooth will learn the right thing to do when they witness his antics. Put out a bulletin or query to the sheriff. Abreast of his car, the cop's head dozed, relaxed and unphased by anything going. The car door shield denoting the official importance of safety, transposing itself on the sleeping body, like a giant insect with a human head. I sped up to legal speed and passed by, feeling relieved. Freewheeling into a service station, an attendant circled the car with a gas hose in his hand and said, "Say mister, ya lost a hubcap on that right front wheel. Whaddyado, run over somebody?"

Three days from Christmas; I spotted the red car, leaning to focus, ahead in a middle lane and my foot leaned. We all inhaled its exhaust and despised it. I eased toward it as it lolled at legal speed. The sensible layers of me wanted to turn back. Something deeper was at work after my travels — a maturing awareness of not needing to act on primitive angst, automatically, from my gut — such as, 'assassinate the tyrant' — rather than reasoning first about what gives rise, and how, to the bone-headed idiocy of enraged drivers. I saw the licence number. The speed was only a trickle compared to my sorrow for all the red car's victims. Only a length behind now. Suddenly, the layers of me were less distinguishable; then the ventilated smooth was gone. There was one clear image on earth's face and in the universe and it was in focus now: the Gargoyle was in that car. It was him. He locked-in behind my car and glared in his side mirror, switching lanes. I switched, too.

Clap hands. Let it go, let go of my thoughts of his kin and their unspun minds sickening to steal our grapes. Very little traffic. But watch out. "Clap hands. Clap hands and sing. Radio on — Righteous Brothers singing *You've Lost That Lovin' Feelin.'* Do not let the him smash your wits. Where does he go? Let the devil follow and take what comes; for the sake of others, let wickedness out of his system. Find where he lives, make a donation, let him follow me and avenge himself like a fire inside his goggles."

We are in a group of three cars. The red cuts in front of

one. He backs up cars, neutral cars, behind him in three lanes. Checkmate? The cars, from the salt of the earth, steady and stable, yet it's all in flux; that's the only constant. Going anywhere, traveling, fluxing, passing through. Red pulls ahead of the steady folks. Moving behind one traveler and motioning to lay off the horn, shifting from one side of the lane to the other, as though I'm a warning flag. Are they blind to red's intentions?

His license plate is visible now, edging closer to the car in the middle lane and nudging a concrete island, banging it pretty good, and, as if I'd knocked something loose, the car slows, swerving to the right under braking. Shifting down a gear and slipping into a space, past the unbroken unfaltering smooth of the other two cars and closer to the red. Straightening my leg, pressing the accelerator; my toes are numb: "Don't go to war, just move on, away from the danger and take danger away from the steadies."

Pushing with my hip; the car's roaring crankshaft shakes with anticipation and screams until its shiny skin rips at the seams. I pause in the red car's blind spot and then edge alongside and salute: "Goodbye." He looks at me, as if shocked or offended.

My eye pranced at his, from one corner to the next, and his pranced at mine, like caged cougars. My left eye went out for a time, the right eye doing all the work, fingers exerting individual jerky pressures on the wheel. I hollered at both for us, "Let it go. Mistake, no prancing, let go!" The Gargoyle opened his mouth as if in disbelief and instinctively drew away from my car, into the right-hand lane of the freeway. I think as this happened, his hand fiddled with something under the dashboard. Radio off. I expected a nervous laugh of relief. Was it shock, the numbness? Was this the right? Embarrassed?

I never got a good look at the person behind the goggles. Lots of people wore sunglasses or ski goggles. Lots of people with red cars. The Gargoyle, who was forward a few lengths, edged ahead of a group of cars. I entered a passing lane and accelerated a bit. The red car put on speed. Not panicked, but concerned with his erratic speed and my tit-for-tat falling back, then positioning to race away for good, I smiled warmly, in the hope of easing the pain he must be suffering with all this monkey business and the load of his ancestors.

"There is nothing here for you. I have a big-engined car. You in that fast red tart with no headlamps. You can save many other victims now and for all time. You can survive your fury." Suddenly close together, the Gargoyle gesticulates wildly, like a person trying to extinguish a fire in his hair. Clutching the wheel in a stranglehold, my feet kick, as if something is grabbing my kidney, and gas shoots into the engine and explodes through the car's skin. The machine rockets away from the smooth, splitting the freeway and breezing away from the red car.

The Gargoyle stared, or so it seemed, in a very serious way and sped up. The experimental cars were out of sight. Three children held hands as they skipped across the bridge. He wore brown gloves, with both hands on his wheel. We now approached the face-placid nerve-ridden city. The first exit was ahead. I watched him from a distance, no one else on the bridge but him and the rain. You could play tennis out there or walk along and feed the gulls, but one factor there with the rain was the exchange between him and me, or more poignantly the furtive exchange of my glee for his god-forsaken wow.

We swap glances, nearly abreast of the first exit — this led to China Town and the shipyards and to the older part of the city and the Oriental mosaics. Gargoyle goosed his car. I fell-back. Now, abreast of the exit, he slams his brakes on and I shoot past. He reverses at 30 miles per hour, then slams the brakes again, hits the exit and disappears.

Meantime, my car slid sideways and screamed as I cut through gears trying to slow down. The car straightened as I started backwards. When my eyes flashed in the side mirror, the experiments were coming at me like geese. I laid a wall of rubber and exhaust, launching forward again. The cars behind flapped their brakes as my acceleration barely missed a tail end collision.

Christmas Eve, after a late shift at work, feeling upset, walking in the last minute shopping crowd. I wanted a little something extra to put in Nancy's stocking, or navel. She surprised me last night with a wonderful bunch of carnations arranged in a spray of mixed wild flowers. The crowd moved in all directions. People like tinsel on buildings with their hurrying. If they slow down just a little, there's time to say "Hello." Anyway, they had their own gift ideas. In a bar off Market Street, in part of an old hotel, I thought about a stocking gift for a weekend at Half Moon Bay. "What'll it be?" "What've you got that's good?" "Everything — Irish coffee?" "Sure." The Irish coffee was stronger than I expected. Several others were in the bar. A TV was racketing, unwatched, at the end of the bar. "I've been a soldier wounded in my head long enough to think now that it's bad strategy to..." someone was saying, as I sipped at my drink. This group was like others in bars: connected one to the other, each with something to contribute to the whole, a basic human way. They sat clustered around the military strategist and discussed post-traumatic stress, home and away. I listened to their shreds of reason, their bits of common sense and their religious homilies, observing the discombobulated Brobdingnag ghosts of several great causes cut up and transplanted on each other in the air around the gossip and speculating, which began with a statement: a gross-thundering postulate. Each of us evaluated it according to his bent and tossing it into a whole, some verbally, some silently. When the shouts grew loudest, politeness returned, long enough for another statement. Then a few sparks of sentences returning to the thundery whirlpool of talk, with nobody considering collateral damage, the less well-off or the vulnerable.

Outside, Christmas reigned, pressing on everyone like an opening door to people on the go, walking in the city. Traffic heavy. It's a kind of pressing that favors people on a night like this. A pressure designed and closely connected to any eve. There is no Christmas on the back of the bridge. Amber lights are on, as usual. They wail at the darkness. Even behind me and under me and in front of me. They are the spirit of the night. As I looked into the spirit, it was pierced by headlights on the bridge. Sky-lit darkness surrounded me and my own ventilated smooth, which somewhat mirrored the amusing glow of a Cezanne painting. Then, a certain extra bright light in my rear-view mirror. Strong beams coming closer and closer, coming up behind and hanging there in my wake, lights without a vehicle, tailgating, anxious to arrive at Christmas stadium, in time for kickoff of the big game, at all costs. The lights felt ominous, burning coldly on my neck, pinching my eyes through the mirror. Their beams fell back, drifting farther behind me. I lost them in the slobbery glow of traffic lying around and behind the smooth. They must have approached from Frisco Island, away from the illuminated hills and the electric humor of the city. Now on the tense footing of the bridge at night, traveling across the span and feeling it wider and higher. The bridge was a marvel of engineering. The result of split-second timing — physical, financial, environmental — considering the social needs of whales and ships free in the harbor, and men tied on the Rock, prisoners and detainees, seeing the dawn from far below this height, through bars, hidden from our ubiquitous faces, looking at eyes in watery depths.

The cars abreast of me remained for some time, unnoticed. The smooth was momentarily less than perfect. A ferry showed Nebraska traders round the harbor and taught them the tricks of its currents, the ferry which let them feel the waves walloping its shore, brandishing the reverie of angles. Reverie, reverie and — clicks off the concrete bridge slabs at night: tires clicking on the slabs and the whirr of rubber on concrete, and planning. Tires whirred and Christmas Eve was almost gone. In fact, technically it was over — after midnight.

Today was a day of salvation, according to some beliefs. The rebirth of the world, affected in a stable, more or less. Such was the man's disciples, sensing it must have all gone on millennia before them, such that the idea of a holiday must have made them tired. Looking forward, sleep late tomorrow, the world and its inhabitants unattended for a day, leave the car in its driveway and stay home.

The Gargoyle's legs will be restless, even the knees. He'll just plain loaf, be bored by his own rules rather than any company's rules and not, for mischief's sake, hire help to assist him being bored. Just rely on good ol' TV to do the trick — click — trick. Pull his head into a web of sumac in the long-ago fall. Just relaxed, forgetting about the spider badge, if that is what it was, on his car, and calling the booth that collected coins all day long a nickel-faced ghoul. How did life bites warp him? Did he feel them in his sleep at night? Could he get the jingle of change out of his little grey cells when he heard the boards of his house creak in the rain on Christmas Day? So nice to relax, to sit at home and relax. Let others run round and visit. Forget foolish imaginings and mad suspicions.

Then a car — in a flash like a bat out of hell I'm sideswiped — my car is thrown against the rail and bouncing onto the sidewalk in a rally of screeches toward a vertical girder with the guts of my vehicle flying out in sparks and scraping metal and both tires on the right side blowing into deformity and somehow in the whole mess of bent machinery the broken side window glass and chrome stick straight out ahead of me like a lance — and my only injury is a sprained thumb.

I climbed from the car and gazed at the glazing water and cars whizzing by. One stopped. A person ran toward me, held me, and was friendly. Bay air filled my mouth, eyes leaning out over the water while rain started again. Gently, being held very gently: that was something, a precious gift?

About the Author

Bill Lemmer was born into an America at war in the 1940s and raised during the seminal decade of the Civil Rights Movement. He received a Wall Street Journal Scholarship during the Vietnam War years of the 1960s and began a career in journalism before leaving his native land for England. *Freedom from Trauma in America* is a novelistic expression of an America which lost its heart, causing mayhem in everyday life; one aspiring character in the book describes this as like being: "...a little one in the greater scheme of things, baying for a mother's wisdom and a student who struggles to be free in a bestial world. Scattered between are fragments of whatever it takes to be a writer, ranging from metaphysical poet to autobiographer to humorist."

Dr. Lemmer lives with his family in the UK. He is the author of *Freedom from Trauma in Dementia*. This non-fiction caregiving guide was written on his retirement as a Professor of Mental Health and Learning Disability and Founding Director of the Dementia Center for Southeast England. Bill writes about trauma and caregiving on his website: www.dementiaonourminds.com

14808199R00183

Printed in Great Britain
by Amazon.co.uk, Ltd.,
Marston Gate.